ALSO BY DAVID LOZELL MARTIN

Tethered

The Crying Heart Tattoo

Final Harbor

The Beginning of Sorrows

Lie to Me

Bring Me Children

Tap, Tap

Cul-de-Sac

Pelikan

Crazy Love

Facing Rushmore

OUR AMERICAN KING

DAVID LOZELL MARTIN

Simon & Schuster

NEW YORK · LONDON · TORONTO · SYDNEY

SIMON & SCHUSTER
1230 Avenue of the Americas
New York, NY 10020

Copyright © 2007 by David Lozell Martin

First Simon & Schuster hardcover edition September 2007

For information about special discounts for bulk purchases,
please contact Simon & Schuster Special Sales at
1-800-456-6798 or business@simonandschuster.com.

Text designed by Paul Dippolito

Manufactured in the United States of America

10 9 8 7 6 5 4 3 2 1

Library of Congress Cataloging-in-Publication Data is available.

ISBN-13: 978-0-7432-6731-1
ISBN-10:   0-7432-6731-1

To Pearl

OUR
AMERICAN
KING

CALAMITY

As a social calamity dismantled the United States, our richest citizens, the top tenth of one percent, purchased and seized massive quantities of every imaginable commodity, trainload after trainload of fuel oil and pharmaceuticals, generators and gin, coffee and clothes . . . and sugar and flour and spices, herds of cattle and flocks of chickens, armaments and munitions, sufficient for the rest of their lives and their children's lives and their children's children's lives. That was the goal: enough for three generations.

Then, to guard what they had amassed, the very rich hired private armies and made deals with generals to gain the protection of troops. But not Marines. Early in the calamity, when negotiators for the wealthy arrived at Camp Lejeune in North Carolina, coveting those 156,000 acres as sanctuary and storehouse and potential golf courses for the very rich, they were met by hand-lettered signs hung everywhere: DEVIL DOGS NOT FOR SALE.

The top tenth of one percent of our wealthiest Americans

needed defensible places to live while they (and their children and grandchildren) fed off what they had pillaged. Across America, they moved onto army bases and airfields. They took over vast cattle ranches in Texas and Montana, and they settled in gated communities throughout the Southwest. In New York, billionaires made a fortress of Montauk at the end of Long Island.

The Hamptons were too sprawling to defend but Montauk was on a narrow peninsula that could be plugged at any number of places, a half-mile bottleneck between Napeague Harbor and the Atlantic Ocean, for example, where you could pile burned-out buses and stretch razor wire and position rapid-fire weapons to keep at bay the starving mad million hordes to the west.

The Montauk rich hired the U.S. Navy to guard against oil-barrel rafts overcrowded with desperate families, to halt these craft before they could land and then tow them into the open arms of the sea where the sacrament of starvation could be completed in privacy.

Supplementing the navy, fishing captains signed on to patrol Montauk's long and varied coast. One of those captains was known as Boat, a family nickname given to him when *boat* was the first word he spoke as a baby. He was a big slab of a man with massive forearms covered in thick blond hair, arms powerful enough to unbend horseshoes. Inarticulate with the spoken word, Boat sang sonnets to diesel engines and spoke in rhymed couplets to the sea. Back before the calamity, he had converted the diesel engines in his beautiful red boat to run on used vegetable oil that he collected from restaurants. He had made his vessel sufficiently seaworthy to sail anywhere in the world. She too was called *Boat*, a name in white cursive, reversed out of vivid red, written in his fine hand on prow and transom. Back in the day, tourists thought it was wonderfully whimsical for someone to name a boat *Boat* but the locals were pretty sure Boat didn't have much of the whimsy in him.

This dawn he's departing Montauk, trying to explain the decision to his first mate, trying to apologize for leaving him without a job.

The first mate says don't worry about me, plenty of vessels looking for hands—but why is it you're going, we got it cushy here.

As if to answer, Boat looks up at geese V-ing across a morning moon.

You're going south? the mate asks.

. . . how to explain this, Boat had been *feeling* something pull on him that must be like what those geese feel, a kind of migratory tug-tug that won't leave you alone, asleep or awake.

Then he startled both himself and the mate by saying, I'm looking for the king.

Boat was unaware these words were inside of him until he, along with the first mate, heard them spoken aloud.

Praise Jesus, the mate said.

No, it wasn't a heavenly king tugging Boat to sea—it was the prospect of an *American* king.

While abed in Fortress Montauk, the very rich awaken from a recurring dream, of glass breaking, of bare feet padding hard and fast across imported tile, of midnight and machete and the stench of the very poor standing over your bed.

1

How did I meet him? That's what everyone wants to know. You come here white-eyed and open-booked, pens poised, needles to prick memories, pretending interest in an old woman when I know what you think of me, living relic whose value lies in the fact that I happened to be there, before the king was king.

I met him at the White House. Actually, at the fence surrounding the White House, he was hanging dead politicians by their ankles, turning their faces toward the fence. "I hang them the way they spoke their words," he told us. "Upside down and backwards." We cheered him and knew without stained fingers that this was our American king. But if you don't mind, before you ask the next two inevitable questions, because there are three questions everyone asks, first I want to tell you about John. My John. I realize he's famous in the history books, but the history books don't know him the way I did.

It was John, my John, who took me to see the king, who discovered the king, who made the man a king, John who talked rivers in which I bathed most of my life—rivers deep and fast you can barely follow the flow, or rivers Everglades slow, over topics you can't see the bottom of, cutting deep into a subject's bedrock, John smart articulate well-read wise enough to float coal barges on what he knows, maddening never boring, always talking, always knowing, while I listened and listened and inner-tubed down that half-century river, eyes closed, my bottom wet, head back, trailing a hand in the watershed of words John spoke.

I'll start the story with John and me in a tree. Oh, yes, scribble, scribble. You don't get many of these remembrances of the calamity that start with people in a tree, do you? We were in a tree in our own suburban backyard and John's river is choked sewage and invective pouring down on a terrible pig. No, not Canadian, this was years and years before we realized Canada was our true enemy. It might be better if you just let me tell it.

John named the pig a corpse eater. "Mud wallower. Disease carrier. You ruined Eden! Satan! Snake! Wormer, garbage grubber, walking disposal unit. Titan of trichinosis and tuberculosis! Get out! Away! Leave us, damn you, leave us!" John went on.

And the pig grunts rapidly as if toward a nasty ejaculation. It was ugly with open wounds and black bristles, a source of stench, equal parts death and shit, drifting contamination up through the limbs of this tree, which John and I love, our backyard tree, Mother Oak we named it years ago.

Pig is four of me. More than three hundred pounds, six feet long, tusks dirty and broken, nose muddy, and eyes, yes, pig-like in their pigginess. I cover my nose with one hand, the other holding tightly to Mother Oak, as I look out at what's left of suburbia. Before the calamity I would've heard children on a day like this, softly warm and windless, and if I had smelled pig I would've smelled pig grilling on a grill is how I would've smelled pig on a day like this, softly warm and windless. And even now, even in my starved condition, I would take comfort in this day's blessing if not for the pig consuming every morsel of my attention. I believe heart and soul he is intent upon eating John and me.

Bizarre to see such a creature, huge ugly tusked, in our suburban backyard but then again the world by that time had lost its old realities, leaving us strange new fantasies, the bad ones, being eaten by pigs, and hopeful ones of heroes, warriors on stallions, I wait for him to come rescue me.

"Why won't he look up?" I ask John as I drape myself belly down along a limb leopard-like looking toward the ground at pig whose head is without benefit of neck.

"He *can't* look up," John says. "He's built like a shark, a big body with a mouth in front. Shark and pig, mindless machines for consumption, mascots for America. Rip open a swimming shark's belly and it will turn to eat in a happy frenzy its own unspooling intestines. Capitalist! Corner a pig in a trap, stab it, provoke it, no matter what, the pig will turn from his torment to eat a handful of corn thrown through the wire. Consumer!"

If I could've laughed I would've—John the old-time radical Commie red-diaper socialist liberal professor. Irish to boot.

I tell him I cannot stay in this tree much longer, there's no meat on me. The rough bark chafes paper skin, bruises my bones, hurts so bad . . . not that I blame Mother Oak, for which, an hour ago, I was grateful her limbs grew close to the ground because when pig made its terrible appearance I was too weak to climb anything ambitious. But now Mother is bruising my bones with hardwood and I want down. "I want down."

"That pig will kill you and eat you."

I say something about the irony.

"What?"

"The irony, John—of me starving to death, then to be killed for food."

"You're not starving to death, Mary."

John says the most astonishing things. I remind him, "There's nothing left of me."

"A million years of evolution designed us to be hungry. It's more natural to be hungry than it is to be full. The last fifty, sixty years of America, before the calamity, that was a historical aberration, for us to be fat."

"*I* wasn't fat."

"More's the pity."

Which is true. If I had been fat to start, I'd be in better shape now. "Where did this pig come from? John, we live in *suburbia* for crying out loud."

"That forest preserve we were so proud of, a mile away, four hundred acres of nature intertwined throughout these freaking tract houses, that's pig's heaven."

These aren't tract houses. They're practically mansions. At least when compared to the bathtub-in-the-kitchen flats where John and I lived over the years.

"Horrible houses," he says, looking around our neighborhood from the vantage of Mother Oak. He's always hated living here. John said suburbia undermined his credentials as a poet. Me, I liked living in a nice house. "Horrible, soulless, vacuous houses," he goes on.

"You live in one," I remind him.

"More's the pity."

John and I couldn't afford to live here on our own, we got to suburbia by way of the university's policy on mixed-income housing.

"But, John, where does a wild pig *come from* in the first place, to get to the forest preserve and then here in our own backyard?"

John's river follows the pull of this question's gravity, John sitting upright on his private limb, one row higher than mine, bracing back against Mother's trunk, the better to talk the river through gates I have opened, generous me, wife, ready to raft.

John tells me that no large animal in the world is better situated than the pig for rapid reproduction and adaptability, five million were feral in the United States at the time of the calamity. John tells me that pigs destroy everything, anything on the ground, they eat turtle eggs and quail eggs and Bambi fawns that don't scamper away quickly enough and salamanders, shrews, voles, moles. "They are master rooters, nose diggers." John even knew the name of their nose bone, the nasal sesamoid, and he told me some of the many diseases pigs are heir to, scabies and lice and ticks and liver flukes, worms of the kidneys and worms of the lungs, tapeworms, rabies . . .

John not only remembers every fact and theory he has ever read or been told but he connects each with others in his vast library of memory so that living with John and listening to his river is like having the knowledge of the world on open tap. I love listening to the rivers John talks, truly I do, but people don't believe I do. Women friends at the university and our neighbors here on the cul-de-sac privately ask me if I don't want to throttle him sometimes just to get him to shut up. They don't understand. I am by inclination and long years *a student, a listener.* I was John's student when he seduced me, more with words than hand or sword, John speaking a seduction river that floated orchids. How many poems did that man recite and write for me, a thousand more than that. For a student of words, to be seduced by John's river of talk was to drown in, drenched and quenched by, love.

"Look at that terrible pig!" John shouts down at the ground.

It has shat and turns now to root through its own debris.

I close my eyes and wish the world was nice again, the way it was when we moved to suburbia and nice young white people with nice white smiles added caramel to my latte and I wore cashmere.

"Disease carriers, rabies incubators, full of muscle worms, unclean meat, on this Jew and Muslim agree, a meat it is said that most resembles in texture and taste our own sweet flesh."

I cover my face with both hands and balance on my thin ass and can't bear any more talk of flesh eating. Not because I am squeamish but because it makes me hungry. I am quite literally starving to death. Neither one of us has eaten regularly in a long time, we've had very nearly nothing this whole past month, but John started out overweight, a hedge fund against starvation.

That morning we ate grass. John said when the Irish died in An Gorta Mor, The Great Hunger, children were buried with green-stained mouths, you couldn't get the wee bastards to stop eating grass—they watched the animals grazing, didn't they now?

Friends of mine enviably thin before the calamity, sizes one and two and looking great in little black dresses, thin-necked and walnut cheek-boned, they're all long dead by this time, starved to death, no reserves.

"John, why do people who are starving get bellies that pooch out?"

"You're not starving."

John's in denial because without me his river would dry up.

"Fluid accumulation," he says. "Dropsy it used to be called. The cellular mechanism that pumps fluid out for eventual elimination, that mechanism weakens with advanced or chronic starvation. Fluid accumulates, especially in the abdomen."

"When Connie was down to nothing, she said, 'I can't believe I still have a belly.' " I'm referring to a woman who worked with me at the university.

John says, "She kept asking men to encircle her arm with a finger and thumb like it was something to be proud of."

"She struggled with weight all her life."

"Not anymore."

"You don't know how it is to struggle with weight. You never struggled, you just gave up and got fat."

He laughs. "You can never be too fat." In the calamity, these words have become truth. "Every pound of fat is worth thirty-five-hundred calories, equivalent storage to thirty pounds of fish or almost two hundred pounds of carrots." He pats his now-nonexistent gut. "I was carrying a little Kroger's, I was. Look! Damn thing's eating all the acorns."

Our acorns. The reason the pig almost caught us, John and I were down on all fours, distracted from eating grass by gathering acorns. You can make flour from acorns if you soak out the tannic acid. Why hadn't we thought of this before? Because, prior to the calamity, *food* meant grocery stores and cans in the cupboard, dinner parties and drives to restaurants, it had nothing to do with little brown things lying on the ground under a white oak tree.

I tell him, "I had my heart set on acorns for dinner."

John laughs and I wonder how can a man in his condition laugh, it's the goddamn Irish in him.

I say, "You wake up next to me some morning I'm dead, then it won't be so funny."

Let me ask you a question. Have you interviewed people and asked them if anything strange happened, back when they were starving to death, anything strange happen to them first thing in the morning, at the very moment of awakening? Because I awoke every morning back then with my mouth chewing imaginary foods that had starred in my dreams—and I wonder if that was a common experience of people who went through America's own Gorta Mor.

Back in the tree, John promises he's not going to let me die.

"How're you going to prevent it?"

"Need be, I will slice chunks of my thighs and cook them for you, if it comes to that."

"It's come to it. Start cutting, start cooking."

"First we got to get rid of this pig so we can get down." He shouts at it, breaks off a little switch, strips leaves and throws everything to the ground floating like confetti to no effect on the terrible thing below.

John said, "When passenger pigeons darkened American skies by the multibillion and roosted in such numbers that tree limbs broke, pigeons as voracious as hogs, pigeons that wouldn't stop eating even when they were full, too full to fly, and hog farmers would go into the woods and cut down the trees, the pigeons too fat to waddle away, landing on the ground and sometimes bursting they were so full, hogs scrambling to eat the adults, feathers and all, but prizing the little squabs, morsels to be snuffled up barely tasted—"

"John, why do you torture me with talk of food?"

"I don't sleep anymore, Mary. I watch out the window at night and see things."

"I see them too."

"It's the hallucinations that come from starving."

"I thought we weren't starving, is what you said, John."

"I'm searching for someone," he tells me. "I'm on a vision quest."

John says this because I'm Lakota, teaching Native American studies at the university. But I don't admit to being Indian anymore. John says I should tell people I'm Israeli.

Diarrhea cramps my guts like how childbirth must feel, though I haven't had children and can't make the comparison with any authenticity. But I know this, that what I felt in that tree hurt like hell and threatens to double me over and drop me to the ground.

"What is it?" John asks.

"The diarrhea."

"From that grass. Go ahead and go."

I'm at a loss.

"Mary, nothing you do disgusts me."

"I disgust myself." How ugly the world has become. I remember when I had nice things about me, a nice white porcelain toilet in a nicely painted room, paper soft and a spray of sea breeze in a can, and, most important of all, the ability granted to me to flush all my nastiness away.

John and I often rank what we missed most from life before the calamity. Somewhere in the top five are flush toilets, along with the foods we loved, coffee, staying warm, and alcohol.

"Diarrhea will kill you faster than almost anything," John tells me.

"Not as fast as slipping off this limb to drop down there." I make a move as if to do it, causing John to catch his breath.

For a moment he thinks I will indeed commit suicide, terror on John's face, and I feel a flush of guilt for having provoked him. I tell him, "I'll drop down *on* the swine. Break its back. Then you can climb down and cut off a piece of pig and then neither one of us will starve to death. *Barbecue*." I speak the word with reverence.

"A barbecue sandwich would give me the strength and the inclination to make love to you," my husband declares.

I snort. In the ravages of this calamity, John stays soft, I remain dry.

"Do you realize we're back where we began, Mary? Chased up a tree by a predator intent upon eating us, that's what our ancestors were doing a million years ago. There was a long run of progress, telegraph, telephone, television, Internet, space travel, the electric guitar and five-dollar lattes . . . but now here we are, starving, bug-eyed, and chased up a tree by something that wants to eat us. Full circle. Who would've thought?"

"John, I can't sit on this limb much longer."

"Get to your feet."

"I can't."

He hollers down at that terrible pig, "Ham I am!"

I am weary. I have no blanket and will be cold the whole night through. Our chiefs are dead. Our old men are dead. The people are cold and hungry and they have no blankets.

"John, do you remember those beautiful wool blankets we had, the Chief Joseph robes?"

"Of course."

"We should've kept one."

This is mainly what we do when we have time, when we're not consumed with the task of staying alive, such as we were earlier, eating grass and collecting acorns and then climbing Mother Oak when pig threatened. When we have time, mainly what we do, we remember all the things we possessed once upon a time.

John says, "If we'd kept blankets, the terrible Patagonians would've had an excuse for ransacking our house. The blankets would've been stolen. And if we had tried to keep those blankets, tried to hide them, we would've been killed. Only by having nothing," he reminds me, "do we continue to survive."

In the beginning of this calamity, people all around us were getting beaten and killed for the things they had, head bashed in for a sturdy pair of shoes, throat slit for a can of Campbell's turkey noodle soup hidden under a couch—and the more you had, the more danger you attracted. The first became last.

And yet people wouldn't, couldn't, give up their *things*. When we were first forced out of our houses, families wandered around pulling wheeled suitcases—big ones for daddy and mommy, smaller ones for the kiddies. Full of what? Cans of food, lotions, clean underwear, medicine, books, electronic games and extra batteries. Marauders took what they wanted from these rolling stockpiles and killed anyone who tried to stop them. Even after watching families murdered for their wheeled suitcases, the people still couldn't give up their stuff—packing it in pregnant backpacks, stuffing their pockets, and then *still* getting robbed and beaten for the things they owned.

John's solution, brilliantly counterintuitive, was to discard or give away everything: canteen, flashlight, cans of food, assorted knives, tarps for sleeping on and tenting under, aspirin, disinfectant, coats, blankets, gloves. By divesting ourselves of anything anyone else wanted, no longer were we of interest to thugs and marauders and the great unwashed displaced persons who stumbled across America like so many million undead. We had nothing for none of them and, in our utterly deprived state, we found safety.

"Twenty-one, twelve, twenty-one," I tell John.

"Stand up," he replies. "Your legs are going numb and you'll drop off that limb whereupon the pig will gobble you up. What did you mean, 'twenty-one, twelve, twenty-one'?"

"I was twenty-one when you seduced me. You were, are, twelve years older than I am. And now we've been married twenty-one years. Twenty-one, twelve, twenty-one."

"I love you," he says softly.

Pig trots off like the self-important running late.

"Guess it got tired of waiting for me to fall," I say.

"No," John says, " 'Twas love repelled the beast."

We were both wrong, it was our neighbor, Tom.

2

Tom doesn't get much credit in the history books, except for a foot-note, being the one who started the business with the string. People don't know he was haunted. I mean that in the sense of how a house is haunted, a tomb. Before the calamity, he was a retired army officer and a successful investor who loved his wife and doted on his twin daughters, age twelve when they died of starvation, limbs like sticks, each in her turn lying across his lap to die. After that, his wife wandered off and was taken we think by the terrible Patagoni-ans, leaving Tom haunted. At night he talks to the ghosts of his wife and daughters and if you were to look up at his windows you could see the candle he carries through the rooms of his suburban mini-mansion.

On this particular day when John and I were chased up a tree by a pig, Tom stands for some time beneath Mother Oak.

"We're up here," John finally says.

"In a tree?" Tom replies without looking up. Like the rest of us, he is starving and muddled, has trouble making sense of the world.

"Tom, we're right above you," John says.

"Who?"

"Mary and me, the people who live here for chrissakes."

"In a tree?"

"Oh, Tom, help me down," I tell him.

"Are my daughters up there with you?"

"They're not, Tom."

Which is when he finally turns his haunted face and looks up.

Climbing down, John is careful the way he moves. In our condition, a broken bone is a death sentence. And death sentences fill our book—drink the wrong water, get the diarrhea, suffer an infected cut. "The pig treed us. You saw the pig?"

Tom says no, he didn't see no pig.

"It left right when you got here," John says.

"Left right?" Tom asks.

John is trying to hold on with one hand and help me out of the tree with the other. "It was a terrible pig."

"They come out at night and feed," Tom says as he comes over to lower me to the ground.

I'm embarrassed to have his hands on me, I am of such a smell and my skin flakes off onto everything, I have mouth sores, and there's so very little of me. Starvation has nothing on vanity. I think of Connie complaining about her stomach pooching out even as she lay dying.

While still holding me, Tom looks close into my eyes. Nothing stirs.

I am Indian, dark and slightly taller than my husband. My hair has thinned in this calamity, once it was thick as rope and black as something very black and was beautiful down all the length of my back. I had large dark eyes and a heavy mouth that men watched when I talked, they watched my mouth as much as they watched my breasts. I have nothing now that a man watches.

I should tell you something about hair, you youngsters who didn't live through the calamity. When you're starving it falls out and breaks your heart to look at a brush and see all that hair. My husband was losing his, too, the former ginger head, formerly thick and red. Fairly handsome he was, my John, a small-featured Irish man with blue eyes and a wicked expression. He stopped shaving during the calamity, so did I. Hair grew all over our bodies while falling out of our head.

Tom used to have thick brown hair that I admired, perhaps too openly. Once at a party, before the calamity, Tom followed me outside in the dark where I had gone to fetch lemons left on the picnic table and he caught up with me in the yard—near Mother Oak— and tried to kiss me, did kiss me, though I did not kiss him back. He put a hand on my left breast, hefting it gently, and told me he'd been in love with me ever since John and I moved to the neighborhood. He called me beautiful and held my left breast with his right hand in the most curious manner as if someone had asked him to hold a sleeping kitten.

In deference to his being drunk and a kind soul at heart, I didn't laugh at him or cut him with my lemon knife, held in one hand behind my back, just in case, in fact I didn't even ask that he unhand my sleeping breast. I just stood there and listened to him ramble, Tom saying John and I were the best things that ever happened to this neighborhood, an Irish poet professor and a beautiful Indian woman who could look at a man in ways that made that man feel like a king.

"Here's the deal, neighbor," I said, taking Tom's arm to walk him back to the house that wonderful drunken evening before the calamity began and I remember the elaborate food and plentiful drink, how gentle the summer's night with mosquitoes its only vexation. "When John and I got married, I gave him a Lakota blood pledge. I told John that no matter what happened, what he did to me, how I might fall out of love with him, in love with another, if he got sent away to prison or crippled in an accident or if his heart turned bitter and he treated me like dirt, or maybe nothing bad happened except we just grew bored with each other over the decades, or if we stayed deeply in love, whatever life might hold for us, I promised John that as long as we were both alive and married, I would never cheat on him. I might leave him, divorce him, marry someone else. I might cut him if he dishonored me because I admit to a fondness for blades. I might do many things. But *while we were married,* I would be true to him and only him and forever. I promised him that he never, ever had to give *that* particular aspect of marriage a thought. Because no matter what else might transpire between us, I would never cheat on him. I gave my husband the gift of fidelity. So Tom . . . not with you or with the Holy Ghost . . . not with no one except John will I ever sleep."

By the time I finished, we were ready to go into the house and Tom was crying openly, drunkenly, telling me I was the most beautiful, honorable person in existence and how lucky John was to have married me and how fortunate he, Tom, was to know John and me both and all the other things an emotional drunk man would think to say.

We stepped into the kitchen, bright and hot with dinner's scents, as John was making another round of drinks for guests laughing off in the living room. Seeing Tom's wrecked condition, John said, "For the sake of a suffering Christ, have a whiskey, man!"

I said, "Tom loves us both and thinks we're the most wonderful friends a person could ever be blessed to have."

"Have a whiskey," John again told Tom.

"Thank you," Tom replied thinly, spilling whiskey to embrace John who said spilling whiskey was a sin.

I patted both of them on their shoulders.

Broad shoulders back then, not sharp and skeletal.

Now we're in that same backyard where Tom kissed me. John and I are freshly down from Mother Oak when Tom points out the tracks marked across our grass by pig's trotters.

"Yeah," John replies. "I told you. A terrible pig chased us up the tree."

"We should catch it and cook it."

"I've been thinking about that."

I tell them frankly, "Neither of you can catch no goddamn pig. You can barely stand upright."

"We could build some kind of trap," Tom says.

John murmurs agreement.

"Look what I got," Tom says, pulling from his pocket a wind of white string.

"What in God's name are you going to do with all that string you're collecting?" John asks.

"I was out this morning scavenging but mostly I had to hide," Tom told us. "Marauders, this time on bicycles. They had people with ropes around their necks, making them trot to keep up."

"Terrible Patagonians," John says.

"Do you have any food?" Tom asks.

A crazy question asked without irony and left unanswered, neither John nor I passing judgment on him for the madness in asking.

"I don't sleep at night," Tom says.

I suggest we should go in. "I'm freezing."

In the living room, we three share a couch next to the dead fireplace. I suggest a fire.

The men say no, it would attract the wrong kind of attention.

I am weary of being cold. I think I hate being cold as much as I hate being hungry. "I'm hungry."

John says, "I'll go out in a minute and get those acorns."

"They have to be soaked," I tell him, "and then *dried over a fire.*"

"If you guys decide to do that," Tom says, "I'll help. You know, for a share."

We're all three nodding at what a grand idea it is to collect acorns, soak them, dry them over a fire, then grind them into flour and make hotcakes.

One of us suggests butter, which we don't have.

Another mentions maple syrup, which we also don't have.

Bacon from that terrible pig would go nice with those acorn hotcakes.

And coffee.

Hot steaming coffee with half-and-half.

And orange juice.

A banana.

Eggs scrambled with cheese and scallions and bits of that ham what am.

Biscuits.

We pleasure ourselves like that for some time, fantasies of food, and then it's dark out and Tom's gone and John and I are on the couch in this overly large house that is without light or heat or hope.

"What happened to Tom?" I ask.

"You fell asleep."

"Build a fire, John."

"Not a good idea."

I don't care, I truly don't care. I'm cold and my teeth rattle. Did our human ancestors really exist like this, cold and hungry, for a million years?

Early on, John saved our lives with his realization that during our first experience living outside, we were more likely to die of hypothermia than of starvation or thirst. When a group of us broke into a Target store, the others rushed to grab food and drink, but

John said we can go three weeks without food, more for those of us who are overweight, and several days without water, but we'll die *tonight,* the very first night, if we can't stay warm. He hoarded matches. He took Vaseline and cotton balls and made fire-starters. He grabbed extra sweaters for us and socks and wool hats. People thought he was crazy, it was only forty degrees outside, not the depths of winter. But they died that night and the next while we lived. They died well fed and well watered, they died like flies on a November windowsill while John and I snuggled in our extra clothing and next to our little fire that had been started with cotton balls soaked in Vaseline, a petroleum product.

When I beg again for a fire, he says we're fine. "We're inside. We're dry."

"Yonder's that nice chair you broke up the other day, oh, John, look how its wood yearns to burn."

"All right then." He shuffles like an old man to the hearth.

I'm too tired and hungry to be actually happy but I do nod approval at this movement toward fire.

"When the Patagonians smell the smoke and come in the front door—"

I interrupt him by declaring that in exchange for fire I will gladly welcome the terrible Patagonians into our home. "Let them share the warmth."

John snorts. "Easy to be brave huddling there on the couch. You see a Patagonian in real life, you shake like a leaf." He's got paper going and is putting on the first sticks, the rungs from that very nice oak chair his mother gave us.

"Tell me when it's warm enough I can come over there."

Before John can reply we hear someone at the front door. I can't remember if we keep it locked or not.

Unlocked . . . because now that someone is coming down the front hall.

"I don't care," I tell John, who has his back to me and is still working on getting the fire going, apparently he doesn't care either. "I don't care if it is those terrible Patagonians."

But it wasn't them, it was Tom.

"You guys are building a fire," he observes in a careful voice, fearful of being wrong about this. "Are we eating acorns?"

"The pig's back in the yard," John says, adding more sticks to the fire, which is now sufficient for me to feel face-warm from where I sit. It's a good fire. I have on a pair of cheap polyester pants, an old shirt, and a cotton sweater full of holes. Our coats were taken from us and we long ago gave away our blankets.

John and Tom are talking in front of the fire, blocking its heat.

"Move!" I tell them.

They make way and I come to sit on the bricks in front of the fire. This is heaven. "What're you two talking about?" I think they talk about me, about eating me after I die—because surely I'm the next to go, just look how little there is of me.

"It's Kyle," Tom says.

"Has he died?" I ask. Kyle Henderson lives down the street and lost his whole family, wife and daughter and son, back when the weather first turned cold. Except they didn't starve or die of hypothermia, they got raped and killed right in front of Henderson's eyes and he kept the bodies, wouldn't bury them or put them out for the scavengers. Rumor has it, the bodies are in Henderson's basement still. Rumor has terrible things to say about Henderson and the bodies of his family.

Tom and John are still talking, whispering to keep something from me.

"What is it?" I demand like the starving shrew I've become.

"Henderson has invited us to dinner tomorrow night," John finally tells me.

"How can that be?"

"We don't know."

"If he has food to give," I say, "then I say give it to us now."

"He's asked us over for dinner tomorrow night, the three of us."

"Dinner?" I repeat. Food was serious, but a dinner invitation was a ridiculous proposition. "Does he have food or not?"

"We don't know."

I move to the couch and, as the fire goes out, drift to a troubled sleep.

At some point in that night, I hear voices in the next room, in the kitchen where Tom and John conspire as to my hocks and loins while blades get sharpened, I can hear the scrape of steel against stone and I understand now, Henderson's having me for dinner. I see Tom's twin daughters sitting on the bricks by the cold fireplace, looking as beautiful as they did when they sat there several Christmases ago wearing red velvet dresses with red velvet bows in their soft blond hair . . . while I am here and I am now and I am freaking ugly and sparsely haired and cold and hungry. I wonder if the boys—Tom, John, Henderson—plan to boil me and, if so, will they please boil me alive so at least I can die warm.

I don't have the strength to worry about it and finally sleep, *dead.*

3

To awaken to a day, cold, hungry, alive and to find that, of the three, *alive* is hardest, is most like the stone, adamant.

Did you wake like that this morning, your life adamant? I know. I can't seem to get out from under it either.

4

I think if I find John dead on the kitchen floor, I might cut a strip from his droopy ass, this old man I've loved for twenty-one years, and skewer that John flank steak to a green stick, threading Mother's sharpened finger through softened flesh, and barbecue him over an open fire I'll make in defiance of Patagonia. Wouldn't I be *honoring* him by eating his flesh, like he was Christ and I, supplicant? Like he was Ruth's Chris and I, hungry? This is the argument I'll use against whatever part of my mind wants to argue the point as my little finger knife cuts a V-section of John, starting from waist down left buttock, ending in upper thigh, a good pound of John, uncooked weight.

"Oh there you are," John says as I see him walking around all upright and unbroiled.

"I'm hungry."

"Ah," he says. "There's that."

We stand awhile, dumb. I notice John looking at me.

"What?" I ask. I saw a mirror the other day and I know the

answer, that I have become a crone, eyes sunken and skin dark in streaks across my ghastly face.

"How can this be happening to people in America?" he asks. "In *suburbia* for chrissakes, starving to death, college-educated white people."

"I'm Lakota, John."

"But in *America*."

I tell him, "I wish I had a hot dog and a slice of apple pie, that's how goddamn American I feel."

He stares wide-eyed. "I dreamt the other night of what I'm searching for, a king. A king who will lead us out of calamity."

"John, Americans don't believe in kings."

"You mean, like unicorns?"

"You're talking crazy." Then I remember something *I* dreamt, that Tom said last night Henderson was feeding us dinner. I tell John of this crazy thing I dreamt and he says, casual like dinner was a daily thing, he says, oh, no, that was no dream, Tom really did say it, that Henderson really has invited us to dinner tonight. So I'm all, like, oh my God we're going to eat.

John says he's not so sure. "We think Henderson's playing a joke, toying with us, getting back for the way we made fun of him over the years."

"*We?*"

"Well, Tom and I."

"Exactly. Tom and you. Not me. I'll go alone and bring you a doggie bag."

"Bring me a fricking dog, I could eat the Lamb of God."

"And this from a Catholic."

"Lapsed."

"John, please. I see you secretly crossing yourself all the time."

"Anyway, Tom and I think Henderson is playing a joke on us and there will be no dinner."

"No dinner tonight?"

"No, none."

"I'm thirsty," I say, looking around as if I expected water to appear magically, out of a tap or something.

My husband scarecrows to a granite counter and pours me out a glass from a plastic gallon jug.

I smell the water, it smells of minerals. "Where'd this come from?"

"The Littons' water heater."

I drink down half a glass of the Littons' water, which I can feel sloshing in my shrunken stomach.

The Littons lived a few doors down, they disappeared weeks ago. We don't know what happened to them. A lot of people just walk off, figuring there's got to be something better somewhere else. John and I have talked many times of joining a migration. But there's chaos out there in the calamitous world, divided as it is between Nice People who follow the old laws and hope for the best and the Takers who have armed themselves and steal whatever they want from Nice People. Gangs abound. Patagonians everywhere. Three million felons have been released from prisons.

That's something the history books don't cover, the decision some states made to keep their prisons locked down, to starve thousands of inmates in their cells, drinking water from toilets, eating one another raw, until, finally, mad, starving, dying. Or was it a better decision that other states made, to unlock those felonious millions, those murderous thousands, tattooed and weight-trained, penned up long enough for even the formerly normal among them to become sociopaths, mad at the world, released upon that world to prey upon us sheep? That's why the history books don't cover it, what's the right answer?

"I broke into their house yesterday," John tells me, speaking of the Littons. "They never tapped their water heater so there's another forty gallons for us."

"I guess they weren't around when Randall explained how to tap the hot water heater. I wonder what happened to him."

"Randall?"

"Yeah, there's another one you and Tom made fun of when he was trying to help."

"Brought those pigeons over."

"We wouldn't turn our noses up at pigeons now, would we?"

"No, Mary, we wouldn't, not now we wouldn't."

We grow quiet as time passes. I don't know how much, where it comes from, where it goes, I am starving to death and my limbs are sticks and I walk stiffly. I think I remember John talking again of an American king. I remember asking about Henderson and dinner.

John sits at the table. His eyes bulge even as the cavities around those eyes are sunken and the skin around those sunken eyes has darkened. Had his starvation begun abruptly, overnight? Or have I lost days, weeks?

"John? Are we starving to death?"

"It's come to that, yes, probably, I don't know. One day without food, that's not even worth the mention. Your liver releases glycogen, from which glucose is produced and Bob's your uncle. Glucose is the brain's preferred food, of course. But after the liver's supply is gone, fat and muscle have to be metabolized. It's all an efficient process, fine-tuned over a million years of evolution. We're born hungry, Mary. We *evolved* hungry. We can do a month without much food. Cases have been documented of people going more than a year without food, without a single morsel of food . . . *fat* people, I grant you, but all the same—"

I ask John where this river is going . . . is this a pep talk . . . pepper talk . . . peppercorn steak . . . but riddle me this, John, how long am I going to live without eating, because I didn't start out fat, John knows that, and my glycogen is long gone, what little fat I had, gone, most of my muscle. "I'm not an angel, John, changing colors on the power of prayer."

"I think someone's out there . . . waiting for us."

I look at the window.

"I want to go into the District and find a king, our American king."

"You know what I want, John, I want fried chicken."

"Hunger's always been the province of the poor, our burden to bear, our weapon to wield. Gandhi! Bobby Sands, sixty-six days, the poor sod."

I catch John once again surreptitiously crossing himself, the old fraud. Slinking back to the Church in your final days, suffering Christ, for this we pray . . . a little communion bread, some protein next time, you poor crucified sod.

"Just as starvation scours the arteries clean, this calamity is scouring America."

"I don't know what you're talking about, John—"

"We should walk to the White House, see who's in charge."

"You're a crazy man. The District is full of Patagonians!"

"You don't know that. Let's walk into the District."

"People said—"

"Mary, listen to me. I was up all night and it came to me. We have to go to the White House. He's there. The one who will lead us out of this calamity."

"*The president?*"

"No, Mary, *a king.*"

"You're mad."

"I think we should—"

"You know what I think we should do, John, we should accept Henderson's dinner invitation."

We sat at the table, I had finished my water. The kitchen was easing toward dark, I heard a faint humming-ringing in my ears. Had the day gone? What else had happened besides drinking a glass of water that John had drained from the Littons' hot water heater? What else had happened during an entire day? We live in a dream world, which must be why John talks of kings. If our ancient ancestors lived like this, no wonder they thought up God. But this current drift through a world of delusions and dreams could be ended by a plate of macaroni and cheese. So I say again. "Let's go to Henderson's house and see if he'll feed us for real."

"It's a trick."

"What kind of trick?"

"Some kind of trick he'll pull because of the way we tormented him."

"I didn't torment him, it was you and Tom."

"You laughed at the Henderson jokes we told."

"You know what I think, I think on the off chance that Henderson is serious about feeding us dinner, let's go see, is what I think."

"It'll be a trick. He'll cut out pictures of roast turkey and show us the pictures, prop them on our plates. Ha, ha."

"I know what you're really afraid of, what he'll be serving us . . . not roast turkey."

"Tom is nodding, he agrees with me."

"How do you know Tom agrees with you, John . . . are you having another vision, like your vision of a king at the White House?"

"No, Tom's standing there in the doorway and he's nodding."

I turn to see Tom haunting our kitchen with his bent thin height.

"It's a trick," he says. "To get back at us for making fun of him."

John says, "We should walk into the District, I think our king is there."

Tom points out what I pointed out, America doesn't have a king.

John says, "I dreamt America had a king."

I say, "Let's go to dinner at Henderson's."

"It'll be a trick," Tom says. "If he serves meat, you know what it'll be."

There had been rumors ever since his family had been killed.

Nonetheless, John finally says, "Nonetheless, let's go."

I wondered if I should bring something, a gift . . . and then I have an imaginary conversation with Henderson's dead wife, asking her, Anything I can bring, honey?, and she says, Just your appetite.

This is wrong, Tom says . . . as he follows us out the door and into the dark cul-de-sac.

In the night, cold, I try to smell what might be for dinner. It takes us forever to get down the block. We walk funny.

5

Like movie zombies, feet sliding, walking carefully as if walking on wet slick ice, our arms out for balance, our natural sense of position gone, forearms parallel to the ground, and our hands, which now seemed overly large at the end of our stick arms, drooping limp from bony wrists . . . funny weird like movie space aliens unsure of this brand spanking new gravity.

The boys, John and Tom, had been trying to convince themselves that Henderson, good old Henderson who was about to feed us if this wasn't a joke, that he wasn't so bad after all, pretty good egg when you come to think about it. The mention of egg led us to a conversation that ranged from hard-boiled to sunny side up, leaving us wondering if Henderson might serve omelettes.

The boys say maybe Henderson wasn't really a total martinet, just a man who believed in following the rules is all.

"And he got skinny like the rest of us, didn't he?" John asks.

"Like a rail," Tom agrees. "At least he was last time I saw him. But that was a long time ago."

I asked, "You didn't see him when he invited us to dinner?"

"No, he called to me through a window. It was dark, I didn't see him. Have you guys seen him recently?"

Neither of us had, and I worried that this dinner invitation, called out through a window at night, came from Tom's haunted imagination.

Though I don't specifically remember any of the three of us knocking, Henderson opened the door to his house and there the four of us stood, neighbors. We hadn't seen him for such a long time, maybe ever since his family was killed, so his condition was shocking, standing there in the doorway of his suburban mini-mansion.

Henderson was fat.

6

Fat and both ears missing, head shaved, Kyle Henderson is a sight our eyes work up and down back and forth to make sense of, most especially the wee dimpled stubs of his ears like fetal remains, made all the uglier by his bald head because while some men are blessed with pleasingly shaped skulls, Henderson wasn't. Serious scratches and deep gashed cuts adorn this bumpy skull, like maybe it had been left on the playground where kids kept kicking it idly.

Though remnant ears are ugly enough, what offends most is the fat, the Henderson fat, ringing his neck, bulging his shirt buttons, overhanging his belt. Not counting his fat ass, Henderson had never been fat-fat before, how did Henderson get fat now? We knew, we three dinner guests knew the answer to that question, but none of us would speak the accusation, *pervert,* or the condemnation, *shame,* 'cause we were hungry, hungry hippos.

Standing there fat in his doorway, he zeroes in on my husband. "Are you hungry, John?"

"I am, Kyle."

Calling the monster by his first name, what a fraud hunger has made of my husband.

"How hungry are you, John?"

"Hungry, Kyle. We all are."

Henderson tormenting my husband, asking, "But *how* hungry, John?"

"Truth is, Kyle, I could eat a baby's arse through the bars of his crib."

Henderson doesn't laugh. "Always with the quip."

"You invited us to dinner."

"You all made fun of me," Henderson says, still staring at John. "But you mainly, John, you were the one."

"Just having some gas with you."

"Always so clever, putting down the government bureaucrat."

"Well fuck you then," John says, turning. Starving to death but still Irish.

Tom and I turn to follow and there ensues a hopeless moment when it seems we will go without dinner.

But Henderson calls us back, "No, no. Come in, come in. I have dinner waiting for you."

John doesn't hesitate, he reverses and goes right in, I follow him, then Tom, who says, "God bless this house," an oath to ward off the evil of dinner.

At the atrium hallway, Henderson plays the host. "I've chopped up some meat with canned potatoes and canned carrots, quite tasty and a lot of it, but I'm sorry to say you'll have to eat it cold."

"I don't mind," I answer too eagerly.

"You look like you're freezing, Mary."

"I'm always cold," I tell him. "My kidneys are cold, there's a chill to my liver."

Henderson laughs, Tom suddenly demanding, "You going to eat this cold dinner with us?"

"Of course," Henderson says, patting his ballooning belly with both padded hands.

A look in John's eyes I've seen before, murder restrained.

"Here, Mary," Henderson says, taking my elbow. "Let me see if I can't warm you up."

He leads me into the kitchen where Henderson takes an empty two-pound coffee can from under the sink, produces a church key and makes a series of triangular holes around the bottom of the can, flips it over and makes another chain of triangles around the open, top edge of the can. Next, the Amazing Henderson comes up with a thick, generic white candle, which he lights, dripping some wax into a saucer, putting the candle in the wax until it stays upright. Then slick as a whistle he turns the coffee can over on the candle.

"Air is sucked in the holes at the bottom," he explains, "and goes out the holes at the top, most of the heat trapped by the can. It gets quite hot. Go on, Mary, put your hands near."

I cup my hands around the can, which already is blazing hot, and soon I feel delicious heat on my face.

I look to John, wondering why we don't have a coffee can stove, it took Henderson all of two minutes to construct one.

I thank Henderson.

"You're so fucking handy with the heat," Tom says, "how come we can't have a hot meal?"

John and I are surprised by Tom's aggression but Henderson smiles. "I ran out of propane and while a coffee can stove might heat up a cup of water and keep your hands warm, it won't cook a full meal. Food's on the table. Shall we?"

In the dining room, table's set, four places with plates and forks. In the middle of the table is a large pot, covered, and a ladle.

In the corner of the dining room, Henderson has constructed a small shelter, two box springs up on their sides, a third balanced over the top, and then a mattress over that. Inside this little shelter there's another mattress and lots of blankets and pillows, with one heavy quilt rigged to cover the opening. Cozy like.

Seeing that I'm staring at it, Henderson says, "I built it here in the dining room because, with the southern exposure, this room usually gets some decent sun and stays warm enough until I get into my little bed cabin there. I'll bring in a couple hot coffee cans and in that little space with the blankets and all, I stay pretty comfortable. Why be cold in a big house when you can be warm in a little shelter?"

Brilliant. I should move in with Henderson.

"Go on," he tells us, motioning toward the dining table, "sit wherever you want."

After we're seated—me in shameless anticipation, John looking down at his lap, Tom glaring at Henderson—our host opens the pot, revealing a huge mound of meat hash. You can see the white potatoes in it, the bright orange of blessed carrots too.

I nearly swoon.

Our host stands, grabs up the ladle, and walks around to fill our three plates with great heaps of hash, placing a more modest amount on his own plate.

Before I can dig in, Tom scrambles across the corner of the table and clamps his hands around Henderson's thick neck, demanding of our host, "Show me the cans, you rotten bastard, *show me the cans!*"

They roll onto the floor with less drama than you might think, Henderson fat and Tom weak.

John raises both hands and covers his face.

I dig in. Yes, I did. It was good. It was protein. I am a woman, I survive. Let the men go to war and anguish over poetry, we women keep the people alive.

They fight, Henderson and Tom, while John weeps and I eat.

Tom is choking Henderson, still demanding to see the cans, I don't even know what the hell he's talking about, John finally standing as if to break up the scuffle, while I stay where I am and eat.

And then the precious protein which I just got down starts to come up. The hash is good but cold and heavy and gluey and I've shoved it in without liquid and now there's a knot in my stomach that feels like a heavy ball, threatening to pitch up while I try my damnedest to keep it down, because I will not by God lose this protein before it does me any good.

Henderson rolls fatly away from Tom and waddles to the kitchen, Tom lurching Igor after him, and my John, face anguished, following, while I sit there shoveling it in again, trying now to get more protein atop the protein that's already unhappily in my stretched stomach.

In the kitchen, a commotion.

I must get something to drink, to break up the clot of hash . . . and I rush into the kitchen to see the three men standing together looking at the contents of a trash can that's been overturned, spilling a dozen cans—corned beef hash and boiled potatoes and sliced carrots.

"Where's the water?" I ask a stricken Henderson, who points to a jug.

Tom opens a cabinet that's absolutely full of cans of food.

John finally speaks. "You've been hoarding all this while your neighbors are starving to death, you are an embarrassment of a man."

Henderson weeping and yet exulting, madness in his eyes, remnant ears bright red, his bald and bruised head glowing with the madness. "Storing up for a rainy day!"

Tom opens another cabinet, more cans of food.

Henderson wailing, a split lip opening to bleed down his multiple chins. "I started a savings account for each child when they were born and put money in on each birthday. I collected gold coins. I was a good provider, small percentage increases in my salary but I got them each and every year and they accumulated because the government's been my only job out of college. I kept going to work during the calamity. I never took sick leave. When the marauders came, I was the only one still on the job. I said, 'May I help you?' You know, in that sarcastic voice you use when someone's doing something they're not supposed to be doing. '*Excuse me, may I help you?*' A lot of people went insane in this calamity. The marauders thought I was one."

John says, "All this food makes you a target for the Patagonians, no wonder they kept hitting your house."

"Each time they wiped us out, I went back to where I had buried the coins and silver and other things I had squirreled away . . . and traded for more food. I didn't intend to let my family starve."

"Instead you got them killed, you idjit. And risked our lives, too. Attracting the Patagonians who knew where food could be found and that's why they kept coming to our neighborhood—"

"*Patagonians!*" Henderson screams with wet eyes, wiping his face and smearing the blood, turning purple with a dangerously elevated blood pressure. "Why do you call them that? Everything has to be clever with you, doesn't it? Can't call them by the names everyone else uses, marauders, rioters, gangs, no, you have to make up a name."

John and I did give them that name, we had no idea it would stick and make it into the history books. From Joyce, yes. Our Patagonians were real monsters, I can guarantee you that. Above all else, they prized showing no emotion, completely without expression no matter what they were doing to you, what you were doing to them. Some of them were children, not even teenagers yet. All of them deadly. During attacks, they wore bizarre outfits, shower caps and wedding veils and sometimes they would dress in a button-down shirt and jacket but then no pants or underpants on. They carried pistols and rifles but their favorite weapons were those machetes and their specialty was lopping off limbs.

Henderson, clearly unhinged, went on screaming at John. "And that fake fuck Irish accent of yours, how it gets thicker and thicker the more you drink, you fake fuck lush."

Henderson obviously didn't have much experience with the cursing.

"What did you do with your family?" Tom demands. "With their *bodies?*"

"What did you do with your daughters, Tom?"

This question shocks Tom and he answers meekly, "I buried them."

"That's what I did. In the backyard. At night. You and I aren't so different. We were friends before these two moved in."

Tom insists he's nothing like Henderson. "I wouldn't've hoarded food while my neighbors starved. I wouldn't've got fat while everyone else was starving into stick figures. Look at you, you pig of a man."

Henderson, grinning now, rubbing his ear stubs like they itched. "But I invited you here tonight, didn't I? Served that hash, didn't I?"

"Can we take some back with us?" I ask him.

"I'm surprised they haven't killed you, too," John says. "The *Patagonians.*"

"I started trading with them. I get tobacco for them, I know where there's a guarded warehouse and I still have gold coins left. I got a plan. Coins for tobacco, tobacco for food, and then I'll get really fat so I can last through the next famine."

"They murdered your family," Tom says, "and you trade with them?"

"I don't trade with the ones who did the killing."

"But—"

"I'm getting fat, you guys are starving to death—you tell me who's the fool."

"But they killed your family!" Tom shouts.

"Killed yours, too, Tom, and now you're dying so I ask again, who's the fool?" Henderson turns to John. "Who's the fool, Mr. Professional Irishman Poet Smartass Everything's A Joke, huh, who's the fool now?"

"They're not to be trusted," John says.

Fat Ass Henderson has become Crazy Ass Henderson, eyes wild and a mad grin stretching his bloated face. "Oh, they knock me around a little, they shaved my head, and sometimes I have to take off my clothes and dance for them, they cut off my ears, but they can be trusted to show up on the nights we're going to trade . . . like tonight."

"You're expecting them *tonight?*" John asks.

"That's why he invited us," Tom says.

Henderson laughing manically. "Come back for dinner anytime."

John and Tom turn to leave the kitchen, a cackling Henderson on their heels, as I ask anyone who will listen, "Can I take some of that hash with me?" Before exiting the kitchen, I grab into a cabinet and come out with a can of pineapple rings in heavy syrup.

We make it to the front door in time to see Patagonians coming up the walk, terrible in their attire and silent demeanor, carrying machetes, one in a full wedding dress including even the veil and two others wearing dress shirts and sports coats but no pants so you can see their half-tumescent dicks.

John turns to me and knocks the can of pineapple slices out of my hand, then leads me and Tom right past the Patagonians, who stare at us with little interest, we are among the starving, and while a few hands come out to run over our bodies, their searches are cursory and, with nothing to our names, we are allowed to pass.

Henderson calls out a panicked welcome to the Patagonians.

Down the block, John tells Tom, "Tomorrow, Mary and I are walking into the District." Which is news to me but I hear the resolve in his voice. "To see if America has a king."

Tom looks back at Henderson's house as we hurry—or hurry as well we can considering the funny way we walk—toward the deeper darkness of our cul-de-sac, getting away from the Patagonians who terrify us, Tom saying to John, "I wouldn't think much of an American king."

"I would, Tom. I have a great wish for him."

Then, just ahead blocking our way, the red eyes of a terrible pig.

Tom has the martyr's look shining in this darkness as he hands John a small roll of string and says, "The rest of it's in my hallway closet. Rolls and rolls of string. Tell your king about me."

"*Our* king. You'll be our first legend."

I have no idea what they're talking about, I'm still shaking from our close encounter with the Patagonians and even more afraid now of the pig in the street . . . when Tom quite suddenly launches himself toward the pig.

John and I flee as Tom decoys the pig, there's a fury of sound, snort and shout, John taking my hand to lead me safely home.

7

All night long demons fresh from hell take turns, and you have to be starving to death to understand why I wasn't at that window screaming—why, instead, I lay very still and tried to sleep through the ravishing of Tom . . . because when you're starving to death the world is dream and nightmare and each hour another mountain, everything hurts, but mostly a sense of bony deep dread pulls down everywhere like extragravity gravel filling all your pockets.

For this new day, my largest concern, instead of poor Tom, is keeping hash down. I had eaten! And now protein must do its work, nourish my starving cells, repair the breaks, put back some small portion of what had been used up. So when I prayed to God last night it wasn't mercy for shrieking Tom outside my window but for me not to vomit, please, Lambchop of God, I pray forgive me my selfish, oafish, eaterly nature.

I wish to brush my teeth, a wish that starts each day unfulfilled. The food weighed heavily on me, no pun possible in my condition, like I was suffering a hangover, but I had kept the hash down and by now it has started to move into bowels, vomiting no longer an issue, next comes the threat of diarrhea.

John in the living room up all night.

"He's gone," John says.

I take a moment to make sure I can speak the name. "Tom loved us both."

"There is no greater love."

"He was a good man."

"Pig finished all of Thomas, all of what he was and had ever been, father, husband, officer, *friend,* all he'd been in all his yesterdays will be pigshit tomorrow. There's a lesson in that, Mary."

"I heard them last night."

"I heard *him* last night. Are you ready?"

"For what?"

"We're walking to the White House."

"You're serious about this?"

"I am, Mary." He comes to me. "We'll find jackets along the way. And better shoes."

"No we won't. There's nothing left." I meant in America.

"Look." He holds up a ball of string the size of a big fist. "From Tom's house. Remember he told us where it was? I went to get it early this morning. There were a dozen rolls in his closet. I'm taking this one with us."

"Why?"

"Give it to our king."

"Oh Christ."

"With our king we will talk of many things, Mary. Of sealing wax and, yes, of string, of parliamentary procedures and the death of American dreams."

"You're crazy. And I don't mean that in a nice way."

"We've both gone crazy with the starvation," John says. "Should we just stay here and die? Die here in this suburban cold house?"

I am tempted to do exactly that but instead I tell my husband, "Let's go."

Once outside—the day bright, brisk, sun warm, though I'm freezing—I look to where Tom was killed by the pig, there's nothing of him to mark the spot, not blood or guts or mangled clothing, just the ground rooted up ready to sow.

"Let's walk over to the parkway," John says after a while. "Some safety in being out in the open."

Hurrying past Henderson's, we give the house our evil eye.

No one's out or about in suburbia, no uneaten dogs bark, children aren't riding on bikes, no vehicles roll. John and I are the last two humans on this particular earth. The standing people still stand, however, and many are in bud.

The capital of America seems far away and walking there must be impossible so I ask John to tell me again why we're going.

"I don't know, Mary," he says, exhausted. "Nothing's left for us back there."

I turn around. Back there is only a few blocks back. Progress is slow when you walk funny.

"Our neighbors are dead," John continues. "Either killed by Patagonians or starved or eaten by pigs. Except Henderson, in trade with the Patagonians. I have the strongest sense that in the District of Columbia, our nation's capital, people have gathered there to put America back on her feet. And that the people are being led by a great man. Not elected. Not commissioned. But born, Mary. A king."

"If there's a feast at the king's castle, maybe we'll get invited."

"You ate last night."

"I could eat again."

"I don't see a cat or a squirrel even."

I tell John that I'd eat a squirrel. "I have relatives who eat squirrels."

"That America has come to this, hard to believe."

I point out to John he's been making a lot of wistful references to America lately, John the left-leaning poet professor who loves to bash these United States.

Astonishingly, he declares, "I'm full-blood American."

I can only pray he's being sarcastic.

"Second-generation Irish," he says. "American through and through. Born in New York City, no joke."

"John, you're playing with string."

He looks down at his hands.

We walk. I think we're making our way over to the George Washington Parkway. I'm not sure. As we walk, we don't talk and often I close my eyes. It is most unusual for John to go so long not talking.

Old Town Alexandria, Virginia, an original port and warehouse district, once officially part of Washington, turned into chic restaurants and tourist shops with expensive, old town houses on cobblestone streets—Old Town burned now and in ruins. Fires are everywhere smoldering, the stench makes my eyes water. Smoke is over the Potomac, sailing upstream. During the last several weeks we had smelled these fires and we had seen their smoke. These fires were among the reasons we gave ourselves for not leaving suburbia, convinced that everything else was burning. And now in the middle of all this devastation, John's river starts flowing again.

"The Soviet writer Vasily Grossman wrote about Stalingrad after being bombed by the Nazis. Stalingrad is burned down, he wrote. Stalingrad is dead. People are in the basements. The walls of the buildings are hot like the bodies of the people, dead but not yet gone cold. It went something like that. Tipping points, Mary. We weren't smart enough about tipping points. A society doesn't run out of gasoline gradually, a little at a time, fewer and fewer able to buy gas, until nothing is left. Instead, as gas is used up, eventually a tipping point is reached and the oil-based fuel system can no longer be sustained, it's over and collapse is instant and inevitable. Especially when the rich people seize everything."

We walk through a ruined Old Town, who could've known it would come to this, not a downturn, not a depression, but a collapse so complete that our American renaissance has become another dark age.

"Nothing happens," John continues, "and then everything happens. A million years go by without a meteorite striking the earth, nothing happens, then one day it happens. And everything changes. Same in our personal lives. Nothing happens, nothing happens, then something happens, and everything changes."

We note everywhere the bodies of rats, pink foam about their mouths.

"The plague," John says. "It races through the rat population until the fleas, the plague carriers, are desperate for new hosts and jump from dead rat to living person."

Vigilant now, I watch for rat bodies and avoid them like something.

"When's our next meal?"

"The questions you ask, Mary, are too hard for my head."

We walk down King Street toward the Potomac River, I am too tired and gracious to comment on the name of the street we walk . . . while John notes lengths of rope tied about the tops of the old-fashioned lampposts. Just under the glass light atop each post are two decorative spikes, and these have been used here and there to hold loops of rope with trailing ends that are frayed.

John says the people have been hanging the rich from the lampposts. "The poor outnumber the rich and come in hordes to pull the rich out of their mansions and hang them from lampposts."

"Wishful thinking, John. I think it's looters who were hanged."

He's not listening. "We'll use our numbers against the rich, that's how we'll win in the end. One thing the poor can always do better than the rich, breed."

I am too tired and hungry to be hurt by this reference, that John and I never had children when once upon a time I desperately wanted a child with John.

We pass a sign, NATIONAL STONE, SAND & GRAVEL ASSOCIATION, and John says, "Oh, look, Mary, they've even organized the wee little rocks into an association."

He used to make this same crack pretty much every time we passed this way back before the calamity, except this time I don't laugh as I always did before.

We walk past ruin, past rack, past royalty cross streets, a majestic restaurant, all the shops looted and torched except a big bookstore, largely intact with the books unstolen on their shelves.

"There you go, Mary," he says, "the value of literature, no one will even bother stealing it."

In the next block, I grab John's arm. "I smell french fries."

He sniffs the air. "My Dear God . . ."

"Somebody's frying something."

"Let's go see."

We walk straight down King, past former warehouses that were converted into expensive restaurants, to the Potomac River, to a pocket park where John and I would on occasion, back before the calamity, sit on a bench in this tiny park to contemplate the life we lived while watching the river, always going, never gone.

Sitting now on that very bench, I contemplate nothing but the fried food we can both smell. Where is it coming from? This is maddening, these phantom fries, those bastard French.

We sit awhile longer, sun warming on our faces. Occasionally, along with the odor of fried food I get a whiff of my unsoaped self, smelling like the river smells right there a few feet away only more personally rank. "Look at that boat, John."

He studies the boat tied at the end of the park, a dashing motorboat, thirty feet, bright red in color, and finally John says, "It doesn't
look abandoned like the others."

"You see its name?"

"Maybe that's where the French fries are being fried."

"You think they'll give us some?"

"We could ask."

We walk to the boat and stand there. It floats even with the land.
A fence has been torn down, allowing us, if we chose, to board the
boat. Without discussion, John steps onto the boat, then turns to
me as if to say, see, easy as pie. I reach out to join him across the airy
gap when from below comes a big white man with blued gun.

Managing to stop in mid-step, I stumble backward and fall on
my bony ass while John is caught there aboard. Big white man holding long blue gun points muzzle at John's anguished face.

We've seen killings. Since this calamity began, half a dozen
human beings John and I have seen murdered in front of our hollow eyes, a throat slit, one baseball-batted, others shot and
chopped. We will forever remember how people die, their individual ballets, the way they dance with hands to throat or holding the
part that got shot. From the killers, we've also come to recognize a
certain stance, an attitude, *a commitment* to death that the killer rep-
resents shortly before using bat, blade, gun. Forget the colorful
curses and grand gestures, when the decision to kill is made, there's
grimness in his eye.

Grim with gun to shoulder, this white man is a short trigger pull
away from killing my husband when John says, "Mercy." He doesn't
plead it or beg it, he simply speaks the word.

The white man lowers his weapon, then puts it again to cheek,
then lowers it again. I think he once upon a time was a big slab of a
man, thinner now but still with the look of roast beef and red potatoes. Thick forearms, thick wrists, the hair on his arms bleached

blond by the sun. He's missed a few meals lately but is not starving to death. Light brown hair, big round face, ruddy complexion, clean-shaven, and the devil's own blue eyes. He's wearing khaki trousers, boat shoes, and a red hooded sweatshirt, without sayings or logos on it and the hood down.

"Mercy when you're at the end of a gun," the big white man finally says, speaking haltingly like he's translating in his head, "but I'd wager not so much mercy for me if you'd gotten below and slit my throat."

"We're starving."

Remarkably composed and quiet-voiced, this big white man with long gun looks over at me and agrees with my husband. "You're the hungriest people I've seen so far . . . especially her."

"The quality of mercy is not strained," John tells him.

"What do you mean by that?"

John teaches poetry and loves recitation so now he opens the gates and when he gets to the part about the fear and dread of kings, the man abruptly points the gun skyward and says, "Hold it right there. What you said about kings."

John telling him, "We've come to find our American king."

The man puts the big gun on the deck as across his wide face spreads a look of astonished love.

John tries to explain. "I believe America has a king now."

"So do I!"

While I think, good Lord, men everywhere mad on this royalty.

John says, "Even now he prepares a table for us."

"I agree with you but I don't understand the way you talk."

"Let me try to explain it in simple terms. When the Sultan Shah-Zaman goes to the city Ispahan, even before he gets so far as the place where the clustered palm-trees are . . . the pet of the harem, Rose-in-bloom, orders a feast in his favorite room . . . glittering squares of colored ice, sweetened with syrup and tinctured with spice. Also, creams and cordials. Sugared dates, Syrian apples. And wines known to Eastern princes."

The man weeps to hear it, telling John to take a seat, indicating a canvas chair, then offering me his hand, "Come aboard, lady."

John asks his name.

"Boat."

"Yes, it's a great boat. And you're a wonderful boatman not to shoot us."

"How long have you been living on your boat?" I ask.

"A year. More." He looks at John. "And we all got this idea separately about a king, huh?"

John says, "There's a theory of how certain things, great ideas and important insights, how they occur simultaneously to many people in separate places without any of the usual means of communication."

The man nodding, agreeing. "People everywhere in America getting tugged here thinking of a king. Like geese flying south, I know exactly what you mean."

I want to say, so far it's only the two of you who are migrating on behalf of an American king, but I keep quiet and wait for the french fries.

John says, "I think what we have here, here in America, is a general *assumption* of a king."

The boatman speaks wistfully, like a man in love, telling my John, "Everything before was a dream and now I'm awake."

I have exactly the opposite feeling.

"Excuse me," I finally interrupt. "May I please have some of those french fries?"

"What fries?" the boatman asks.

"I smell fries, don't be coy."

He nods, finally understanding. "My diesel runs on vegetable oil, that's what you're smelling—the exhaust. I stop at ports, take a cart and a barrel and a pump, break into restaurants and fast-food places. All the food's been long ago stolen but there's plenty of old oil . . . there's practically an endless supply of the stuff."

"That's what brought us to you," I tell him. "You smell like french fries."

"Thank you, ma'am." Then to John, "Where's the king at this moment?"

"In D.C."

John has dreamed all this up.

The boatman asks what he can do.

John says, "Do you know where the steps come down to the water?"

"I do."

"Lay off there under the bridge and wait for a signal."

"I will."

What the *hell* are they talking about?

"I won't keep you any longer then," the man says. "I know you have to get to where you're going." He helps us make the step from his boat to the ground.

I've missed half of what they were talking about. "About those fries . . ."

John says, "There are no fries, Mary."

This is terrible news.

The boatman tells us to wait a minute as he hurries below.

I take John's arm and complain, "I don't know what's going on."

Boatman returns with a brown paper bag, which he hands across to me.

"Fries?" I ask.

He smiles enigmatically, like maybe fries, maybe not fries.

John hands him a length of string. "Tie this around your left wrist. By this string, the king's people will know you as one of us."

The guy accepts the piece of string like something holy.

By the time we leave the park, I have opened the paper bag, bringing out one of several little packages tied in newspaper and rubber bands, hoping against hope to find french fries. When I finally get the first package open, I yell.

"What is it?" John asks.

"Baloney and cheese!"

"The way you hollered, I thought you'd seen Jesus."

"To the starving, John, God appears as a sandwich."

"I've heard that before, where's it from?"

I couldn't answer, my mouth was full.

8

We walked a biking, hiking path between the river and the parkway. No one is about. The Potomac flows on our right without a burden of boats and, to our left, the parkway's pavement is empty of cars. America had run out of oil, the remaining gasoline confiscated and stored underground by the Federal government or in depots guarded by mercenaries in the pay of rich Americans.

Near the path, everything is grown up. Fallen limbs stay where they have fallen. Here and there are wrecked cars. A big Greyhound bus looks as if it had been used as living quarters, trash all around and clotheslines to nearby trees. But the bus is empty now. John and I walk.

I worry what'll happen if we encounter Patagonians. Even with nothing to steal, we're vulnerable. They might kill us for sport. Or cut off our arms. And all without speaking a word.

"We'll walk up to Memorial Bridge and cross there," John says. I think the boatman's unexpected enthusiasm for the idea of an American king has knocked John off balance, making him wonder if he's stumbled onto something truly magical.

I eat from Boatman's bag, offering portions to John who is deep in a calculation of possibilities. I don't know how the idea of a king can be bigger than baloney and cheese, but John clearly is distracted.

We're losing the day. Although I've finished Boatman's food, still I'm running out of energy. "Can we stop for the night?"

John looks at me as if he'd forgotten I was along.

"Stop? Yes," he says. "We don't want to go into the District at night. Let's sleep by those trees."

Here we are, two Americans of the modern era, stopping to sleep by trees the way my migrating ancestors might've done a thousand years ago at this very spot.

Except my ancestors wouldn't be looking in the sprung trunk of a wrecked car, which John does, finding a cheap plastic blue tarp. I ask him if we can put it over us for a blanket but John says the tarp will serve better as a ground cover, to keep the damp and cold from seeping up into our frail bodies. He says he'll look for something to put over us.

"No fire tonight?"

He doesn't think we should risk the attention it might bring.

Fire's a wonderful invention, I think, but, unlike our ancestors, we can't use it. For security reasons. Such is life in the modern era.

I ask John if someone can die of misery. "I know I don't have hypothermia but I am so tired and miserable of being cold. My feet hurt and itch and, last time I checked, the skin was cracking."

He pats my leg.

"No, John, the question wasn't rhetorical. *Can a person die from being miserable?*"

He said he didn't know, then he explained I had chilblains, that's what was causing my skin to crack and itch and hurt. "You have to keep your feet dry."

"I'm cold."

"Didn't Boatman's food help?"

"I suppose. Yes, it helped. I would've been colder without that food. I ate it all, John. I'm so sorry."

"No, you offered. I'm just . . . distracted."

"With thoughts of kings?"

"Yes."

John spreads the blue plastic tarp on the ground to the lee of a burned-out Mercedes SUV. In the twilight we can see fires here and there, across the river and down the way. In deference to John's somber mood, I don't start in again about how we should build our own nice, warm fire. He saw me shivering though and John said he would bring over dead leaves, there were tons of them around and they were dry and would make good insulation.

"How are you going to get them?"

"Stand up, I'll use the tarp."

"I'll help you. John?"

"What?"

"Are you okay?"

"Fine."

"If I lost you, I couldn't go on."

We took the tarp to the trees and filled it several times, bringing each load to the burned-out car, piling leaves there until we had a mound large enough to cover both of us. We spread the tarp on the ground again and repiled the leaves on it. He put some spidery limbs over the top to keep the leaves in place, though the night was thankfully windless.

We burrowed in. Primates make a simple leaf nest at night, we are primates. This den had none of the comforts of a real bed, I don't want to give a false impression, but the leaf-mound offered a nesting feel and filled my head with a powdery scent.

John and I had leaves between us but we could touch each other if it came to that.

"Cozy now?" he asked through the leaves.

I was a million miles from cozy but told him, "It's pretty nice, actually."

"The human body at rest produces two hundred and fifty BTUs per hour. That's about the energy from a seventy-five-watt bulb. You'll be taking off your clothes next."

I laughed.

He said it's been a blue moon since he heard me laugh.

Yes, put a baloney and cheese sandwich in me, I become a party girl.

I think if you start out your life sleeping in a bed, you never get used to sleeping on the ground. I hated it during all those years of the calamity. And on that cold hard ground under leaves and next to a Mercedes, I remember Tom's death. Pigs scavenge at night. Now every sound I hear will put a fist in my throat. My stomach churns and I pray to keep Boatman's sandwiches down.

"Tonight's the calm," John says. "Tomorrow we open the hinge of history."

"You mean meeting that king?"

He says yes that's exactly what he meant.

Here I am worrying about pigs while John has kings and history hinges on his mind.

"John?"

"Yes."

"How will you know him?"

His answer comes quickly. "He'll be magical from first sight. It won't be one of those situations like when you meet someone of note but the person is so unprepossessing that later on you say you had no idea he or she was important. This one, this king, he will prepossess from the git-go. Something distinctive about him. An aspect of the man. A sense of possibility, of danger, of magic. There will be about him a certain magnificence. The loose and confident way he walks. His eyes are green."

Later in the night I hear John whispering prayers and I feel sorry for my husband, a lapsed Catholic yearning for grace and praying for the impossibility of an American king. His Hail Marys are heart wrenching.

"John," I say, reaching through the leaves to find his papery hand.

"I have such a great wish for him, Mary."

"I know you do."

9

Another adamant day depressed me awake, shivering, needing to pee, a terrible rumble in the bowels. This next hour will be nasty. As if to offer a hopeful answer or mock me, I'm not sure which, clouds separated and light broke across the river to flood our little grove. John reached through the leaves and pulled me close. He spoke with fetid breath, which didn't disgust me, this was, after all, my beloved John, but which did make me feel bone sad for the man. We were both such wrecks. What he said, however, stood in vivid and hopeful contrast to the way he smelled. John called me his little darlin' and told me not to worry, here comes the sun.

10

John waited patiently for me to get over my bowel sickness. I washed off in the Potomac River. Moving upstream from where I had just cleaned my hands, I leaned to the freezing river and drank directly as one has learned to do in this calamity. God knows what's in the water and what it'll do to my tortured innards.

"Ready?" John asks brightly when I return to him.

I nod.

On Memorial Bridge we encounter the first people of the District. They've been propped in sitting and leaning positions along the concrete railings and sidewalks of the bridge. When we see that many are missing hands, missing arms, we know it was Patagonians that made these killings. A few of the bodies have been decapitated and propped into sitting positions on benches, holding their heads on their laps. Thus are we welcomed to the nation's capital, by a boulevard of atrocities. The cool weather has preserved the bodies in fair condition but with the sun warm today and spring coming, the stench will be unbearable soon enough. They'll be tipped over the rail and into the river, a burial that thousands have undoubtedly already received—and when I recall drinking downstream from here, I get stomach sick and soul sick.

John puts an arm around my shoulder and we walk like that across the bridge. The first living people stare at us strangely. They seem relatively normal. No one appears prosperous or fat but, still, compared to John and me . . . and that's when I realize they're staring at us with repugnance because we are walking skeletons, their own personal forecasts, which they find appalling.

An older woman in a heavy coat offers me an apple. I shrink back. Something must be wrong with that apple, people don't give food to strangers. She's crazy, she's a witch. But then I see her eyes, wet with pity, and I take the apple and am ashamed.

As if I am committing some perverse act, I eat half the apple with my head turned away from the other people we see on the bridge. I offer the other half to John.

He shakes his head.

I tell him, "You're scaring me. You keep turning down food, first from Boatman and now this apple. John. What's wrong with you?"

He shakes his head but I insist.

"It's my teeth."

I look at his mouth, which he's keeping closed. "What's wrong with them?"

"They hurt. They're loose in their sockets. Like my whole jaw is coming apart."

"Oh, John."

A dental problem in our current situation is horrible.

"You need vitamins, you need the citrus in this apple."

"If I try to eat," he tells me quietly, "my teeth will come out."

I chew a bite of apple until it's mushy and then finger it over to my husband, telling him to suck on it and swallow the juice—

which he does eagerly, wiping his mouth and weeping just a little. I feed him another piece. "Why are you crying, you big baby."

"Exactly. A baby, toothless, fed by hand, *a baby.*" He wipes his eyes with filthy hands and cries openly as people gather around us to gawk.

"Can you spare some food?" I ask, apparently shameless.

They are horrified, not at my request but at our condition.

John tells me, "Don't shame yourself."

"The shame is on them," I say, loud enough to make sure they hear. Still, my words don't get us even a slice of bread.

We walk around to the Lincoln Memorial and here, on the steps and filling the great expanse beyond, *here* are the citizens of the nation's capital, clustered in groups, circled around fires, moving in a great swirl of activity that appears aimless . . . we can smell the smoke of their campfires and the stench of their garbage and sewer, we hear their shouts and see small riots break out here and there, one group overpowering another or a single individual set upon by dozens, caught, dragged away. I want to go home and starve in suburbia.

"Come on," John says, taking my hand. "People won't bother us."

"Why are we the only ones starving?"

John doesn't know. "Is there more apple?"

But we have finished it to seed and stem.

"I wouldn't mind having some more even if it made my gums sting," he says, opening his mouth to inhale cooling breaths. What I see inside that mouth is unspeakable.

We pass among the people and John is right, they leave us alone. Although they aren't starving the way we were starving, still they have about them a demeanor that's equal parts fear, bitterness, anxiety.

As we walk down the steps and away from the Lincoln Memorial, John produces two lengths of string to tie around our left wrists.

"John, for crying out loud . . ."

"Indulge me."

I do.

With strings around our wrists, we walk along the Reflecting Pool, which is stagnant. Several cars and one city bus are in the water. None of the usual ducks, however. Have the people been eating ducks and park squirrels, is that how they've put off starvation?

Bodies are strewn around the World War II Memorial, and they have been here long enough to raise a stink.

"John, let's go back."

He shakes his head. "To the White House."

"Oh my God."

"What?"

"Look, someone's blown up the Washington Monument."

When we get closer, we see that the monument was apparently toppled by a plane—the burned wreckage of an aircraft mixed and mingled with charred-black stone from the monument.

"Terrorists?" I ask.

John doesn't know but speculates it was an accident. In the final weeks of commercial aviation, plane wrecks became commonplace as desperate people bribed and bullied flights that should've never taken off as airport services were shutting down and fuel became increasingly contaminated.

As we cross Constitution Avenue, we encounter gathering crowds. This is intimidating, frightening, noise from people incessantly talking, shouting, arguing. As loud people spot us, however, they grow quiet with morbid curiosity for our walking skeletons.

John occasionally holds up his left wrist to show the string.

Embarrassed, I tell him to put his hand down. "John, these people don't know what the string means." How could they, he just made it up yesterday.

The Ellipse is thronged by refugees, the displaced, walking wounded, those who are lost, children stunned into silence, people hungry though not starving, not yet.

Away from the parks it is less crowded, John and I circling around on various streets, eventually joining a crowd in Lafayette Park, across Pennsylvania Avenue from the White House.

"What's going on?" John asks a fellow in the crowd, who starts to answer until he sees our condition and then backs away like we're plague carriers.

A young woman presses a stale roll into my hand and moves off into the crowd before I can thank her. The bread is hard, John will never be able to eat it unless I chew it first. Pre-chewing that apple for him was easy but handing him a warm piece of masticated bread will test our bond.

I'm gnawing on the roll when John announces he's going to work his way through the crowd and see what's going on across the street at the White House.

I tell him we are *not* splitting up.

Holding hands and bracing ourselves against the touch of others, we maneuver among the people who are resentful of being pushed until they turn and see us, then step aside.

I get another chunk of the stale roll bitten off and into my mouth where I chew it like hardened gum.

We are stuck on Pennsylvania, too many people. The crowds spook me toward panic and I hold tightly to John. My bones are kite sticks and my skin parchment paper, too delicate for jostling crowds. And I resent their frank stares.

I'm gnawing on my stale roll when John abruptly shakes my shoulder, causing me to drop the roll. I curse and fall to my knees, thinking I'll have to scrabble for it and fend off others—but no one bothers trying to steal my bread, which I grab from the pavement and hold meagerly with both hands, pressing stale roll to ribby chest.

John is still trying to get my attention, pulling on my clothes and speaking my name.

"What, for chrissakes, John, what is it?"

"*Look*. It's him, Mary. Our American king!"

11

What was he really like? See, that's the second of the three questions people always ask me. Everything you've heard about what kind of man he was in the beginning, when he was still good-hearted and true, it's all accurate and historically correct—he was perfectly formed and magnificent. Not just charisma. That's what everyone says, he had charisma. Yes, but more than that. Certain people in history have about them an aura of greatness, of otherwordly differentness, and these certain individuals compel us. How did Joan of Arc, a sixteen-year-old farm girl, convince the royal court to give her an army and then lead that army to defeat the English? Certain people of greatness have a basic quality that resonates with us, that our genetic makeup remembers from a million years of evolution. That's what Tazza was like.

Sections of the piked fence around the White House had been pushed down, unescorted citizens wandering the grounds, and I asked John, "Have we taken over the White House?" Meaning *we, the people.* He doesn't know, doesn't answer, isn't listening to me—

my husband lasered on the man there by the fence, a crowd tightly around this man John supposes to be our king.

I can see only bits and pieces of what's going on, people moving in front of me as I grasp tightly to John's waistband, which offers a generous handhold.

The man in question is too far away for me to know if his eyes are green but everything else John has predicted seems true enough: a commanding presence.

But nothing obviously royal in apparel, he's wearing blue jeans and a white shirt, a man just over six feet. He moves, the crowd shifts, and I see then several bodies hanging from the White House fence. Short lengths of rope have been tied around their ankles, the other ends looped over the spikes in the fence. Their heads are hanging a few inches above the sidewalk, ashen faces turned away from us and toward the fence. Several more bodies are on the ground as yet unhung. They are all men and they are all wearing suits, jackets open and draped all wrong now that they're dead.

John's king does an extraordinary thing, he grasps a body on the ground, grabbing lapel and belt, and lifts the body into a short arc with such power and grace that you think for sure he's going to toss the body completely over the fence, feet first, if such a thing were possible, but, instead, he swings the upside-down body until the loop of rope catches around a fence pike, then he lets the body hang down while he turns its face toward the fence.

"I hang them the way they spoke their words," he tells us. "Upside down and backwards."

John and I join the cheering even though we are ignorant of the context—who is it hanging there from the White House fence and how had they died and, if killed, *why?*

He speaks to us, answering questions he hasn't been asked, walking the line of hanging bodies.

"This traitor was elected to Congress a poor man representing working families, but after he became rich he could be counted on to vote against unions. He has betrayed us for the last time."

As we cheer again, I glance at John's face—radiant.

"This one's a senator born to wealth," the man continues. "He was given every privilege, yet he would not open his pockets to help his citizens who were starving."

This king walks from the fence to come among us, people everywhere reaching out to touch something of him, a sleeve, an arm, his hand.

He returns to the bodies on the ground and nudges one errant arm, French-cuffed. "We have lobbyists with their fists full of dollars, we have the wealthy who never gave anything back, and, here, this one, he was a consultant who specialized in firing people, downsizing they called it, he got bonuses doing it, firing with equal fervor the newly employed with young familes and the old people with no hope of getting another job, and he became famous for a technique he called, 'Listen, nod, nothing.' When someone came to him to talk about being fired after twenty years of loyal service, he would listen, nod sympathetically, and then do absolutely nothing for the person. He would brag about his work and make fun of grown men who cried to lose their jobs. We know all this because one of the workers he fired brought him here and as you can see we downsized him good."

This speech he's giving is not loud, no broad gestures, it's more like he's talking intimately to a small group of us.

He grabs the one who's French-cuffed and lifts him to hang him by the rope around his ankles, upside down from the White House fence.

We cheer, he comes among us again.

When I can see him up close, it's like falling in love. His head seems large, his face heavy. He has even features. I enjoy looking at him, it's a restorative, and my empty stomach feels the full excitement of his presence. The mood among us is as if anything can happen—miracles or fistfights. His complexion is dark but not like mine, more tan than blood, his thick hair, fingered straight back, is black. John was right, lucky guess or not—the man's eyes are green, green like seawater is green on those days when it looks like green paint. When the man passes closest to us (he doesn't notice or speak to John or me), his scent is strong. Not body odor but something distinctive. I'm not repulsed by his smell, in fact I felt a twinge of something long dormant.

Speaking now to people who have circled close around, the man says, "We have measured their offenses. And they have been weighed guilty by the hundred-weight and by the penny-pound." Cheers! "At a time when leaders were needed most, they abandoned us and looked after their own, after the power brokers and money holders. Where are our real leaders? Not among those hanging from the fence and ten thousand more like them, haughty and high and mighty—where are *the people's leaders?* Where are our poor kings with stars in their eyes?"

At the mention of kings, John squeezes my hand, but it proves to be a passing reference.

"Instead of great chiefs with fiery visions, we were given small men on fat accounts. We were given men and women who know nothing of us, who instead of spinning stories of our greatness, they spun the truth to suit themselves. Where are the presidents and ministers who leave public service impoverished because they were rivers to their people? No wonder we hang them upside down and backwards. They are America's shame and we don't want to see their faces."

We repeatedly cheer this voice.

He moves away and says things down the line that cause others to cheer as wildly as we had. This is the most exciting moment of my life—of John's, too.

He hollers at a tall man near us, "What's his name?"

In the din, we don't understand the shouted reply.

"Who is he?" John asks, hoping to hear *king* in reply.

But the tall man shrugs and moves away from us, crazy skeleton people.

John is trying to drag me through the crowds to get closer to the king when *again* there he is right in front of us, except this time he sees us, looking right at us. He stops everything and takes John and me by our stick arms, moving us gently out of the crowd, leading us back to the fence, and then turning us to face the people.

"Do you see this?" he asks, his voice soaring. "These are *Americans*. Starving to death. Millions across America have already starved. There was enough to go around but everything was confiscated by our leaders, by the rich, the power class. They holed up on military bases and on islands and on peninsulas and for a while there in the White House, staying well fed while *this* is what happened to America." Again he indicated us, putting powerful arms around our bony shoulders. "This is what they want for us, America. *This* is the plan those hanging from that fence had for us. We are better than this!"

John and I are horrified to be paraded as a terrible fate in store for the rest of them, yet we're thrilled to be in the center of this great man's attention.

The people shout. "Tazza! Tazza!"

Hearing it clearly now, John whispers that name, repeats it, rolls *Tazza* in his mouth like something hard and sweet.

The man strides back and forth in front of the people, exalting them and smiling and holding out both arms to figuratively embrace his people. He is bold, magical, dangerous, commanding, magnificent. People love him. John and I love him. We love Tazza.

He is such a natural king that we *assume* this love for him and hope he loves us back, are thrilled when he says he does.

Americans never felt our worth, the true weight of our own worth, until this man spoke to us.

He takes John and me with him, Tazza mobbed by those who wish to speak a word or hear one from him, to touch him, to ask a favor, to tell of some loss, to see if they can see in his eyes that he loves them.

He's tireless and we follow in his wake, joyous people weeping.

12

When we get to the Executive Office Building where Tazza has set up headquarters, John asks constant questions as people bring food.

"I could keep you as my hunger artist," Tazza says when noticing John is too busy talking to eat. "Parade you as what should never be, an American starving to death."

"You know the story?" John asks. " 'A Hunger Artist'?"

Tazza smiles, he has big white teeth and is so magnificent up close that once again I feel a sexual tug, it's a wonder he can produce such a feeling in a starving woman.

Tazza finally orders to John stop talking and eat, here comes more food.

I don't have to be told twice.

Tazza talks . . . of what happened here in Washington and other cities across America, the rich and power classes grabbing storehouses, commandeering food and supplies, fuel and medicine, everything cached on military bases or large complexes of defended buildings, defended by armed government forces. It was like when those hurricanes hit New Orleans back in the day, how the people were abandoned by the government, by the police who took care of their own.

When a bowl of soup is set in front of John, he attacks it with a fist-gripped spoon, causing Tazza to laugh. I smile too and we eat, this is wonderful, we've been delivered. Bread. They give us bread. Oh my God, there's butter.

John asks Tazza about his name.

"It's my mother's maiden name."

"Italian?" John asks.

Tazza is considering the answer when on a lark I ask him, "What's your nation?"

He doesn't answer the question but says, "People mispronounce my name . . . they go, '*Tahhh-zzza.*' When actually it's more *Tat-sa.* But I think people like saying the *z,* stretching it out."

John asks him if it's his given name.

"I use just Tazza."

I say to John, "Explain to Tazza why we're here."

John bends to the soup without speaking.

Tazza asks, "Why are you here?"

Knowing I won't let this slide, John fesses up, "To speak to a king." He brings out a length of the Tom string, which he ties around Tazza's right wrist and tells him, "All those who follow the king tie string around their left wrists." John holds up his left wrist and asks me to do likewise, showing off our string. Then he points to Tazza. "The king ties string around his *right* wrist."

Tazza considers this a moment, I expect him to laugh, but he asks solemnly, "How many are there with string around their wrists, what are our numbers?"

John won't answer him but I tell the truth, "With Boatman and you, that makes, let's see . . . *four.*"

Tazza laughs loudly, others in the room looking over at us.

I feel sick from eating too much too quickly and Tazza, seeing this, directs that the food be taken from John and me. I watch my soup leave and pray for its safe return. Tazza tells us, "Let your bodies digest what you've eaten, get some rest, clean up, then you can have another meal."

"It'll all be gone," I say, panicked.

"No, there's plenty."

John asks how can there be plenty. "We were starving to death in the suburbs, not ten miles from here."

"I liberated warehouses of food, that's why I'm a hero." How can a man speak without irony of himself being a hero? "Did you know I was a hero here in Washington? Is that why you came looking for me?"

John doesn't answer so I tell Tazza, "No, he thought you were the king."

Tazza says he is. He's the hero, he's the king.

It can't be that easy, can it?

I have handmaidens. Two young women, one black, the other white, dressed in jeans and clean white blouses, padding around on clean bare feet, young women who talk incessantly of Tazza, how people weep to hear him speak of hope and how he could inspire the dispirited to take up arms and hope and how he protects his people from rioters and marauders—and here I take them to mean Patagonians—and how hot he is and what they would do with him given half the chance . . . as great as any rock star, this Tazza . . . so say my handmaidens as they bring buckets of warm water to half fill a fifty-gallon barrel.

I expect them to leave me alone so I can strip and use a chair to climb into the barrel of warm water but, no, they are handmaidens and they proceed to unbutton and pull apart my old, torn, body-odor-stiff rags that pass for clothing.

Weeping with the shame of the way I look and smell, especially as I see my condition reflected as pity and disgust in the mirrors of their young unlined soft faces, I try to push their hands away even as the warm water beckons.

"Now, mother," the black one tells me. "Be good and let us help you."

The other one adds, "After your bath, you'll get new jeans and a nice white blouse."

Later they explain to me that Tazza commands an army of scavengers who can find anything, who just last week liberated a warehouse of clothing, mostly jeans and white shirts and white blouses.

The prospect of being clean and wearing new clothes is akin to the promise of salvation so I surrender myself to their nimble fingers and soon am naked. Now it is the young women who weep.

I apologize repeatedly.

They say it's nothing I have to be sorry for.

The young women help my naked, ravaged, bent, stick form mount a chair and, from there, they lift and lower me into the water. I feel churlish for wishing it was hotter.

"We have soap," the white one says.

I look at her blue eyes. "You have hope?" I ask.

"Soap."

It's the same thing, does she realize that?

"We're going to wash you."

I don't think I can permit that.

They insist.

It's three sets of sudsy hands, mine and theirs, that plunge into that warm water barrel to soap me.

"There was no water to bathe in where we were," I say, to

explain my filthy condition. "Sometimes we barely had water to drink, draining it out of hot water heaters."

"Tazza and the scavengers," the white woman tells me, "located wells and rigged up hand pumps. They chlorinate the water and distribute it everywhere. Then we have this other water, which you're bathing in, which is probably okay but hasn't been chlorinated."

When we have soaped my pitiful body from face to waist, I pull their hands out of the water and insist I'll clean the rest of the way down. I ask the women if we can dump this barrel and then fill it again so I can wash a second time in clean water.

They discuss my request, the white one goes out to ask about this rare privilege of double bathing, while the black woman helps me shampoo my matted hair.

The other woman returns carrying two buckets of water, which she pours into another barrel there in this large conference room.

"So it's okay?" the black one asks.

"Anything she wants," the other one says, indicating me.

"Tazza must really like you," the black one whispers conspiratorially as if we are harem mates and word has come back of the master's approval.

The women fill this new barrel and, after a second bath in clean water, I am renewed. Handmaidens dry me, murmuring *you poor thing*. I am dressed in clothes so clean I want to hug myself.

While trying to fit me with shoes, the young woman who is white asks about John. "Is he your husband?"

"Yes. We've been married twenty-one years."

"He's a talker."

"John talks rivers," I tell her.

"Instead of taking a bath or eating again, he's still sitting out there talking to Tazza."

"About being a king."

"A king?"

The young black woman comes over to deal with my hair, humming as she brushes and untangles. She has to pull hard enough that tears fill my eyes.

They finish with me, ravaged but clean.

Handmaidens ask what else they can do.

"A sandwich and a glass of milk."

"We haven't seen milk for some time," the white woman says. "But we can definitely get you a sandwich. What kind?"

"Peanut butter and jelly."

"Okay."

"Tuna fish. Do you have cans of tuna fish?"

"Actually, we do."

"And ham and cheese?"

"There's salami and cheese."

"Perfect," I tell her.

"Which one did you want, the peanut butter and jelly or the tuna fish or the salami and cheese?"

I look at her with some embarrassment but then the other woman laughs and then the woman I had been talking with gets that I want everything.

After I've eaten, I go back to where I left John and Tazza, sitting in their same seats. I expect when my husband sees me all spruced up and hair brushed, he will comment favorably, but John has eyes only for a king.

"Mary," he says when I sit next to him, "America is upside down. Those who had everything, they turned their backs on the people and went behind walls. When the people came to those walls, they were told there was nothing for them. In the name of public safety, the military had already confiscated all guns. We were left without arms to bear, without hope or the possibility of hope. Some of the people, desperate, stormed the gates of army bases and were shot down like dogs. American soldiers killing American citizens, Mary. Our great cities have been abandoned to chaos and terror. Washington was a mess, too, the federal government left the city to anarchy, until Tazza here, until he organized the people and they took back the city and set up distribution systems for food, for water, to get medical care to the people, blankets, Mary, *blankets*." He grasps Tazza's forearm. "Go on, tell her."

Tazza laughs. "Sounds like you just told her."

I say to John, "We knew these things, about the people being abandoned."

"No, we'd *heard* about these things. Tazza here has seen them, has fought against them."

I asked Tazza if he is a revolutionary.

He said he saw what he saw. "I saw people who worked in this city, Mary, and had good-paying jobs and were self-important and had fat retirement plans and expensive cars and their million-dollar houses were commonplace. These were the people who would stand in Starbucks and take five minutes ordering a latte exactly the way they wanted it, foam or no foam, skim milk or soy, *exactly* the way they wanted it or getting peeved if it wasn't perfect . . . these were the people, Mary, I saw them after the calamity, they were using straws to drink dirty water from footprints. Meanwhile, the very rich and the highest echelons of government commandeered everything and left, abandoning the rest of us to die. Being merely rich wasn't good enough . . . being a corporate vice president making half a million a year didn't mean shit, you were out there with the riffraff trying to pretend that a chunk of meat on a stick roasting over a fire wasn't rat . . . or cat . . . or dog."

I turn to John and tell him to go bathe, get clean clothes. "Hand-maidens will help you."

He shakes his head, he needs to listen to this man and see if he's a king for real.

"We were under a viaduct during the worst of it," Tazza is telling us. "And this little boy, I don't know, four or five, he's whining and crying and cursing his mom because she hasn't given him whatever it is he wants, something we don't have . . . his mom has somehow kept him well fed but he's crying and complaining from petulance and a personal history of never having been told no. The rain is a deluge, the rest of us can't leave from under the viaduct without getting soaked or maybe caught by the marauders and this kid is making a bad situation all the more intolerable—until a man steps out of the crowd and walks over and, without saying anything, knocks the boy to the ground. The mother tries to intervene but the man pulls a knife and says he'll slit her throat. Meanwhile, the boy stands up and screams at the man, tries to kick him, and the man hauls back and slaps the kid to the ground again. Kid gets up in a rage, man knocks him down again, slapping across his head, knocking him across the shoulder, enough to put him on his ass without breaking any bones. Now the kid is raging, screaming, but won't dare get up again, so the man lifts him to his feet and knocks him down again. This goes on without the man saying a word. Until finally the boy shuts up and stands there, staring hard young eyes at the man who stares back and finally tells the kid, 'Whatever you're feeling now, hold on to it because it's that feeling that'll get you through these bad times, if you can stop complaining and start being as hard as the times are hard, being mean and ruthless and adamant no matter how many times you get knocked to the ground, then you might survive.' And the man was right, those who developed a hard core survived while those who complained and waited for help, they died from exposure or got killed for being tedious."

Much later we learned it was Tazza who kept knocking that boy down to shut him up and teach him to be hard, Tazza a notorious liar when it came to history.

A young woman puts a soft hand on John's shoulder and tells him his barrel bath is ready. Before John stands to leave, he says to Tazza, "I can make you a king."

"No one can make a king."

"You're right, of course. What I mean is, I can advise you, teach you speeches, help you sell the idea."

"Of an American king? I don't think so, John."

"But you said—"

"Americans won't tolerate a king."

"You're wrong. In this calamity, the way things are now, the people will embrace a king."

"America doesn't have kings."

John tells him, "You're already a king, Tazza, what I'm offering to do is help everyone see you for what you are."

"A king, is what you're saying I am?"

"A king, yes. Our American king."

"And if people accepted me as their king, what then?"

"You'd make America a promised land."

After a dramatic pause, Tazza, the actor, announced in a booming voice, "I am Tazza, *king*."

"Good."

Tazza says, "Go take your bath, I'll sit here with Mary."

John left us alone, not fearing to leave his wife to the powers of a king because I had given my husband a pledge of allegiance, just as schoolchildren once pledged allegiance to the American flag.

13

I remember the first morning of this new era, waking to a soft day with my well fed husband next to me on a forgiving bed. We are both clean. We are under wool blankets. I am warm. Our bedroom is an office, our bed a mattress on the floor—this is the Ritz and John and I are wealthy beyond measure. Last night we laughed about not being hungry and about the noises our bodies made as stomachs and intestines kick-started mechanisms long idle and produced all night an inelegant symphony, growling and gurgling, burps and hiccups and funny foul farts. I fart, John laughs—this is a truth as reliable as sunrise. Last night we both laughed, delirious with food-full stomachs, on a mattress, under warm blankets, in awe of this human body, to endure so long without food and then be so ready to resume production, this wondrous tube within a tube, distiller and boiler, fermentor and factory. I ask John if we can spend the day in bed.

But something else is on his mind. "What did you and Tazza talk about after I left?"

"I asked him again what was his nation."

"He's Indian?" John seems surprised. It didn't occur to him?

"He says Italian."

John asked me what I thought and I said I thought it was safer in those days to be Italian than Indian. "But Tazza was fascinated that I was an Indian, he wanted to know if we had any kids and when I told him no he asked if there was a problem with my machinery, is what he said, or yours."

"What did you tell him?"

"I told him it just never happened and we never tried to find out why."

"Do you wish we'd had children?"

The insensitivity of this question astonishes me.

John continues, "Maybe Tazza wants a baby from an Indian woman. You know the calamity rumor, that only Indians will be able to have children. Did he ask you if you knew any qualified Indian women?"

"Qualified? You mean eligible for marriage?"

"No, *able* to have a baby. Did he say anything about wanting a baby?"

Rather than lie to my husband, I remain silent and John doesn't pursue the matter except to say, "At least we know he won't try to tap you to carry his baby." John swings around to put his feet on the floor, his back to me. "He'll need a young woman for that. You're too old, huh?"

His words sting so quickly and so hard that, in an instant, I am weeping quiet fat tears blurring my eyes and wetting my face . . . oh, John, turn around and see how you've hurt me.

14

Over the next days, John advised Tazza on speeches, stage presence, and Stirring Commentary. I know what the history books say but personally I'm not sure how much credit John deserves for making Tazza a king. Tazza was already organizing D.C. before John and I got there. Tazza already had the genius for speeches, for convincing people of his truth. Mainly, John helped *motivate* Tazza, who tended toward laziness, who was more interested in women than in matters of state.

John begged Tazza to change his name, choose something less foreign-sounding, he could still make it one name but something solid, *David*, because there would be Goliaths to fight and David, king, would slay giants, but Tazza wouldn't be moved.

John and I took up residence in another office-room, this one with a real bed, not just a mattress on the floor, and a toilet down the hall we could flush with a bucket that was refilled for us. We ate real meals at regular intervals. Water was for the asking. In just a matter of days, as the necessities were met, they receded into the background, the very same necessities that once dominated our lives. I think something like this must happen to long marriages, whereby the man who once wrote you rivers of poetry and was the light of your life, fire of your loins, becomes, with time, just the husband.

John and Tazza planned to take their show on the road, they would travel across America preaching how the government and the rich turned their backs on the people and now it's time for us to seize our birthright, seize the wealth of America from those who hold it and then we'll return that wealth to those who produced it . . . collecting followers along the way until a vast *population* accepted Tazza as king and, with this population, Tazza would return to Washington and rule the country.

The problem with this plan was that Tazza had never yet claimed to be king. Not in a speech, not in public. He told John that democracy was so ingrained in Americans that talk of being a king would turn the people against him. If he was taken seriously, if anyone thought he really had a chance to take over as a king, he would be reviled as a danger to our democratic heritage. But if people *didn't* take him seriously, they would laugh at *King Tazza* the nutcase. John kept insisting Tazza was wrong, the people were ready for a king. "Democracy might be part of our history for the past two hundred or so years," John said, "but the need for a leader people can trust and love, can pledge their loyalty to, the need for a chief, a lord, a king, this goes back thousands of years, it is in our very DNA."

Tazza gave speeches John wrote for him, exciting all who heard him, but Tazza never declared himself to be king and John asked what was the point. "To have more and more people show up at your performances? To increase your fan base? You've done a great job of organizing scavengers, they keep finding warehouses and malls that haven't been raided, but eventually all that'll run out and what then when you can't supply the people with food? And what happens when the government returns?"

Tazza listened intently, made a *performance* of careful listening, then went out and gave speeches, sang for the crowd, recited famous scenes from plays and movies—but still never declared he was king.

"I think he's interested only in being an entertainer," John complained to me one night. "I think he was an actor or an aspiring one or maybe he worked on a stage crew. He says he was in the field of entertainment. With his voice, maybe he had a local radio show. He's very cagey. I think most of the scavengers he recruited are former stagehands."

"But he's smart. You told me that."

John nodded. "He's brilliant. He could make up his own speeches if he wanted to, he's just lazy and reads the ones I've written for him. The guy can do anything onstage. He's a hypnotic storyteller. And when he starts singing, I mean, Tazza could've been a recording star, the people go crazy. But, Mary, when the government comes back, they're going to pat him on the head and put him in a USO show for the troops."

"Maybe you're the only one who thinks Tazza could be a king."

"He *is* the king, born a king."

I disagree with John. "Tazza is a born entertainer. Someone else will be born a king, that's the one who will lead us."

"I know that's what Tazza keeps saying but, meanwhile, what we got is, we got Tazza."

On a beautiful day in May, Tazza addressed his largest crowd yet, must've been five thousand. He stood on marble rubble from the toppled Washington Monument and spoke to the people all around him. We were accustomed to modern gatherings where voices are amplified and, usually, the speaker is televised on scattered screens so that we in the crowd learn to pay less attention to the actual figure there in the distance and more to his video presence. The day at the toppled Washington Monument, however, Tazza's unwired speech was a throwback to ancient times when a leader stood among his people to speak. Those within reach of Tazza's powerful voice become his minstrels, his heralds. They move back through the crowd to speak to people who heard the sound of Tazza's voice but were too far away to make out his words. "What did he say?" the people would ask—and those who had been up front but are now moving back, they respond, "He said we were all brothers and sisters, regardless of race or religion. He said when the people become united, they're unstoppable." As these former up-front heralds move back, they put their own spin on Tazza's words (on John's words as spoken by Tazza), emphasizing aspects they agreed with and ignoring those parts they disagreed with—but there were hundreds of these moving-back minstrels so the overall message, trimmed and tucked as it might be, is based on the original. This was how the Bible was passed down, how our ancient stories were delivered, handed down and altered to fit the times. The crowd churned and during the hours that Tazza spoke, almost everyone eventually heard him directly and almost everyone eventually heard from someone else what the great man had said.

On this May day Tazza told the people that racism was unnatural, that left to our own devices we would not divide ourselves by color. People were skeptical, hadn't there always been race hatred, hadn't the Bible talked of the banishment of the dark races? Tazza said people will naturally align themselves by where they live (neighbor joining with neighbor) and by their station in life (working folks with working folks) but that the split on race (black neighbor against white neighbor and white workingman against black workingman) was *introduced* and financed by the classes in power to ensure the people would never unite. He told how, in Colonial America, black slaves and white indentured servants would form alliances that the power class broke any way it could, by giving white indentured servants jobs overseeing black slaves, placing one brother above another, or by passing miscegenation laws to prevent alliances based on sex and marriage. And when white workers struck in the early days of the Twentieth Century, when unions were illegal, factory and mine owners brought in black workers to scab the strike, offering up black faces for white workers to hate, to keep blacks and whites from uniting for their common cause.

What you have to understand about Tazza is that his skill as a speaker, his overwhelming power as a speaker, made these issues electrifying even for people who hadn't given the topics much thought or might not even have agreed with Tazza's and John's egalitarianism. The *words* were true, I'd heard them from John in one river or another at one dinner table or another for twenty-one years, but it took Tazza to transfigure those words into something people heard as holy truth.

"He has a gift but he's wasting it," John said afterward. "He doesn't follow up by saying he's king and taking charge of the people, which he could do. At the end of that speech today? He could've led people into the Potomac River, they would've followed him."

John did convince Tazza to start handing out string, encouraging people to tie lengths of it around their left wrists as symbols of their support for him, but without Tazza telling them why, without declaring himself king, the string became an affectation.

Meanwhile, I became disgusted with Tazza sampling all those string-wearing girls who came to him with their big American breasts and oral talents. Was I jealous? I think I *wanted* to be disgusted by him as a way of keeping him at a distance.

Tazza became fascinated with symbols and accoutrements, wanting a regiment of bagpipers to precede him to whatever makeshift stage he was speaking from. John told Tazza he was getting it all wrong, seeking the attributes to awe and majesty but avoiding the essence of kings.

In a speech a week after the one he gave from atop the Washington Monument rubble, Tazza told the crowd of seeing the president of the United States being executed along with other high officials. People asked how the president died, did he weep and plead. Tazza said, "The man died begging for his life, begging that we don't hurt him. He died like a sissy. But let me clarify that. If you think dying like a sissy means dying like a girl, you're a fool. Sissy means weak. Our women are strong. Our women are the people's power. Without them, we can win nothing. With them, we are unstoppable. The people have a saying. *No nation is defeated until the hearts of its women are on the ground.* The hearts of our women will never be on the ground, we will never be defeated."

Women of all ages bevied around Tazza, the young ones shamelessly aggressive, getting close enough to whisper in his ear their outrageous offers. John, my old John, got some of this young attention by virtue of being Tazza's advisor and it was pitiful the way he goofed and grinned when some young tart rubbed up against him during one of Tazza's speeches, asking John were those really his words, did he really write everything Tazza says . . . John telling the tart (and I'm standing right behind him, isn't he aware of my presence or doesn't he care or is he delighted I can overhear all this?) that Tazza doesn't know how to say "Good morning" without John writing it for him, the girl laughing and leaning into John, who later told me with little boy's delight, "Her big boobs were right up against me and she didn't even know it." I assured the old fool that a woman knows where her breasts are at all times.

John questioned Tazza about seeing the president executed, did he really witness that and more to the point did he participate? "Those politicians you were hanging upside down on the White House fence, were you part of the group that killed them?"

Tazza hesitated.

"I'm not going to condemn you, I just want to know."

"I wasn't worried about you condemning me, I was worried you wouldn't have any respect for me if I told you that I had nothing to do with it, the killings, even though I sort of tried to take credit, the way I was hanging them upside down, people naturally thought I helped kill them. But, no. I don't believe in killing. I want to be the kind of king who's known for mercy. Instead of executing my enemies, I'll, like, you know, *exile* them somewhere. Vanquish them."

"Vanquish your enemies? For chrissakes, this is not dinner theater. Tazza, listen to me. When the government comes back, they're going to be deadly serious about treason."

"I haven't committed treason."

"Is that why you won't declare yourself king, you think you'll be accused of treason?"

"I just don't think the time is right."

Tazza meanwhile was giving two speeches a day, John warning him against overexposure and saying that people shouldn't feel overly comfortable with their king. "We'll pass around word that you're not going to speak or even appear in public for a few days," John said. "Then we'll say you have the most important announcement of your life to make. We'll set you up down by the river. There'll be a hundred thousand people, they can watch you from the bridges."

"And that's when I announce I'm their king?"

"It's time. God hates a coward, Tazza."

"And it's God who makes a king, John, not you."

15

"Are you sleeping with him?"

It was a woman who first asked me this question. I can't even tell you her name. I had seen her around but we hadn't spoken beyond saying hello. She has come to bring our buckets of water, the water John and I use to wash in. John is with Tazza, working on the big speech. Like the rest of us, this woman wears jeans and a white top. She has dark hair and a sharp face—not unattractive but strong features and I think it would take a confident man to love her, a man who didn't need a woman to have soft, unthreatening baby features to make him feel safely masculine. She and I have this in common and I also remember her being about my age.

"Tazza," she says.

I knew who she meant, of course—speculation was rampant around that man.

"I don't know you," I tell her. "I'm not going to gossip about who's doing what with whom. And, by the way, *no,* I'm not sleeping with Tazza."

"I know your husband is his advisor or speechwriter or whatever he is, but when I see you and Tazza together, there's something . . . I don't know, something *furtive* about the way you both act. And with your coloring being so similar to Tazza's, you know . . . your heritage or whatever . . . I was just wondering."

This woman needs to be careful, talking about my heritage—she has no idea who I am, what I'm capable of. I grew up on the rez. I had to toughen up my soft parts if I wanted to get out of there without kids and an early marriage, without drugs or being raped. I told you earlier I had a fondness for blades, did you think I was joking? In high school I carried a knife and if a football player wanted to drive me home, that was fine, and if I wanted him to touch me, that was fine, too, but if he grabbed my hair and tried to force me down, he would draw away bleeding—not enough to require the emergency room but enough to respect me. And now this woman thinks she can be familiar enough with me to talk of my coloring?

I feel around to my back pocket where I keep the new folding knife Tazza gave me, there's something off-center about this woman. Maybe she's in love with Tazza and wants to kill off her rivals—which considering everyone he's banging would be a huge undertaking.

She smiles.

Her creepiness pisses me off. "Keep your speculations to yourself," I tell her, slipping the knife into my hand, ready to unfold its keen blade.

Then she fools me completely by apologizing, crying softly. "I'm so bad at trying to make friends. I thought some girl gossip would be a way to break the ice with you."

Girl gossip? She's crazy.

"Have you heard of tipping points?" she asks, picking up the buckets that a moment before she had placed on the floor.

"You can leave the water. And, yes, it's a topic my husband discusses."

"I was working for the Commerce Department. We held endless meetings on how things were to be handled during what we were calling at the time, The Emergency. How files were to be downloaded to flash drives, which were to be properly labeled, duplicates stored according to elaborate procedures. I kept coming to work. We held special meetings and attended team-building exercises on managing human resources during a time of crisis. We were prepared for some disruption but not for a calamity. We trusted in the government. The United States of America government, the most powerful on earth, I was happy I had the job I had. They told us our salary would accrue even if we weren't able to come to the office, and then after The Emergency there'd probably be bonuses. We felt pretty good about everything. Sometimes traffic was bad and I was an hour or more late for work but the supervisor understood and nothing negative ever went into my jacket. I was concerned with maintaining a good work record. You know, twenty years with the Commerce Department, good benefits, job security—"

"Why are you telling me this?"

"Are you in a hurry?"

"I've never even talked with you before."

"I'm sorry. Isn't it permitted?"

"Permitted?"

"For just a common person like me to talk to someone like you."

"Don't be silly."

I can't figure out if she's facetious or malicious or what. And again she gives me a look unsettling enough that I keep the knife in hand as I tell her to go on.

"So we thought there would be a gradual slowdown, maybe we'd be put on four days a week, then three, then told to work from home, then maybe we would monitor some Web site or call a phone number for more information. But it didn't go like that. We were working, my husband and I had a nice house in a great neighborhood in Rockville, it was worth three times what we had paid for it, I mean we could've sold that house and been able to place nearly a million dollars equity cash on the table, who would've guessed that about us? So one day I'm at work and I guess the tipping point had been reached because these people, these *hordes* came into the office, trashing everything."

"Patagonians?"

"Who?"

"The marauders—those terrible people with machetes?"

"No, this was before they even existed. Have you heard the latest rumor about them? I think they've all been killed."

"Killed? By whom?"

"I don't know, that's what I heard. But the people I'm talking about, these hordes of people who came into our offices, they were dirty and angry and hungry and they're enraged at the whole government and everyone who worked for the government because of what was happening and I couldn't get my car out of the garage and of course the Metro was out of the question, I saw people getting beaten, it was like old newsreels they played in school about things that happened in Europe last century during the World Wars. That's how it felt, like America had suddenly slipped into the Third World. And I'm, like, a refugee."

She's embarrassed, as if confessing she was an alcoholic.

"So I start making my way home, *walking* home, thinking I'm going to be raped or beaten, there were so many of us, I just got in the refugee stream that was heading for Rockville. And all the time I'm walking, I'm thinking what Pete and I, my husband, Pete, what we had been planning, to leave town if the trouble got too bad, move to our beach house in Bethany. We'd made a list of all the things we would take with us. That little stainless steel barbecue grill we'd just bought, it would be great for roughing-it situations. Some books. All of our L.L. Bean camping gear, of course.

My jewelry, Pete's coins—because now suddenly having a portion of your assets in gold coins and good diamonds didn't seem paranoid, did it?"

I still don't know where this story is going, why I'm being told it, or if there's something mentally wrong with her that makes her speak in a disengaged monotone with a faraway look in her spooky eyes.

"Pete wasn't home. I never saw him again. *I never saw my husband again.* I stayed by myself in the house. A couple days later I walked back to my office but *people* were living in the building. And the government of the United States of America was just, like, *gone.* Whatever that tipping point was, it had been reached. *No systems were set up, no contingencies, no procedures.* When I walked back home, people had taken over my house. I got in the front door and saw, like, a whole dirty family sitting at my dining room table and I said, 'Excuse me, this is my house, will you please tell me what you're doing here?' And the man walked over and hit me with his fist. Didn't say a word. Didn't tell me to be quiet or leave, didn't announce that they had taken over my house or anything, just hit me. I lost a tooth from where he hit me. You go along in life and think it's always going to be what it is or some variation on what it is but then there's a tipping point and everything is profoundly different."

"I don't know what you want me to say."

"Is Tazza forming a new government? Because if he is, I have a lot of experience and I could really help organize things. He could put me in charge of a team that's tasked with outlining formation protocols."

"I don't know anything about that."

She looks at me with a servant's petulance—and I respond with the master's arrogance. "Put those buckets over on that desk and bring in two more."

The woman nods and leaves.

When John returns I try to tell him about the woman but he can think of nothing, talk of nothing, but Tazza's speech. "He's magnificent, you tell him something once and he can recite it back to you verbatim a week later. But I still don't know if he's going to declare himself king. He's so scared of it backfiring."

"John, that woman I was trying to tell you about, she said she'd heard all the Patagonians had been killed."

"A rumor a day."

"But we haven't seen any since we've been here."

"Mary, listen to me." He grasped my forearms and made me look into his eyes. "Tomorrow at noon, a hundred thousand people by the Lincoln Memorial, and Tazza's going to tell them we are the new America and he is our American king."

"John, he's promised that before."

"Tomorrow . . . he'll do it tomorrow."

16

Tazza began speaking at noon on the steps of the Lincoln Memorial, not nearly as many people in attendance as John had hoped but on this clear, warm day in May hundreds more arrived every hour. You have to understand, we Americans had been the most constantly entertained population in human history and all of that stopped during the calamity and we were desperate for something to watch, listen to, attend. In fact, Tazza's audiences would've been even larger if people hadn't been afraid of the fighting that always broke out when crowds gathered. There'd be different factions with long-standing feuds, they'd curse each other and throw things and then, often as not, there'd be a melee. Or if families were carrying food, swaggering toughs would rough them up and take everything. Young women couldn't go out into those crowds unaccompanied. This violence wasn't deadly, like that from the Patagonians, whom we hadn't seen for months. The violence in Tazza's audience came about because there was no one strong enough to stop it. Tazza had his army of scavengers but they were freaks and geeks who wore fedoras and talked like pirates, they weren't a police force.

We're standing halfway up the steps leading to the memorial. The few thousand people who've come to hear Tazza are on the steps with us, and on the concrete down below, and scattered beyond that. No one will have to move back and forth in the crowds to convey the message today, we'll all be able to hear Tazza directly, especially if he uses one of the bullhorns that the scavengers found last week. So far, no fighting.

I asked John, "You think he's going to pull the trigger today, declare himself?"

"He says he is. Look at him working it."

Tazza up there pointing to people he knew, hugging everyone who came to say hello, whispering in certain ears—and each person who has contact with him, each man and each woman is grinning as if given an injection that induces grinning. Even from where we are, halfway down the steps, you can sense an energy surrounding Tazza as he meets and greets and seduces people. He has a remarkable way of laying on of hands. He touches a forearm or drapes an arm around a shoulder and leans in so close to hear someone that it looks as if he's trying for a kiss. Sometimes after shaking hands with a man, Tazza will continue holding on so that after a few minutes of conversation it seems that Tazza and the man are a dating couple. For the most part, Americans aren't enthusiastic about touching but these Americans couldn't get enough of Tazza.

"He wanted to wear a cape," John tells me.

"No!" I laugh.

"Yes. And he claims he's organizing a regiment of pipers."

"An ermine cape?"

"I don't know. He'll probably want a crown."

I told John that kings have crowns.

"Not an *American* king," he said.

"John, is this all written somewhere, the attributes of an American king?"

"You shouldn't ridicule what you don't understand."

"But you're making this up as you go."

"*Of course I am.* We need someone to lead us out of this calamity. He can do it."

"Does Tazza understand that? I think sometimes he considers this a lark. But if the people do finally accept him as a leader and then they end up not liking the way he leads or if someone else wants to be king, did you explain how kings get turned out of office? They don't lose an election, John, they lose their head—does Tazza realize that?"

Instead of answering me, John points. "He's starting."

Tazza isn't using the bullhorn, starting as he always did with a paraphrase from James Joyce by way of John. "Come all you gallant Americans and listen to my story!"

He speaks now of the greatness of Americans . . . how each of us carries in our blood the heritage of warriors . . . Celtic warriors and African warriors and Spanish-speaking warriors. But in the past we went astray. Instead of leading strong lives, we watched television. Our grown men dressed up like little boys in their favorite team's jerseys. "We ended up cheering ball teams when once we cheered kings!"

John squeezes my hand but Tazza goes on without making the declaration.

"Things are different now. You survived a calamity. Your government abandoned you but you have not abandoned each other. There is greatness in each of you, in each of you is the soul of a poet who died young. Do the drops of water in the Potomac River down there realize they are part of a mighty river? Do you standing here today realize the power you are part of? When the people fear their government, there is tyranny. When the government fears the people, there is liberty. So I tell you this, when the government returns to this capital, let it find *liberty* here and be afraid!"

People cheered and John told me Tazza's speech was full of quotations from great people, including Thomas Jefferson. "Anything I can remember, I stick in," John says.

"Is he saying what he believes or what you can remember?"

John waves me off.

As Tazza spoke and moved in and out of the crowd, the few thousand grew to five thousand and then more and still the hooliganism hadn't started. Now he used a bullhorn and began his speech all over again for the newcomers, climbed back up the steps, descended into the crowd, then back up again. As people moved back and forth telling one another what Tazza was saying, the excitement intensified. People called for him to sing and Tazza told them that today he was singing the truth.

But then he *did* sing. He got people close to sing with him, old protest songs that pledged, like a tree planted by the water, we will not be moved. He made extravagant promises that caused these previously starving people to cheer, we will feast on fat things full of marrow, he promised, and when you ask me for a blanket, I will give you a home, and when you ask for water, I will give you wine and honey.

The people became wild with their love for Tazza and his love for them. They did not always know what his speech meant but they aspired to know. All their lives the people had been talked down to. The marketplace offered them things easy to operate, simple to know. Teachers told them there were no stupid questions when in fact the people knew that stupid questions outnumbered smart ones. Television was played for idiots who had to be cued when to laugh. Politicians assumed the people were cretins who cared about nothing greater than the price of gas and the sanctity of their social security. And now here comes a man who speaks to them of a true and abstract greatness, who uses French and Latin and refers to passages in Shakespeare. Did the people always understand what he was saying—no, not literally. But just as they got the message that others took them for idiots, the people got the message from Tazza that he held them in high regard, a great people who could be trusted to do what's right and noble. They were aware of and inspired by the assumptions he made on their behalf, that they had a capacity for what was hard to know, that they yearned for the cosmic. All their lives things had been dumbed down for them, Tazza smartened up everything he told the people.

Antoine de Saint-Exupéry, author of *The Little Prince,* said that if you want your people to build ships, don't teach them how to work with wood—instead teach them to yearn for the vast and endless sea. So it was with Tazza and these Americans, he kept encouraging them to raise their eyes, believe in their own greatness, and hope for a vast and endless future.

On the steps of the Lincoln Memorial and beyond, Tazza kept speaking, the people kept cheering, John and I kept waiting to hear some declaration of royalty.

Then comes the commotion toward the back of the crowd, off to our left. People are screaming and shouting, and we assume a fistfight has broken out but then the crowd parts and sweet Jesus here come the terrible Patagonians dressed for murder, some in shower hats and skirts, all of them quiet, and all of them carrying machetes. They marched toward the front of the fleeing crowd, toward the steps, toward Tazza.

The armless among us wept.

The Patagonians were terrible because they were senseless, as meaningless as the shrieking of the mindless wind, to quote John quoting Whittier. These were not muggers who wanted your money or rapists who wanted your humiliation or an army who wants your surrender. These were young men with machetes who cut off your arm just to see how you act when your arm is cut off. Terrible because many of them *are* kids, some as young as eight or nine, mutilating people alongside their adult comrades. Terrible because of the bizarre way they dress, in wedding gowns, without their pants on, in flamboyant wigs, bangles about their wrists. But terrible mostly because of their demeanor, their total unimpressed blankness. They cut off an arm with no more than curiosity showing on their young faces, rape a woman with only an expression of concentration, kill a man and never blink except when the arterial blood splashes back in their eyes. It seems nothing you can show them would surprise or shock or impress them; nothing you can teach will bend them toward the quality of mercy; they are the uncivilized nature of man.

And we know nothing of them, how they got organized, if they have leaders, why they are so terribly violent, why they don't speak, or what their sign language and finger snaps mean. Rumor has it they're on powerful drugs that make them disaffected and sociopathic. Rumor has it their ranks formed among the orphans of the displaced millions and they've been so brutalized during the calamity that they've become brutality's own essence.

Now here they were among us, fifty of them cutting through the crowd, sometimes literally, as people who didn't move out of the way quickly enough were hacked with machetes. With no obvious leader, they moved as a mass up the steps toward Tazza. I think they knew nothing of him, unaware he was the hero of D.C., a popular figure who hung politicians upside down and backwards and who organized the scavengers who kept the people fed—I think they saw Tazza simply as the one with the bullhorn, the one speaking, and that was enough to target him.

John says, "It's over then."

I pull on his sleeve and say we should go. When these Patagonians finish with Tazza they will turn on the rest us.

Indeed, hundreds are already fleeing the coming bloodbath, not Tazza though. He does the strangest thing, he descends the steps lightly, a dancer about to break into song, heading right for the Patagonians, who halt their ascent to watch expressionless his approach, Tazza's face radiant, Tazza holding out his arms as if to embrace all fifty Patagonians. Thus positioned, perfectly positioned in fact to have those arms cut off, he moves right among them and starts talking.

He tells them, first thing out of his mouth, he tells them he is the king of America. "I am your king," he says. He repeats it a dozen times.

I've contended all along that this talk of kings is catnip to boys and men, more so to the boy in the man—and here at this moment the king talk proves beguiling to the Patagonians as Tazza tells them excitedly that he is their king and they will be his Vieille Garde. He says this in French, they seem mesmerized. "It means Old Guard and I will keep you close like this at all times." He is there among them, clasping their shoulders and placing a hard hand to the backs of their heads, sometimes even touching his forehead to theirs, repeating over and over he is their king and the king will keep the Old Guard close. One of the younger boys rushes to Tazza and uses both hands to raise a machete and seems fully prepared to bring that machete down on Tazza's skull. Watching this, John grabs at my hand. Tazza's own hands shoot toward the boy's face, which Tazza holds firmly as he says, "I am your king." The boy lowers his blade in obedience.

They are seduced, mesmerized, confused. You would think that keeping your message simple is imperative when talking to barbarians but Tazza goes into a baroque explanation of Napoleon's Old Guard, Vieille Garde, and how it was fifty of the Old Guard who accompanied Napoleon on his return to France (actually it was thousands). He tells the boys that Napoleon was an emperor of such greatness that he marched on Paris with a band of no more than the fifty we have here and the government sent out armies to stop him and every army sent to oppose him, instead of firing upon their emperor, they pledged to Napoleon their loyalty and thus the armies sent to oppose him joined him and became *his* armies. And within the great armies of Napoleon remained this elite core called Vieille Garde, the Old Guard.

The terrible Patagonians crowd around to hear what he's saying, each in awe that one of their own hasn't yet cut this man.

Tazza named them the King's Own Patagonian Old Guard and told them, "When all else is lost, you will gather around me as you are now—and none will pass until all are dead."

They like hearing this story, animations of joy transforming their previous stony faces, storytelling an invention more wondrous than fire. Tazza dumbs down nothing, he tells them British artist Benjamin Haydon described the Old Guard as having the look of thoroughbreds, of veterans, of bandits. Depravity, recklessness, and bloodthirstiness were burned into their faces. They wore giant bearskins and ferocious expressions.

"You are my Old Guard," Tazza tells them again . . . and then again. Do they even know who Napoleon was? Knowing or not knowing apparently doesn't matter to the terrible Patagonians, boys, who crowd around Tazza to hear his every not necessarily understood word. Is this what they've been searching for the whole bloody time, a king?

"At Waterloo," he tells his enraptured audience who must guess at what a Waterloo might be, "Napoleon committed the Old Guard, who were decimated, those still alive forming the final defensive square, futile it was, surrounded they were. When asked to surrender, the commander of the Old Guard apologized. They'd *like* to surrender but they cannot. They are *Vieille Garde*. 'La Garde meurt, elle ne se rend pas.' " The lost boys around Tazza nodding their heads, some with tears in their eyes—none having any idea what he'd just said but all knowing in their savage hearts the essence of what this king is telling them. " 'The Guard dies, it does not surrender.' " Tazza's green eyes bore aggressively into their dark and willing eyes. "Who among you will die for me?" They silently raised their arms in assent, not only willing to die for Tazza but yearning for the opportunity. "Who among you would ever surrender?" They bark denials, bark like dogs, and look ferociously at their fellows, ready to descend on any brother fainthearted enough to contemplate surrender.

Even though John and I watch at close hand what Tazza did with the Patagonians, we couldn't understand it—how by force of will a man takes command of others.

"All these people . . ." And here Tazza indicates the crowds, which have stopped moving away to linger and watch the Patagonians kill Tazza and, when that didn't happen, to see what comes next. "These people are your charges, are the ones you will defend. You are my Patagonians, my Old Guard, and you must never let harm come to our people. Soon a great government army will arrive here and I will call on you to defend us."

Tazza held his right hand aloft. "The king wears a string around his right wrist. All the people wear strings around their left wrists. Show us your string!" People tentatively lift their left hands. "But you, my Guard," he tells the Patagonians, "you will wear this string around your right wrists and you alone will be allowed this privilege. Because this is how close you are to your king."

As he pulled lengths of string from a pocket, Patagonians crowded close to get theirs tied around their right wrists by the king himself. Tazza called to John because John always carried extra lengths of string.

"Just as you predicted," I tell John as he goes to join Tazza among the Patagonians, "a kingdom held together by string."

17

Word spreads among the people of the taming of the terrible Patagonians, whom they knew as marauders or gangsters but who will be known henceforth as Patagonians, the name John and I had given them long ago, a private joke in the privacy of our home, now become universal—Patagonians and Old Guard and whatever else Tazza declares them to be—as crowds flow like an unbanked river toward the monument. People who didn't have strings around their left wrists became desperate to get the string, word being that the string gives protection against Patagonians. John sent for more string, a hundred rolls of string that Tazza's scavengers had collected and John stored in an office near where we slept, white string and colored string, the people making up stories what it meant if you had red string around your left wrist instead of white or purple.

Tazza is crowded off the monument steps, the Old Guard keeping close to him but treating the people gently as Tazza had instructed.

John wept when he heard Tazza telling the people again and again, "I am your king!"

I look at my husband who is crying and I weep, too, to hear Tazza repeat it, "I am your king! *I am your king.*"

I apologize for becoming so emotional about this after all these years. My talk of loving a leader must seem quaint to you, who make your leadership decisions based on voting records and position papers. There was a time though . . .

Word spreads far back into the crowd and then that word returns to the front again, told and retold a thousand variations among the fifty thousand who gather here as the afternoon grows long, we have a king. Tazza is our king. Go see him. Tazza. Go see if you can touch him, he's our king, wear his string, Tazza, *king.*

In their euphoria, people crowd Tazza and the Old Guard around the side of the memorial, the Patagonians protecting their king from accidental injury as the river of people move us toward the Potomac.

I was terrified that a stampede would crush us but Tazza laughed, talking as we moved, shouting speeches to people who couldn't get enough of his voice, shouting stories that John had taught him from Booker T. Washington speeches.

"A ship was lost at sea for many days when it sighted another vessel and sent a signal, 'Water! Water! We die of thirst!' And the friendly ship signaled back, 'Cast down your bucket where you are.' The lost ship didn't understand and signaled its distress a second time, 'Send us water! We die of thirst!' Yet again the other ship instructed, 'Cast down your bucket where you are!' The men on the lost ship became crazed, why don't they send us water? Finally, the captain of that lost ship issued the order, 'Cast down our bucket where we are!' The men obeyed, casting down the bucket and bringing up fresh, drinkable water and shouting, 'We are saved!' Unknown to this ship, it had sailed into a part of the ocean where the mighty Amazon empties its fresh water far out into the sea. So to those of you who have waited and waited for the government to return and restore your lives, I say, wait no longer . . . *cast down your bucket where you are.* I am your king, we are saved."

The crowds went wild. We were so euphoric I expected to take flight and sail around Washington in the glory of being saved and having a king.

As this and other speeches and stories and exhortations from Tazza were passed through the crowds, ten thousand more joined us, those in the back pushing forward to see the king, Tazza's fifty Patagonians keeping the king within their hive but unable to stop the river of people pushing us back across one highway, then another, then down steps to the Potomac.

"They'll push us into the river!" I shout at John, who has an armload of string as do a dozen aides around him, trying to pass the string out to the people as fast as they can. "John for chrissakes stop playing with that goddamn string and do something before we all drown."

Tazza is in fact about to be pushed into the Potomac, several of the Old Guard having already been knocked into the water, when from beneath the Memorial Bridge churns a sleek red motorboat, the only vessel on the river, smoke billowing from its stack, reeking of french fries, water foaming at its stern.

"Boatman!" John shouts.

I ask, "He's been waiting all this time?" But John doesn't hear me.

Tens of thousands of newly kinged people are fascinated by this red boat, the Potomac's one and only. Ah, this must be what it's like to have a king . . . red boats appear from beneath bridges to mark his presence. The pushing stops as we watch the red launch swing close enough to drop a plank, which Tazza uses to board. Seeing their king being picked up by red boat alone on the Potomac, the people ease back to watch. No one else is pushed into the river, and the boys already in the water climb out. We've just witnessed a miracle.

From the boat, Tazza continues addressing his subjects, shouting speeches, repeating his declaration, "I am your king."

John meanwhile has started handing out entire rolls of string, telling each person in turn, "Hold tight to this end, don't let it go. Tazza will be given the other end. When you feel him tug, you'll know you're connected to your king."

People are enthralled to do this, crowding around to get rolls of string.

With the free ends being held by members of the crowd, John gives the rolls one by one to Patagonians, instructing each to unroll the string as he makes his way to the river, then swim out to your king and give him the roll. The ferocious boys do this without hesitation, into the freezing water, dog-paddling to the boat, pulled aboard with one strong heft from Boatman.

John passes out a dozen rolls of string, then a dozen more. The people helping him also give out string, handing free ends to those in the crowd, giving the rolls to Patagonians willing to swim out and hand them to Tazza. Eventually there were fifty, then a hundred lengths of string, the ends here on land each held by someone in the crowd, by three or four or more, a dozen people with their hands on each roll of string. The rolls are still being delivered to Tazza in the boat. Eventually so many strings came to him that he couldn't hold them all and had to tie the ends around the boat's railing.

We are laughing, we are crying. Even I, a royal skeptic, couldn't resist the charm—lengths of string, white and red and purple, stretching from people on shore to a king in the boat. Strings leading from land to water, some dipping *into* the water, others pulled tight and then allowed to slacken and then pulled tight again as people reached to touch a string and feel on the other end the tug of a king. And as we tugged, each pull on each string contributed to a power sufficient in their unison to bring the red boat closer to shore, drawing our king near.

How long ago was this, fifty years, more, don't tell me—I remember it not like yesterday but like right now, I see hundreds of strings pulling that red boat to shore, all of us weeping and shouting, drawing our king closer and closer, string by string, and I tell you this with a cold eye, that—except for the birth of my son—it was the most glorious event I ever witnessed in my long and eventful life.

18

I should tell you about the scavengers because history books have
ennobled them in ways I don't recognize from knowing them back
then. Before John and I arrived in D.C., Tazza was known largely on
the basis of the work done by his scavengers. They were a collection
of stagehands and rock band roadies and computer geeks, young
men who didn't bathe regularly even before the calamity made
bathing a luxury. You're not old enough to remember or even know
what audiovisual equipment was but Tazza's scavengers would've
been on the high school AV crew for sure. They were computer
hackers. They loved sci-fi. They wore fedoras without irony. The
calamity swept away their usual opportunities for computer games
and sci-fi movies and somehow they congregated around Tazza,
geeky young men given to hero worship, and he put them to work
scavenging food and supplies, whatever they could find, and their
pre-calamity skills and knowledge and propensities somehow made
them perfect scavengers. These guys were amazing. They found
warehouses no one else knew existed. They could get into elabo-

rately locked buildings, saving us over and over again by finding the food, the medicine, the sources of potable water, the blankets, the shoes, whatever we needed, they scavenged.

So much for our scavengers, let's now talk of democracy. Are you surprised what little nostalgia we Americans had for representative rule? John wasn't. He said American democracy offered rule by vote, by election campaign, by constituent voting patterns, by focus group, by sample polling, by red state, blue state, television ads, by running mates' dodgy bios, and snappy slogans. By contrast, Tazza offers the fear and dread, royalty and divinity, pomp and majesty of a king. American democracy has been around for a couple hundred years—the people have had kings for ten thousand years. Against the historical sway of a king, what is a ballot but paper? "We crowned him in the old way, Mary—by affirmation of the people. He was the one among us to walk out and meet what we feared most, the Patagonians. He will give us heart, he will speak of light. He is our king."

I teased John about his Arthurian talk, and he laughed, admitted to being carried away—but I had the strongest sense that all too soon there'd be no laughing about such things as king and string.

At first the Patagonians had been ferocious about enforcing the string rule, wear it on your left wrist—with only the king and Old Guard allowed string on the right wrist but after a while as things relaxed and we all got happy, you'd see strings around biceps and foreheads, no one cared. It was summer, tables were laid out up and down the Mall, living was easy. We had pulled our king ashore—and we were happy.

That was the summer I became the king's affinity.

We thousands settled in and around the 146 acres of the National Mall, occupying the nearby government and office buildings that we were able to break into. People had come to the Mall during the last days of the government, because the federal district in and around the Mall was the final area under protection from the

U.S. army. Everything else, the close suburbs and the neighborhoods of Washington, D.C., had broken into anarchy. Gangs roamed. The strong and violent dominated the weak and law-abiding. Then, after the federal government left D.C., people stayed around the Mall in memory of and hope for its protected status.

On beautiful days when he didn't feel like working, Tazza took a group of us to the National Arboretum. Tazza's scavengers had come up with a few dozen bicycles and we'd ride New York Avenue, a broad but ugly street for most of the way, flanked by warehouses and businesses, everything closed up, boarded over, burned, abandoned. Roaming gangs and hollow-eyed survivors followed us at a distance or kept apace on parallel streets. We would've never made it to the Arboretum or back without our Patagonian escort—these terrifying silent boys apparently had made their mark on the displaced hordes because, seeing our machete-bearers, the desperate of D.C. shrank back and stayed at a distance.

At the Arboretum we strolled the network of lanes and slept under stars that, without competition from electricity, blazed in the old ways. Tazza explained how the phases of the moon worked and taught us an easy way to distinguish a waxing moon from one waning. Before the calamity, living in cities, we had forgotten everything we once knew about the sky.

All across the Arboretum and in the trees ringing the Mall, butterflies blue in color made their thin-lunged residence, and we took this as a further sign of our happiness.

We didn't venture into the rest of Washington, beyond the Mall and the open expanses of the Arboretum—the city had been burned and trashed, looted and ransacked, rats and desperate squatters and the zombie displaced people everywhere.

John asked Tazza, how will we keep our people warm come winter? Tazza's reply angered John but made perfect sense within the context of that summer, "All you need is love."

Our scavengers found tents and chairs and blankets, the scavengers as important to us that summer as Patagonians. The scavengers kept to themselves, roomed together and ate together, they grew beards and kept their hair wild and long. In spite of their disgusting habits, I loved them all, they were funny, wise-cracking and pranking and endlessly goosing each other.

I don't know where they kept finding all the stuff they kept finding, but Tazza would never have had a kingdom without them.

We enjoyed unplugged music concerts every night. When summer rains fell warm, we played in the mud, girls taking their tops off with big grins as old men looked but didn't leer, a miracle of their biology. We had magic shows at midday, mimes at midnight battling to walk against powerful winds the mimes made you plainly see by the waxing moonlight only to find themselves trapped in boxes that just kept getting smaller . . . and smaller.

Poetry became important. Without television, movies, radio, video games, cell phones, computers, Internet surfing, instant messaging, and a thousand other mental twinkies, our minds became lean and hungry, receptive to songs that had been sung a hundred thousand years, *poetry*—and poets became our stars. Readings were must-attend events, and the next day people went around quoting poems they'd heard the night before, and if a popular poet wore a floppy purple hat, floppy purple hats became fashionable, and it wasn't how pretty your face or sweet your ass that made you a star but how true rang your words. It was said that even the king trembled before a properly rhymed couplet.

I became the female force of order in our kingdom, John and Tazza and the Patagonians and scavengers playing knights and pledging fidelity . . . while I and my women worked to organize operations that hauled the water and distributed the food and triaged our patients because someone was always getting sick, getting hurt—doctors at a premium. When the scavengers found a few dozen barrels of gasoline, I arranged allocations to trucks that would bring supplies whenever a new and distant warehouse was found and stripped clean. I have been criticized for organizing my women in subservient roles, cleaning and caring for others, but without us there would've been chaos and at the time we believed there was honor in service.

I spent way too much time dealing with Tazza's conquests. He was a king and they were willing. The corps of women I had organized to do the business of our people was being torn apart by jealousy, by fights, hair-pulling and face-spitting and, one time, a short blade buried in a rival's rib cage. I put the king's bed off-limits to any woman under my command. The younger ones still tried to get around me to get to him but I was well fed now and displayed a female energy in full fury—skillful, composed, and deadly.

My ferocity in keeping women away from Tazza convinced people all the more that he and I were sleeping together. And maybe I *was* jealous and maybe I realized somewhere deep inside me that it was inevitable, Tazza and me. But at the time, I told others—and told myself—that I was simply trying to keep order.

One afternoon while John walked the Mall to hear what the people were saying and see what new treasures our scavengers had brought in, Tazza sent for me.

When I got to his room, he was alone and said to me, "I didn't realize I had taken a vow of chastity."

"What're you talking about? You're the most unchaste man I've ever known. By the twos and threes they come to your room."

"Not anymore. They *came,* Mary—past tense. Now the word among women is, the crazy Indian, Mary, she'll go tribal on your ass if you sneak in to see your king."

"I couldn't get any work out of them."

"Are you jealous, Mary?"

"Don't flatter yourself."

He was in a white shirt, opened at the neck, his black hair a tangle, Tazza dark tanned, green-eyed, barefoot. I don't remember all the words we spoke, the real conversation was conducted by our eyes, back and forth, and by the bottom basement of my stomach squeezing hard as I looked at him, handsome and cocky and alpha, looking back at me. My loyalty to John was so long-standing and complete that I had never toyed with what was being toyed with at this moment.

"Come over here and sit by your king, let's talk."

"I'll sit over there," I replied, taking a chair that required me to cross in front of him. I walked with my shoulders back, breasts out, moon tight, like a woman I walked.

"You're beautiful."

"And my husband is your friend who named you king."

"Yes, well . . . there's that, isn't there."

"You need to stop screwing around with my women. I've set up a system of work details and you can't keep sampling among my women, messing up my schedules. And besides that . . . the calamity might've made pregnancies difficult but it didn't eradicate disease. God knows what bugs and bacteria you've picked up this summer."

"I'm clean, Mary. I had a doctor check me out. I've always been fortunate that way. I don't get sick, don't have allergies, don't catch colds. This is going to sound conceited but it's true, my body is perfectly formed."

I laughed at him.

He said he was serious. "My ears match, my eyes are level, my legs straight, digits flawless. Look at my feet, perfect the way the toes match. No monkey feet on me, Mary. And you know what, I bet my internal organs are all in perfectly matched working condition, too."

"I can only hope you're being sarcastic—because otherwise you're a conceited asshole."

He laughed. "Take off your blouse, Mary."

"Go to hell."

"I'm not that interested in your breasts per se."

"Per se?"

"But I have an inordinate fondness for nipples. I wonder about yours a lot. Size, color. I wonder if I would need a finger to stuff one of yours in my mouth."

I looked at him my face hot with embarrassment and anger, telling Tazza, "If this is supposed to be arousing me, it's having the opposite effect."

"And yet . . . your nipples, Mary."

I stood and walked slowly to the door, telling Tazza, "I guess your stupid talk works on the girls you've been screwing, but I'm a woman all grown up and married and you make me ashamed for you."

He seemed genuinely hurt. "In your heart of hearts, you truly don't want to be mean to me like that."

"You don't know what I want."

"You want to walk back here—slow again just like how you walked away, so I can get a good look at what's going and coming— and you want me to kiss you hard on your open mouth, is what you want, Mary."

It's not right he should know what I want and it's not right I should want what I want.

In a wet fever I went out that door and looked for John, who upon seeing me all flushed asked what was wrong, and I lied to my husband and told him it was nothing, an anxiety attack, nothing to do with him—then we got our faces painted with blue butterflies and went to a concert after dark, a white boy, former government accountant, channeling Muddy Waters, miracles on a nightly basis. When John and I got back to our room after midnight, we made love so vigorously that he asked if it was the blues or was it something else that made me need so bad some sugar in my bowl. I laughed but John wasn't making a joke, he was not a stupid man.

A few days later I heard that Tazza had broken off relationships with his girlfriends, news that made me twitch, flattering and shaming myself that a king was preparing his way toward me. And then there he was one night, John gone (an assignment from his king had taken him away) and Tazza telling me urgently I had to come with him, something he had to show me. It seemed important and I went with him straightaway, running a memory check on the underwear I had on and deciding I would wait until later to feel guilty about John.

Tazza took me outside on the Mall, gave me a flashlight. Apparently a truckload had been scavenged, flashlights handed out to anyone who asked, hundreds flashing their lights around the Mall this evening. It was always like this when something new was scavenged—leather vests found in a warehouse by the thousands and, overnight, everyone is wearing a leather vest. Tonight it's flashlights, some people carry one in each hand. It'll be fun until the batteries run out.

Tazza led me to the corner of a building, down into a house-size excavation and then into a hole that had been hacked and cracked through the building's foundation. The inside air was hot and depleted as if it had gone through a thousand lungs before reaching mine. Tazza in a hurry, taking my hand and pulling me along, and when I gripped his fingers in mine, holding hands with a king, I felt at once girlish and estrous, ignoring petulantly the grown-married-woman guilt that stood there tapping its toe and tsking.

We went through tunnels, up ladders. When we finally stopped, I asked Tazza where we were, and he flashed his light to a wall where hung a Madonna. I used my light. Raphael. What a beautiful baby is yours, Mother Mary. The baby has a pudgy baby-boy body but a face old with wisdom and serenity. How long has it been since I've seen something so beautiful?

"The National Gallery?" I ask Tazza, then shine my light on his face so I can see he's nodding yes. I told him, "You'll have to put guards here so people can't steal the artwork or damage it."

"I know, they've already taken some down from the walls. Here, that one leaning over there, it's Saint George killing the dragon."

We knelt, leaned in, shined our lights to illuminate every detail of this painting that was meant to be seen up close. I realized then something else I'd been starving for since the calamity, *art*.

"Do you think he looks like me?" Tazza asked.

I laughed, was he serious? How like children are men—dangerous, mercurial, Patagonian children. I shined my light from Tazza king to Raphael saint. "Spitting image."

"You see the ribbon around his calf? See what it says, Mary? *Honi*. That's the first word of the slogan of the Order of the Garter. *Honi soit qui mal y pense*. Do you know what that means?"

"No, but I'm sure you're going to tell me."

"Disgraced be he who thinks evil of it."

"Who told you that?" I asked, then realized what the answer must be—Tazza came here with John and it was John, my John, who spoke a Raphael river for the king to drink. I said, "I have to leave now."

"See, that could be you over here praying for me," Tazza said, ignoring my request to leave while he illuminated another part of the painting.

But I had already stood. "Which way out?"

"Mary, wait."

I walked off, figuring he'd eventually catch up and turn me in the right direction. When I heard voices, I followed their sound through stifling corridors, some of which had been stripped of their treasures and others having been used as toilets—was Tazza following, I wanted him to catch up and fuck me against some old expressionist, was how bad I had the fever for him.

The voices of children, I followed them around this way and that until I came to a room where dozens of children from toddlers to teens, each with a flashlight, shined those lights dancing across one huge painting: John Singleton Copley's *Watson and the Shark.*

So scary was this scene I took in a sharp breath as I watched light beams follow the painting's various actions, so much going on, the poor lad in the water, in the sea, so very white was he, anguished reaching, and so very naked, his blond hair like angel seaweed floating in the waves as, sweet Jesus, here comes a terrible shark, eye out of the water, shark eye trained on naked boy, evil eye eyeing boy, shark but inches from boy, why don't his friends *do* something . . . wait, there's one with a harpoon, oh look at his face, he's so angry, about to strike the terrible shark but will he strike in time, hurry, shark has snaked around from the front of the rescue boat and is lifting its terrible shark head out of the water, look at those teeth . . . the boy's mates, two of them at least, reach for him, why is he floating on his back all naked and white and vulnerable, why doesn't he grab the hands being offered him, has he already been shark-bit and is he dying? Some of the men in the boat have given up all hope, they've surrendered to despair, see it in their sorrowful faces . . . I can't bear to look at it another second, the painting tears at me . . . and so it tears at the children, too, children watching *Watson and the Shark,* children as shark-shocked and fearful as any man in that boat, some of the kids crying, one boy of eight holding a younger girl, sobbing . . . yet they can't stop looking, proof of this in their lights that play across all the painting's narratives, from harpoon unreleased to shark on the brink to lost naked boy with floating white angel seaweed hair . . . how long have the children been coming here to watch this painting the way they once watched scary movies, does art give them nightmares?

As if by signal all lights turn on me, and I put an arm across my face to ward off such illumination, wondering if they'll attack . . . but, no, the lights are not meant for me but for the one standing behind me. How did they know their king was present, did they smell him, did Tazza give a signal I failed to hear?

They advance on him, an attack of adoration, calling his name in a way that buzzes the *z*, "Tazza! Tazza!," as the smaller ones throw arms around his legs and the middle ones embrace his waist and the taller ones hang around his neck and laugh. He laughs, too, and doesn't tell them to stop, in fact hugs them back and then offers the children a common but remarkable gesture, what you do when puppies jump and whine at your presence, you lean down so they can deliver to your face a thousand puppy kisses, the king kneeling to his subjects.

I back away, envious of the children's intimacy with him.

When he stands again they hang off him like refugees and pepper Tazza with questions about the painting.

"What's going to happen to him?"

"Why doesn't he have any clothes on?"

"Will that guy in the boat get the shark before it's too late?"

"What happens?"

"*Tazza! Tazza! What happens!*"

"His name is Brook. And he's a boy not much older than many of you, fourteen. He was an orphan."

Several children gasped to hear this, *they* are orphans, too.

"And he loved the sea. Took off his clothes to go skinny-dipping in the harbor, Havana, Cuba. In that harbor lived a shark, its teeth sharp and pearly white. See it there, that Gorgonian head, that sawpit of a mouth." The children shine lights on the shark and shudder. "As young Brook swam, carefree, the shark, hungry, swam close behind. The attack, when it came, was swift. The shark bit off part of the boy's body. Who can tell me what part it was?"

They turn as one, their lights examining the naked boy in the painting.

"His right foot!" one of them shouts.

"Part of his right leg!" another excitedly agrees.

"Aye, lads . . . young Brook lost his lower right leg in the first attack, but he was *alive* and shouted for his friends and they came swift as they could, but by the time they reached their mate, the shark had returned to finish its meal. Look how they strain to reach Brook, look at the face of the one with the harpoon, how ferocious."

"What *happens*!" the children demanded, tormented by the suspense. And as Tazza unfolded the story I am reminded of John's river of talk, Tazza's story flowing to this open sea of children who are stricken to know how it ends—as I too am stricken to know how it ends, with my betrayal of John.

By July, Tazza had assembled his brigade of bagpipes, which preceded him to speeches and performances. And around the pipers slouched the totally cool Patagonians.

Dogs, which apparently had been kept in hiding so they wouldn't be eaten during the calamity, were allowed out to play among us on the Mall. Our mood was given further proof, those constant small butterflies, bright blue and barely an inch across, filling the air like windblown blue blossoms from forests of blue. We grew our hair ever longer and smiled from morning to sleep. You hardly ever encountered a face that wasn't painted with flowers and sunbursts and tiny blue butterflies.

Summer weather was perfect, love free.

Tazza wore tie-dyed shirts and spoke of this free love—love is the answer, he said, love is all you need.

Everyone rode liberated bicycles, including the Old Guard who had the hardest time looking ferocious as they pedaled by.

John wrote speeches warning against a sure-to-return government, a government of the power classes, a government to whom we will never surrender, we Americans possessing within us a hard core that will serve us well, loyal to our king, we will never give up. But, instead of those sober speeches, our love king gave soft messages advising that if you can't be with the one you love, then love the one you're with.

Young people dressed in outfits our scavengers found, girls in old-fashioned long dresses of velvet and lace and granny glasses, boys in vests and tall hats. When the scavengers brought back the contents of a music supply warehouse, people wore band uniforms with feathered hats and heavy coats bearing exaggerated epaulets. Brass buttons were everywhere. People old enough to remember said Tazza bore a resemblance to Jim Morrison.

We saw handmade posters advertising love-ins, be-ins, poetry-ins. Teenagers played at being witches and wiccas and wizards and Celtic druids and voodoo queens. Casual sex became so casually commonplace that of an evening you could literally trip over the intertwined. There was no police department to round us up and beat on our heads with their nightsticks, no mommies and daddies to say no.

Summer was a gas.

And then one of the scavenging trips returned with a truckload of cannabis.

We got high and stayed stoned, finding profundity in, like, you know, a single little blue butterfly that just, like, landed on my finger . . . you think that doesn't *mean* something?

Tazza came into the room John and I shared, our love king wild-eyed and happy at 3 a.m. to announce that he and his council had figured out, like, a whole new society where you would work sometimes and then other times you wouldn't have to work, you could just, like, kick back and contemplate the universe or whatever. "It operates on the honor system," he told us. "Like, no one keeps track of your work time but there's this whole big honor system that no one wants to violate, shame yourself, you know what I mean? Hey, you guys got anything to eat?"

I still met daily with my teams of determined women as we laughed indulgently at the potheads and plotted out what had to be done to keep our world livable, but then the scavengers brought back psychedelic mushrooms and later liberated a government lab that had made LSD and as drug supplies from various sources entered our lives, those lives got crazy and then profoundly lacking in ambition.

I was among the minority who didn't indulge. I went to see Tazza only when he was sober and happy to see me, saying I was his destiny as I watched him move about the room, blue jeans and unbuttoned white shirt, godlike in his prowess, the epitome of an alpha creature, his arrogance the arrogance of beauty.

I told him his feet were filthy.

"Yeah, I've been barefoot most of the day."

I brought over a pail of water and told him to sit there on the edge of the bed, I'd wash his feet.

"Wow, this is like, you know, *Jesus* and Mary."

"Don't talk." It was better when he didn't talk.

He watched me washing his feet and said, "See what I mean about being perfectly formed? Usually, people will have toes that are strange. Some are stubby, others too long, some like monkey feet, but my toes and feet, admit it, Mary, they're perfectly formed."

"They're very nice."

"No, *perfectly formed*. Mary, you think I'm bragging but I'm not, I'm trying to tell you there's something to this thing about me being a king. Like I was born to it."

"I thought the child you're always talking about will be born a king while you were made a king. At least that's what you're always saying."

"Here, let me show you my dick, how it's perfectly formed."

I laughed and splashed him with water. "I don't want to see your dick, you jerk."

"No, I'm serious."

I was still laughing when he carried me to his bed.

Our drug culture deepened, the early offerings of pot-LSD-coke joined now by Ecstasy, Special K, tanks of nitrous oxide, PCP, heroin, meth.

I lost to drugs most of the women who did the work and, after that, things that needed to be done went undone. Food spoiled. The Mall smelled like a sewer.

A crowd of stoners trying to break into the welded-shut Pentagon set off booby traps left by our government and seven were killed, dozens maimed. About half of our scavengers were still on the job, ranging ever farther to find supplies, and they came back with disturbing reports. Whenever they traveled more than a few days' journey from D.C., they found open graves and people hanging lynched from trees and bodies lying facedown with steaks cut from their buttocks.

I tried to tell Tazza that there's still a calamity in America, we're living in a bubble, but all Tazza wanted to do was fuck.

The nightly concerts got uglier, people slamming into one another, fistfights commonplace once again, banging heads together as some kind of crazy sport.

John and I seldom spoke except to argue, everything I did or said he found frivolous, ridiculous, a cause for scorn—and I saw him as ever so old, impotent, and poorly formed.

One afternoon, when I returned to our rooms, *when I was expected,* I opened the door to find John in our bed with a young woman, she must've been in her teens, red hair and plump as a hen.

I started to erupt, then went cold in my heart and told her, "Get out!"

She exited my bed all white-skinned and jiggly, red-haired between the legs, too, John, you fucking Irishman, the girl weeping her repeated I'm-sorrys as she fled.

John sat up, making no move to dress or explain or apologize or even look me in the eye.

I told him he should be ashamed of himself, a girl that young.

He said he was trying to give me comfort.

"Give *me* comfort?"

"Mary, now you can justify your betrayal of me—doesn't that lift a burden from your shoulders?"

"John." I wanted to go to my husband and try to explain but the look on his face was hateful.

We stopped sleeping in the same bed after that, still living together but no longer as man and wife.

Thousands of the people drifted away to start communes in the mountains, either to escape the constant drugs, sex, and rock 'n' roll or to indulge them all the more.

At one head-banging concert, someone in the crowd knocked over a couple bicycles owned by the Patagonians who were providing security that night, and the Patagonians went after the guy and knifed him and cut off one of his arms and stomped him to death. People screamed at them to stop, the Patagonians holding up their right wrists to show the strings tied there.

A few mornings later, I was walking back to my room from having spent the night with Tazza, which I did now on a regular basis. The Mall bore dawn evidence of yet another lost night, people passed out, clothes and trash everywhere, vomit splats forcing me to watch where I walked, a reeking smell of urine, piles of dog and people shit covered in little blue butterflies. I was halfway home before my eye made sense of something: a certain pattern to the trash. I tried to figure out what it was, then I saw it: the Mall was sown with sheets of brown paper. I picked up several, they all had the same printed message.

It was sobering to see something recently printed, which meant that someone somewhere had access to computers or other means of setting type and printing. I got a chill when I realized that the even distribution of the flyers meant that they had not been passed out by hand but had been scattered from aircraft. *Last night, a craft flew over us and dropped things while we slept.*

John was up when I got back to our rooms, he was washing his face in cold water, looking like a hundred years ago. The window where he stood faced the Mall.

"Do you see them?" I asked.

At first he didn't acknowledge my presence but then looked out at the Mall while drying his face.

I said, "Those brown flyers everywhere, see them?"

"So?"

"John." I didn't need him to be pissy right at this moment, I was shaking so severely I had to sit.

"What is it?" he asked impatiently.

I held out one of the flyers.

John came over and got it, read the headline, then looked at me with stark eyes.

I asked him, "It's bad, isn't it?"

Tight-lipped, he nodded.

19

SOME THINGS YOU
SHOULD KNOW
WHEN WAR COMES

This leaflet confuses and frightens us. *When* war comes? We had heard no rumors of war. Who's the enemy? What will they do when they reach us? Where are they at this moment? Are *we* the enemy?

The leaflet claims, "Your Federal Government is taking all possible measures for the defense of the United States and the protection of all law-abiding citizens. You, in turn, should do all you can to help your Government. Keep your gas masks and thermal fire-retardant blankets with you at all times."

We have no gas masks, we have no fire-retardant blankets—and the idea that we will need these items is sufficiently terrifying that people sober up right quick. We police the area for trash, druggies hide their stashes, the night's concerts are canceled, and we gather to talk about what the leaflet means.

A second flyer is dropped a few nights later. This time, without drugs and loud music to interfere, people hear the copters. These leaflets are printed on light blue paper.

THE IMPORTANCE OF YOUR SOCIAL SECURITY NUMBER

"Every person must have and know his/her Social Security number and the U.S. Postal ZIP code at which the person was residing prior to this emergency. All Government benefits and protections will be distributed based on citizen identification as established by Social Security number and former U.S. Postal ZIP code. Once your Government has reestablished control, a very nearly painless method of laser application of your Social Security number will be provided free of charge. This service is highly recommended."

John, Tazza, and I are talking near a Metro entrance on the Mall, John displaying his ability to separate his loyalty to his king in one compartment and, in another compartment, the plain fact of being cuckolded by the man.

"Metro can become a vast underground fortress, like the tunnel system the Vietcong used." John is arguing for Tazza to assemble an army immediately, arm the people with whatever weapons the scavengers have collected over the summer, and begin a resistance against government forces.

Tazza's not so sure. "We need to figure out how many people will stand with us."

John looks hatefully at me. "Will your women corps fight?"

"If it comes to that."

"Well that's twenty more *cleaning ladies* we can count on," John says disgustedly. "We know of course that the government stock-piled fuel. Enough for those helicopters dropping flyers—and enough for troop trucks and tanks, too. A few more leaflet drops and next thing we know they're just going to show up here one bright dawn. And then what?"

Tazza says, "The Patagonians want to fight. And my scavengers say they can scavenge enough materiel to supply a guerrilla army indefinitely. You're right about the weapons, they've been collecting and stockpiling them all summer. We got the stuff under lock and key in one of the buildings off the Mall. But mainly it's hunting gear."

John says, "Which is what the Minutemen and other patriots used in the Revolutionary War, their hunting rifles."

I point out that in the Revolutionary War the Americans were fighting *against* a king.

My husband shoots me another hateful look, a thousand a day he sends my way. "Fighting *tyranny*. And now a king can oppose democratic tyranny—if the king chooses to fight."

Tazza said he doesn't think the people have it in them to fight.

"Then *inspire* them to fight," John insists. "For chrissakes, Tazza, have you forgotten the speeches you gave, the way the people responded? You've lost your edge, we all have, after a summer of getting stoned, wearing flowers, and fucking people we shouldn't be fucking."

Tazza started to say something, John put his hand up. "The point is, we can get our edge back. Your people will be inspired to follow you if *you talk to them and lead them*. You haven't given a single speech since the first leaflet was dropped."

Just then we hear a distant thump that quickly becomes louder, scaring us into the Metro entrance and far enough down the stopped escalators to hide from whatever it is flying over us—like prairie dogs diving into a tunnel as a hawk approaches.

Black Hawk. Low enough we see its crew sitting along the open door. And in the Hawk's wake, another ten thousand flyers.

WHAT THE EMERGENCY POWERS
ACT MEANS FOR YOU
AND YOUR FAMILY

Treason normally applies only during times of war but it is applicable now, says the leaflet, because the calamity has been declared the equivalent of war. *Sedition,* according to the leaflet, is any act that any government official could interpret as damaging to domestic tranquility. *Slander* against the government was mentioned prominently. Same punishment as for treason—in fact summary execution and imprisonment of family were the punishments for all the listed crimes:

> *Breach of allegiance.*
> *Betrayal.*
> *Espionage.*
> *Insurrection.*
> *Mutiny.*
> *Sabotage.*
> *Subversion.*
> *Syndicalism (organizing or joining a group advocating overthrow*
>   *of the government).*
> *Terrorism.*
> *Counterfeiting.*
> *Fraudulent tax evasion.*
> *Crimes against the administration of justice.*
> *Crimes against the reestablishment of Government.*
> *Perjury (usually taking a false oath in a judicial proceeding but*
>   *now defined as lying to a government official).*

Subornation of perjury.

Bribery.

Contempt of authority.

Intent (not committing but intending to commit any of the above).

And so on. In the whole long list, one crime was boldfaced: *"No person shall accept, extend, or tolerate any emolument, title, office, or commission from, or make any statement or act of loyalty toward, any person or persons claiming status as King or Prince. Punishment is summary execution. All family members of the guilty party will be imprisoned until such time as the status of their guilt, innocence, or complicity can be established."*

At the very end of the leaflet, in smaller type, were ten footnotes:

1. The Government will until further notice regulate all organized religions and ban practice of those religions not registered with proper Government authority; all speech, publications, and performances must be submitted in advance to the proper Government authority; no more than three individuals may gather in places private or public for more than three hours without a permit from the Government; grievances under these provisions and others will be stored in a database until such time that grievances can be reviewed by the proper Government authority.

2. All firearms must be turned over to the proper Government police or military authority immediately; there are no exceptions.

3. Until such time that Government housing facilities can be renovated, Government officials, including, but not limited to, military personnel, will be quartered in private homes as deemed necessary by proper Government authority.

4. Enforcing the laws against crimes outlined in this information sheet may require search and/or seizure of persons, houses, papers, effects, vehicles, computers, hard drives, weapons not limited to firearms, and other such as determined by the proper Government authority.

5. Laws against crimes outlined in this information sheet will by necessity be enforced directly, without indictment; if new evidence of such crimes is uncovered after a person is acquitted of such crimes, that person will be brought before the proper Government authority for subsequent review, trial, punishment as deemed necessary; various conventions against methods used to collect evidence, including self-incriminating statements, have no authority within the United States; in this time of calamity, proper Government authority may requisition, without payment, whatever property, materiel, and labor as are deemed necessary for the common good.

6. Persons detained under the laws against the crimes outlined in this information sheet will have hearings when time permits; hearing officers and jurors will be appointed by proper Government authority; when national security so requires, the accusations against persons brought to trial under the laws against the crimes outlined in this information sheet will be sealed, as will the identity of witnesses, jurors, if any, and judges; outside counsel is not permitted in hearings and trials involving national security issues.

7. When the backlog of cases waiting to be prosecuted under the laws against the crimes outlined in this information sheet is deemed burdensome, trials and hearings will be processed on a fast track basis without jury.

8. No bail is allowed for persons accused of breaking the laws against the crimes outlined in this information sheet; persons convicted of said crimes will have property seized; international conventions governing punishment are not applicable in the United States.

9. The enumeration in this information sheet and the authorizations under the Emergency Powers Act, of certain crimes, laws, and powers, shall not be construed to deny or disparage other authority retained by the Government.

10. The powers not delegated to the people by this information sheet are reserved to the Federal Government; until such time as order is reestablished, State Governments will work in cooperation with, in support of, and in subordination to the Federal Government.

20

I awake at dawn to a gagging urge to vomit, forcing me to scramble out of bed and find an empty bucket. The thought and smell of food is an abomination to me as my husband and my king plot in the next room over burnt toast and black coffee.

"How many will come with us?" John asks.

"The Old Guard, the scavengers, my pipers."

"Yes, yes, I know—but how many of *the people*? You've been out talking to them. Will we have a credible number?"

"What's credible?" Tazza asks.

"The government is probably still in disarray. If they weren't, they wouldn't be wasting time with those stupid leaflets, trying to intimidate us—they'd just roll on in and take over. I figure if we had a few thousand people, a thousand minimum, a thousand united, armed, determined people, we might be able to negotiate a settlement, get a little piece of territory, somewhere in the mountains where they'd leave us alone until they got their strength back. And then by that time, maybe we have enough people with us that we can stave off the government indefinitely."

Tazza says two hundred.

Which takes the air from John. "Two hundred people out of all those thousands, those tens of thousands who rallied by the river, who partied all summer on the Mall. What's that give us? It gives us nothing. Add in your fifty Patagonians, your fifty scavengers, twenty pipers . . ."

"No, I was adding those in already. Two hundred including everyone. Including even you and me, you and me and Mary and Mary's women—two hundred."

Which leaves John with nothing to say.

"People are afraid of the federal government," Tazza tells him.

"You know what I think, Tazza? I think the people are sheep. I think they can't wait for someone to show up from the government and start telling them what to do."

I come into the room to see Tazza standing behind John, who's in a chair with both hands over his face, Tazza leaning down to comfort my husband.

John isn't crying, he's simply exhausted with despair.

Tazza tells him we'll make a stand. He speaks to us, to me over by the door and to John sitting right there where Tazza stands, he speaks to us of holding tightly to hope, of never giving up. He speaks quietly, his fingers don't jab the air, he doesn't gesture—but there is about his voice an intimate strength and absolute sincerity that make us, John and me, want to believe the impossible story he's telling us.

I walk over and put my arms around the both of them, John glancing up, catching my eye before slipping out from under my touch with a muttered word I think is *cunt.*

21

In the night, tanks and trucks tremble the streets of Washington, D.C., as we few, we two hundred left from so many thousands, we shiver in a summer's pre-dawn chill to organize our blankets and cooking pots and then pull our carts and carry our bundles refugee fashion down New York Avenue to diaspora our sorry asses at the Arboretum.

We hurry along to rumors and sounds of RATs.

The United States Army developed the Rumsfeld Antipersonnel Truck during the calamity to disperse mobs. It was an armored vehicle more tank than truck but Congress, suddenly dainty, refused to authorize expenditures for tanks to be used against American citizens, so the military called this tank a truck. The RAT proved so effective against crowds that it was eventually deployed all across America, used to protect army bases and airfields where the very rich had nested under the protective eye of the U.S. military. We had heard of RATs being sent in to break up demonstrations, we had heard they were wickedly effective killing machines.

It was an eight-wheel-drive combat vehicle, the size of a large panel truck, highly maneuverable on combat-reinforced tires. The RATs looked like drones in that there was no obvious hatch, no openings, no observation portals, and the front of the vehicle differed little from the rear. The turret contained twelve barrels that could be swiveled up and down, side to side. Around the RAT's edge, above the eight tires, four electrified cables were strung on insulated braces, the bare-wire cables about eighteen inches apart. To test its capabilities—and this is all part of the historical record, you could look it up—a RAT in Detroit drove into the middle of a thousand starving, rioting domestic terrorists and then simply stopped with the electrical grid off. People swarmed the vehicle, looking for a way in. Once the RAT was covered with these hunger-crazed domestic terrorists, the crew switched on the grid and fried forty of them—then the RAT took off very fast and stopped abruptly, go and stop, go and stop, making sure that all the electrocuted terrorists got shaken off the wires before bringing the RAT home with zero casualties to the federals troops inside.

How would we defend ourselves against RATs? Escape into the mountains of western Virginia and West Virginia seemed our only option. But for the moment, to collect ourselves, we would camp at the Arboretum.

The first order Tazza and John issue is espionage—that a dozen scavengers should ease themselves toward the Mall and White House, find out what the Feds are up to, then report back to us. The scavengers throw themselves into the assignment, starting with detailed discussions about disguises.

Over the next two days, we set up tents, we women, we organize feeding schedules and sentry duty, aware always of the possibility that the government is going to send in the RATs. The early spy reports are as bad for us as they can be. *The people who abandoned us are happy with their government.* Happy as in iPods distributed widely with generous selections of music. Happy as in generators set up and movies and taped television shows playing twenty-four hours a day. Happy as in half the team we sent there to spy went over to the government's side and never returned to the Arboretum, the scavengers turned traitors in exchange for video games. Of all the bad news, the worst came from a young scavenger who said the Mall was scattered with short lengths of string abandoned by the people. I told Tazza we should go to the mountains and prepare ourselves for a guerrilla war. We'll Castro their asses.

But, against my advice, we stayed at the Arboretum, spreading our camps among the conifers and junipers while planning to take to the deeper woods, hide under bridges in Fern Valley, make ourselves scarce when the government comes for us. We welcomed displaced people who wandered in from the surrounding neighborhoods, we fed them and indoctrinated them with talk of king. We added maybe a hundred to our number—and lost fifty who couldn't resist the temptations being reported back by our spies, that the government had set up stores where you could buy nice clothes and fashionable shoes and cellophaned snacks, where you could buy Coca-Cola, which we hadn't tasted in a year or more, where you could buy cosmetics and cameras. Purchases could be made with tokens that you earned by working for the government.

Then came the development that turned history in our favor. To manage human resources, the government said people would have to be organized by the ZIP codes where they lived when the calamity commenced. Since residence was the basis for the most profound divisions among pre-calamity Americans, with neighborhoods segregated by race and wealth, with the rich in their own protected pockets—using ZIP codes to assemble people began reestablishing racial and economic segregation.

Poor people got pissed, realizing it was the same old shit all over again. With Tazza, no one had been segregated—not by race or riches or rank.

Matters got progressively worse for the poor people under the federal government's jurisdiction. Wages paid in tokens got cut and the cost of goods went up, working people forced to take on second jobs if they wanted to continue eating at tents franchised by McDonald's and shopping at the tent-city Wal-Mart set up on the National Mall under government sponsorship.

Meanwhile, the government issued elaborate instructions written in dense governmentese regarding what behavior was allowed, what was prohibited, these impossible-to-follow regulations enforced arbitrarily, keeping the people perpetually in violation of something. You went unjailed only at the discretion of the government.

In the name of national security, hundreds of citizens disappeared from Washington, D.C.

We started getting our people back. At night when they could slip between government pickets, poor people made their way to the Arboretum where we welcomed them home without recrimination. They eagerly re-tied strings around their left wrists.

Those among us who had had military training or were hunters taught the rest of us how to shoot. Helicopters overflying the Arboretum got peppered with gunfire from eager-to-practice trainees.

We dug bunkers and bomb shelters at the edges of Arboretum forests and expected the bombardment to commence with any given dawn, the government hoping to catch us asleep with our children, but day after day we went unattacked while night after night our numbers grew as more people became disaffected with the government.

Tazza gave speeches rekindling the old fire, telling the people that what the federal government was doing on the Mall was exactly what the government would always do because it was a government established to protect the rich and powerful and, to do that, the working people and common people and poor people had to be kept divided. "They will split us as they have always split us," Tazza said.

"Union against nonunion. Black against white. Educated against unschooled. One will get the privilege, one will not. At times it will be reversed so that the formerly unprivileged become the privileged to lord it over those no longer privileged. The government cares less who is favored, black over white or union over nonunion—the government cares more that we are kept divided so that we can never rise up against government oppression. I tell you this, that if there were but twelve of us left and we were all white or all black, all union or all nonunion, the government would still divide us somehow, by eye color or by height—or alphabetically by our last names so that those after *M* got special favors never enjoyed by those whose names fell in the first half of the alphabet. We must do the opposite of what they're doing on the Mall. Where they divide, we must unite. We must join together black and white, English-speaking and Spanish-speaking, educated and unschooled, former supervisor with former worker—all the people united under their king to establish a kingdom dedicated to the well-being of everyone."

As word spread that Tazza was reestablishing his kingdom at the Arboretum, this time without drugs or promiscuous sex, many of those who had left earlier in the summer came drifting back from their outlying communes.

Tazza's goofy but spectacularly effective scavengers rounded up a hundred pigs and we had barbecues every night.

We had survived the summer of love and returned now to the idealism of our earliest days, Tazza's fiery and emotional speeches making us cheer and weep as we greeted a hundred new converts and a hundred old friends returning each night.

As the weeks wore on, I left my shirt untucked to hide my truth, not fooling the one man on earth I wanted to fool.

Finally the hour we dreaded arrived at midday, a thousand government troops marching, their heavy uniforms and giant helmets and tinted visors hiding their humanity. These anonymous military units carried rifles and, on the ends of their rifles, they had affixed silver bayonets that flashed in the sunlight. They had marched here from the Mall, unaccompanied by RATs or any other vehicle, not even a motorcycle. The soldiers arrayed in straight lines, rifles up, blinding bayonets tilted skyward.

When Tazza saw the intimidating effect these heavily armed and uniformed troops had on the people, he called for his pipers and his Patagonians. With these in attendance around him, he gave us a speech. I tell you now that our situation differed little from that of a thousand years ago, ten thousand years ago. An enemy approached. A leader spoke to his people.

"We will win! We will prevail! If you don't have confidence of that, I have confidence enough for all of us and thousands more. Whatever it is you need, anger enough to fight or courage enough to die—I have enough for each and every one of you."

He was feeding his people and we ate eagerly of our king.

22

The stalemate was reminiscent of the Revolutionary or Civil War. Those thousand U.S. Army soldiers in lines, some straight and some curved to accommodate the landscape. In places, three or four ranks lined up one behind the other; on other terrain, a single rank of soldiers held the ground.

Our people, outnumbering the soldiers, hadn't been armed. We asked Tazza several times about the weapons but he wouldn't give the order for our people to arm. With nothing but courage to protect us, the people arrayed behind hilltops and in whatever copse and thicket would hide us.

Being civil to me for at least the duration of this battle, John took me to a flank position where we could watch the action without being in the cross fire. He didn't know why the government hadn't advanced or hadn't started firing—but he figured they were waiting for us to fire the first shot and legitimize a counterattack. "That's why Tazza didn't give the order to arm."

"Smart," I said, placing my hand on John's forearm. "Was that *your* strategy?" He stared at me until I stopped touching him.

A terrible screech broke the standoff's silence as here come Tazza's pipers, marching all kilted and highland-flinging in one ragged line facing the nearest rank of government troops a hundred yards away. In two groups, one at either end of the pipers, the King's Own Patagonian Old Guard ran in front of the bagpipers playing an old war scream.

The Patagonians wore their outfits, shower caps and wedding dresses, and they carried machetes and they were once again grimly mute.

What did the United States Army soldiers think of this bizarre alignment, mute men with machetes and wedding veils eighty yards away and, twenty yards behind them, men in kilts, playing pipes? Were they laughing behind their face shields?

John and I watched the plan unfold, Tazza coming out from the forest with children, a hundred children around him, children as young as four, as old as eight, Tazza carrying a beautiful baby in each arm, one black and one white, both wearing red dresses. The children walking around him wore dresses and overalls and footed pajamas in rainbow colors, the older children helping the younger, some lingering to examine a treasure in the grass and then running to catch up. This children's crusade walked among the pipers and then through the ranks of Patagonians and then Tazza like a piper himself led the children toward the soldiers.

The Patagonian Old Guard held their position and the pipers fell silent. From around the ends of their lines came a hundred young women in summer dresses. I wondered where the scavengers found such an array of pretty dresses. The girls were barefoot and carried things. Among the things they carried were flowers and fudge and small drawings they had created with colored pencils. A hundred beautiful women, beautiful for being so young—fifteen-year-olds and twenty-year-olds and their hair shiny and they wore flowers in their hair and they smiled white teeth and they were young black women, young white women, young Latina women, young Asian women, many of them laughing, nudging one another as girls do on a lark.

This group of two hundred, half children and half young women, all led by Tazza in jeans and a white shirt and barefoot and I saw now that he wore a garland of white clover blossoms tilted on his head like a Bacchus.

Joining in from the sides marched yet another one hundred women, these were my women—my organizers and workers, my nurses and nurturers. They were my age, forty-two, and they were old enough to be my mother and they were old enough to be my grandmother. These hundred mature women in plain dresses carried baskets of food they had made, preserves from this summer's early berries and bread freshly baked in our camp stoves and they carried cookies, too. I had no idea what the children or young women would do upon reaching the soldiers, but I knew with an absolute certainty what my women would do, they would open their baskets and say to the soldiers, "Here, have something to eat."

When Tazza carrying his babies now laughing got to the first rank of government soldiers stationed along the prairie section of the Arboretum, he simply walked between bayonets and continued to the next rank, making his way between two more upright bayonets, on and on more deeply into government territory while all around him his accompanying children bumped through and around the legs of soldiers. Some of the kids stopped to stare up at the intimidating figures. Some spoke to the soldiers, asking what's your name and telling their own names. Many of the younger children had tired from the walk and excitement and sat at the booted feet of their government. A few of the younger children wept and fussed but most were quiet and obedient to whatever lessons Tazza had given them before the march.

Into the soldiers' ranks behind the children came the young women barefoot and larking while, behind them, came the older women with food.

The soldiers held.

John said, "Their commanders can't figure out what orders to issue and, in the absence of orders, this paralysis."

I said, "There's nothing in the government manual to cover what to do when the enemy comes at you with children and pretty women in summer dresses and older women who remind you of your mother and your granny, where's it say in the war manual what to do about that?"

As Tazza penetrated the ranks with his children, the young and old women continued to follow awhile, then they stopped and talked to the soldiers. A young woman would say to a helmeted head, "I wish you'd come back with me. We have a king now. Every-thing we do, we do to help one another. I'd love to show you how we live. Come on, join us."

The old women would say, "Here, have a cookie. I baked them myself."

A child might hold out her arms and ask to be picked up.

When Tazza and his children got far enough into the ranks that all of the young women behind him and all the old women behind them were among the government troops, he handed his babies off to soldiers, the first several refusing to break formation and accept a baby—but then one did, carefully placing his rifle on the ground and taking the little black baby, who screeched in fear of the big hel-met until the soldier took it off and smiled and the baby smiled back at him. After that, a dozen soldiers laid down their arms and took off their helmets and knelt to speak to the children. Tazza went among these dozen and shook their hands and told them he was their American king and pledged his life to taking care of them. The young men said they were weary of killing Americans.

The young women were pretty and happy and like summer itself, bright and warm and shiny, a hundred of the thousand soldiers taking off their helmets to speak to these girls, accepting from them small colored-pencil drawings and, from the bolder girls, a kiss on the cheek.

The older women put their detergent hands to the cheeks of these boys with guns and told them they were princes—princes who looked like they could use a home-cooked meal. "Come back down the hill with me," the women told the soldiers. "I'll serve you dinner and wash some nice clothes to wear, those uniforms look miserable."

I was amazed to see it, the magic that Tazza made against a government army. John was impressed, too, but he couldn't get over the chance Tazza was taking. "One soldier, one bullet, one bayonet thrust, and our king is dead and our whole movement is lost. Who would take up where Tazza left off? There's no one."

There is one, I thought, a tadpole not yet ready for a throne.

John said, "It's not fair to the rest of us."

"But it's working."

By now, half the government's force, five hundred of them, had taken off their helmets and put down their rifles to talk to the women and hold the children and accept things to eat. A few of the soldiers were being comforted on the heavy bosoms of those older women; many of the soldiers were holding hands with the young women.

Whoever commanded these soldiers finally took action and issued orders through helmeted receivers. The soldiers were to form up and leave the Arboretum. Those who heard the order told their brethren who weren't wearing helmets: saddle up, it's time to go.

Marching gingerly not to step on a child's foot or knock into an old lady, the government troops reassumed military postures and made their way up a hill and out as they had come in.

Except . . . for one hundred and sixty-eight of the soldiers who, instead of marching away, walked down the hill still holding hands with young women or taking an old woman's arm—many came carrying babies. The Patagonians were too aloof to acknowledge these soldiers but the pipers piped them in and the people swarmed them with welcomes and good wishes. These were our brothers, our sons—made to war against their own people. But now they had come home to us.

John and I walked down to congratulate Tazza, who was greeting the soldiers, asking their names, which he would remember, each one of them, such was his talent.

"You took a hell of a chance," John told him when the three of us finally had a chance to talk. "But it's not going to happen like that next time the government comes."

Tazza smiling, telling John that he carries his worries too heavily. "I got a hundred and sixty-eight of them to come over to our side," Tazza said, still grinning. "Next time I'll take their whole . . . entire . . . army."

23

That night Tazza talked to the one hundred and sixty-eight soldiers,
walking among them, a hand on their shoulders, an arm around
their necks, working his magic, whatever inborn quality he possessed that made us love him and made us want to be loved by him,
making Tazza a king. In small groups and one at a time he advised
these soldiers to leave in the morning. In fact, he said, I *need* you to
return to your units. He said he feared for them if they stayed here
at the Arboretum with us—they would be shot as traitors. He didn't
ask the soldiers to spy for us or go easy on us if there's a battle, but
Tazza knew that those hundred and sixty-eight would return with
stories that might make other American soldiers hesitate if given an
order to kill us. He knew this because he knew how they would be
treated tonight.

"For now, for tonight," Tazza said, "accept our hospitality. We
have barbecue. Music. The moon's bright, spend the night. Enjoy
the company."

At the fire, I sat near Corporal Oliver Eric Mor, as he formally introduced himself to me, ma'am. With him was one of our young women whom we called Cap. Their sticky talk made me feel fraudulent . . . I who had a husband to whom I had given my Lakota pledge of fidelity and I who had become pregnant by a perfectly formed king. These adult complications in my life made me sick when I heard a teenage soldier telling an adolescent girl how it felt to touch fingers with her.

"They instructed us back at the base," says the soldier Mor, "that the women hanging around this guy, your King Tazza, that they were all, you know, *easy,* it was a cult and the women had to sleep with King Tazza and the women had diseases and would try to get us to, you know, do it with them so then the diseases would knock us out of action."

"Maybe you shouldn't be holding my hand—God knows what you might catch."

He's mortified she took him wrong. "No, I was just saying what they told us, to show you the kind of lies we've been told about you people and your King Tazza."

She laughs softly. "*You people?* We're just regular Americans. I was in junior high when the calamity hit."

"Yeah, me, too. Well, just started high school."

She suggests they move away from the fire, too hot here and too crowded. "I promise not to seduce you and give you a disease."

"I shouldn't have even said that," he says as they walk away in the night, two fingers of his hand intertwining two fingers of hers.

"Do you like the night?" she asks.

He must wonder what answer will please her, this soldier prepared to despise the night and curse its darkness or, if that's the wrong answer, he will declare love and eternal devotion for this black-browed night.

She is an American teenager, she has a large mouth and large smiles and she laughs easily; a national calamity and months of starving didn't throttle the coquette in her. She has short brown hair and tonight has gone to the trouble of feathering it. Lipstick, at a premium, is prominent upon her generous lips.

He takes her hand fully in his.

"You're being bold, soldier boy."

"I wish I could hold your hand all the time, twenty-four hours a day."

"That would lead to some awkward moments."

"I wish I was a glove on your hand."

"Easy now." She laughs, squeezes back when he squeezes her hand. "Just keep in mind I'm an enemy of the state and you are a soldier of that state, pledged to defend it against all enemies, foreign and domestic."

"You're not my enemy," he says earnestly. "I mean, dammit anyway, do you think of *me* as your enemy?"

"I suppose this hand isn't my enemy," she tells him, squeezing that hand once more. "Or your foot." Playfully nudging that foot with hers. "Or your arm or this face." She touches his face with her free hand (the other hand he is loath to release), a face he hasn't yet grown into, though she can tell, any woman could, that the years will make him handsome and will eventually put his Adam's apple in perspective. "Or any other part belonging to a man."

He gets red, he gets hard.

"I don't want you to be a soldier that fights against the people," she tells him, dead serious now and whispering in that way young women whisper to break a young man's heart. "If you gave up being a soldier, I'd give myself to you."

Delirious he becomes and tells her *yes* a thousand times. "Call me 'love' and I'll be newly baptized."

"The way you talk!"

He guffaws, waits for another lick from poet's tongue, then falls mute.

"You see the moon?" she asks, encouraging him with the possibilities, moon June swoon.

"I see how beautiful it is," he says, looking at her and not the moon.

She laughs and puts a finger under his chin, raising his face to the moon.

The soldier lids his eyes and says, "I know the moon is envious of you, is sick and pale with grief that you are far more fair than she."

"The way you go on!"

"Let's sit here."

They sit beneath a weeping blue atlas cedar, *Cedrus atlantica,* beneath which they kiss, her tongue tip touching his lightly, inflaming him.

"Oliver?"

"What?"

She requires them to sit up so he can see her face in this moonlight, which in fact has rendered words superfluous, though words she nevertheless offers him. "I love you."

He starts to say he loves her too, a rookie's error, but she silences him by touching his lips with a soft finger. "I know you must leave tomorrow, and I know I'm going to cry all day. But I'll be better when tomorrow night comes. Because when it's night, it'll remind me of this moment and I'll think of Oliver cut out into little stars posted in the heavens making the sky so fine that all the girls here will fall in love with the night and pay no worship to the garish sun."

"Okay."

She kissed him, hard.

Coming up for air he isn't sure how to ask this next question. "Are we going to do it?"

"Well, Corporal Oliver Eric Mor, we have already bought love's mansion, I think we should possess it, don't you?"

Of course, in truth I have no idea what they said to each other once they left the fire and went off by themselves. But I imagine.

24

At our encampment in the Arboretum during the days following our victory at what the history books whimsically call the First Battle of the Arboretum, we are euphoric to have turned back the government and as people elsewhere hear about this bloodless victory our numbers increase by hundreds. Yet, none of us believed that the war was over.

We three sit on red canvas chairs outside a large tent where Tazza lives with a dozen Patagonian bodyguards. John has his own tent somewhere, I don't know where, probably living with his chicken-breasted baby redhead. While I live in a tent with my women.

My pregnancy, an open secret, has given me and the women an elevated status; one of them told me that "Mary and her women" are spoken of with a reverence equal to "Tazza and his Old Guard." My women have taken to dressing alike, wearing full-length white aprons that tie at the neck and waist. It is a practical garment—my women still do mother's work, we feed the two thousand or so who live here at the Arboretum with us; we doctor our sick and take in the orphans; we oversee the construction and maintenance of latrines; we settle squabbles; and I meet daily with the scavengers to tell them the commodities we need.

"If a history is ever written of this period," John tells Tazza as we sit here on red canvas chairs idling the day, "the historians will wonder why Tazza dithered at the Arboretum following the government's first unsuccessful attack. Why didn't Tazza take his people and escape into the ruins of the city or into the mountains? Why did he simply wait here for the inevitable second attack? Which he must've known was coming. Which his trusted advisor told him was coming. The government can't allow a renegade group to survive, not when the government is trying to reestablish itself and is having its own problems. You remember what those soldiers told us, the ones who stayed overnight? The ones we should've kept with us instead of sending back, trained soldiers with their own weapons who would've supplemented nicely our Patagonians with shower caps and machetes. Those soldiers told us that the government was not all-powerful, that occasionally the food or fuel runs out and there are no aircraft, no power for their computers. A government that is that *tenuous* is dangerous and for its own survival it must be tough on insurgents before other breakaway groups are encouraged. Yet here we sit."

Tazza eats a small but very red apple. "Are you finished, John?"

"No—but you've stopped listening to me."

Tazza's consumption of the small, red apple is accompanied by a level of enjoyment that I find mesmerizing and that makes me want, actually hanker for, an apple equal to his. "Mary?"

At first I think he's asking me about the apple, it looms so large in my mind, but then I realize he wants my opinion. I tell him, "If the government sends troops again and, if this time they're willing to shoot—how do we fight back?"

John won't acknowledge me directly but agrees that it's a good question.

"I've been in negotiations with the government," Tazza says as he contemplates the apple's core.

John and I are surprised. First, this is huge news, Tazza negotiating with the government. Second, what does it mean that he didn't bring us into his confidence, that he didn't ask our advice or counsel for something as important as negotiating with the government?

"So that's why they haven't attacked," John says. "They're talking to you."

I'm more direct. "Why didn't you tell us?"

Tazza says, "One of my advisors, you know her, Mary—Beverly? She was in pharmaceutical sales before the calamity and has a brilliant way of *seeing* things. At her suggestion and with her help we sent feelers to the government commanders, asking if we might negotiate a surrender."

Neither John nor I had any idea that Tazza was conducting this entirely separate strategy. We thought we knew the man but apparently we had been seeing only small parts of who he was, of what he was capable of doing.

"You wouldn't surrender us," John says.

"The idea being to give us time," he explains.

"Time for what?" John asks.

"They're monitoring us," Tazza says. "If we started to leave, they'd attack."

"So we stay here until when? Are you waiting for something?"

"A naval report."

John and I exchange looks.

"Naval as in . . . ?" I ask.

Tazza sits smug in his ability to keep confounding us.

John's the one who figures it out. "Oh my God, you mean *Boatman*."

Tazza smiles. "You told me he was the second person, next to you, who believed America could have a king."

"What's he going to do, mount a naval attack on government forces—one man, one boat."

"He's gathering . . ." Tazza looked around to make sure no one lurks within listening distance. "Boatman is finding out about the weather. Up and down the coast there are still lots of people with boats, with radios that work—they know when storms are coming."

"I don't understand," I say to Tazza.

"We got word that a hurricane is heading this way."

John asks him if the plan is to use the storm to cover our retreat.

"I don't intend to retreat. This coalition we now have is fragile. You saw what happened, so many of the people returning to the government at the first opportunity. The only way we'll survive is if we defeat the government forces."

"*Defeat?*" John looks to me for support. "We have children with machetes, our men carry hunting rifles and six-shooters."

"A great storm is headed this way. It will count as a division and a corps on our side."

"He's insane," John says to me or to no one as he starts to walk away, then returns and puts his hands on the back of a canvas chair to tell Tazza again that he's out of his mind.

"You forget yourself, John."

"No, you forget *yourself.*" John is as angry as I've ever seen him. "I made you a king and you betrayed me."

"It was destiny, what happened between Mary and I."

"Mary and *me*, you fucking ignorant actor."

"I could have you killed, John."

"You and Mary betrayed me," John says quietly, in despair.

"Then it was your destiny to be betrayed."

Which is when I get up and leave.

For the next hour I work in a garden, tending vegetables I know we will never harvest, our time here is too tenuous—and it is among my heirloom tomatoes, large but still green, that John finds me.

I want to stand and put my arms around him, touch my dirty hands to his old face, try to measure for him the breadth and depth of how very sorry I am—without ever mentioning, of course, what I find bright in this terrible thing, I'm finally having a baby, so late in life but not too late—a king's whelp in my belly.

"It's madness," he finally says. "I've talked to others. You know what his plan is, his whole fucking crazy plan? Boatman is monitoring this hurricane, God knows how they're doing it these days, but apparently the forecast is, it'll hit sometime tomorrow. Tazza is going to break off negotiations, tell the government to come get us, and then during the battle, the storm hits and scatters the government forces and everyone thinks Tazza is divine. He's talking to his inner group about the kamikaze, the typhoon that destroyed the Mongol navy in the Thirteenth Century, saving Japan. Kamikaze means divine wind. *That's his plan.* That we're going to be saved by a divine storm."

I don't know what to say.

"You have to talk to him, Mary. If a storm does hit, we could use it to cover our escape. No aircraft to track us in a storm. That's still a viable plan. You have to talk to him or else we'll be wiped out."

"I heard about the storm plan the same time you did, an hour ago. He doesn't confide in me."

"When the government attacks next time, they won't be held back by pretty girls in summer dresses and old ladies with cookies."

"I know."

"Have you seen the RATs?"

"My women have told me about them."

"They're patrolling around the Arboretum."

"I've heard them, it's terrible the way they sound."

"The government is going to send the RATs after us and it'll be a slaughter, storm or no storm."

"I'll talk to him but—"

"Tell him he has to arrange for us to escape before the government attacks."

"John, he doesn't listen—"

"Threaten him, tell him that if he doesn't order a retreat, you'll abort that bastard you're carrying."

"Oh, John." I reach for him.

He curses me and storms away.

25

For the two-man crew, the psychological brilliance of the RAT was its Battle Command Communications System, which controlled vehicular functions and gunfire and—most important of all—converted outside visuals into computer images. The driver looked at his screen, not out a windshield or portal. He saw a green computer image of the terrain through which he was maneuvering; people were depicted as heat-producing targets—TP or Target, Personnel. The driver could run these down or avoid them, depending on his orders. The gunner operated RAT's ordnance with a joystick and he also saw his targets as TP designations on the computer screen. The system was redundant: the driver could gun and the gunner could drive without either changing positions. Because the crew members could not see the people they were running down and shooting, could not determine if a TP was an armed terrorist or a fleeing child, the RAT effectively took the human element out of the equation. You could fry a bunch of people climbing on your vehicle because they weren't really people, they were blips on a computer screen, and you weren't really shooting men and women with that joystick, you were playing the kind of computer game you'd been playing since you were ten years old. A RAT crew could drive into a crowd, kill hundreds, drive back to the base, and exit the vehicle without ever having seen or heard another human being, except for each other. When asked what they thought of the RAT, most crew members used the same word, "Cool."

For the enemy, that is, for American citizens made homeless and hungry by the calamity, the RAT's terror resided in its noise and in its terrible prospect when the sparking wires were activated and of course in its effectiveness as a killing machine. The noise was created by the RAT's powerful, unmuffled diesel engine and a variety of sirens and whistles designed to deafen people, sometimes permanently, and to make us vomit, sometimes instantly and uncontrollably.

The RAT's only potential vulnerability lay in the fact that the crew had no direct way of looking outside; all visual information came from the periscope cameras. If those cameras could be broken or blurred, the RAT would be blinded. But to reach the periscopes, you had to get past those four wires strung completely around the vehicle. Touching a wire or putting any part of your body between the wires meant a stunning shock or instant electrocution, depending on which setting was being used. When the sparking mechanism was activated, the RAT produced its own lightning—thick blue electricity crackling all around and making a terrible sound, filling the air with the smell of ozone.

The military had determined that one RAT could disburse, rout, or kill a crowd of up to five hundred TPs. Approximately two thousand people were with Tazza at the Arboretum. Four RATs could've done the job, the government sent fifty.

Tazza's storm, his divine wind, did in fact hit on the day of the battle, the Second Battle of the Arboretum, but had minimal effect on the outcome. It's true that the RATs were not quite as agile in the mud as they would've been on dry land. They slid around the Arboretum's pathways and took out benches and pagodas. The heavy rain occasionally short-circuited the sparking device between cables around each vehicle. And the storm prevented air support. But, still, the hurricane was not a decisive factor.

Except Tazza said it was. "The hurricane saved our lives," he would claim in a thousand tellings of the battle. "It arose in the hot seas off Africa and followed a route sailed by a million Africans sold into slavery to build the new nation. The hurricane's name was Deliverance and she zigged and zagged her way to find us as a mother will look in desperation for lost children. And when Deliverance arrived on the day of battle, she was horrified to see RATs killing children and so she struck, as a mother will, with terrible force. She flung herself against our enemy. She howled in rage. She drowned the RATs and swept away the forces arrayed against us. The storm, Deliverance, so cowed our enemy we were able to walk among them."

Each telling of the tale became the grander, the more apocalyptic and spiritual. The storm swept through the Arboretum drowning soldiers, according to Tazza, but lifting the people gently into trees. At battle's end, the storm stopped and birds landed among the people; little children picked up exhausted parakeets, hearts beating wildly and feathers luminescent. The sun came out, the birds sang, and the people gave thanks for Deliverance.

A great story, John pointed out each time he heard it, with one flaw—it isn't true. It's not even close to the truth. A bad storm hit during the battle and it helped us somewhat—but it wasn't a terrible hurricane and it didn't drown or cower our enemies. Tazza said the truth wouldn't matter years from now, when the story of Deliverance, *as he told it,* would be incorporated into our history with all the reverence of Revolutionary War stories and bravery at the Battle of Gettysburg and the greatest generation who saved us from evil in Europe. But, John insisted, people know it's not true, we were there, we saw what actually happened. Tazza said he felt sorry for John, such an educated man with so little sense of history.

Tazza's battle plan split our force into two. He led one force, a raiding party, a couple hundred armed men and women. The rest of us were to assemble near the conifer forest, seven acres of more than five hundred different kinds of conifers. We were bait. When the RATs came for us, we'd have to disperse as best we could. We had dug tunnels, some of which became useless as they flooded in the heavy rains. We would have to hide among the weeping, upright, and mounded conifers. The government commanders, who had set up their headquarters back on New York Avenue outside the Arboretum, would be thrilled to see the people scattering—exactly the situation RATs were designed to handle, scurrying after and rooting out fleeing TPs.

Tazza figured if we women and children scattered quickly and hid well, we would survive the initial assault. In the meantime, Tazza, his one-hundred-strong Old Guard, his four dozen pipers, and another hundred men and women armed with revolvers and hunting rifles, would attack the command post.

What Tazza didn't know was that the government commanders, working out of eight bus-size mobile command centers, had held back a reserve of twenty RATs, fully armed, fully fueled, and fully staffed. Until they were committed to battle, these RATs created a defensive wall around the command center.

It would seem, then, we were destined to lose the Second Battle of the Arboretum. RATs would kill most of the people scattered in hidey-holes throughout the conifer forest while Tazza's raid would fail against the twenty RATs stationed there. It didn't happen that way, however. We were saved not by a hurricane but by O. E. Mor.

In the wind and rain before the battle, Tazza went among the people and told them the truth. The government was coming not to sue for peace or demand our surrender but to kill us all. Not to kill just our warriors and disarm the rest of us but to kill our women and kill our children and wipe us from our earth.

Tazza went among the people and told them, "We are about to die." A modern leader with modern PR might've held out hope— we'll win this battle and continue fighting. But Tazza told men, whom he called brother, that they would die with him during the assault on the command center. "I am proud to die with you, my brother," he told them. He told women, "We will die today, sister— and so will our children." He cradled those children in his arms and told the wee ones, "I will see you when we both go home." The kids knew he meant heaven.

"Here," he told the people, "here in this beautiful Arboretum and out on New York Avenue, history happens today. Here is where a great people stood their ground and would not be moved by oppression wrapped in a blanket that had once been democracy."

He went among the people and spoke fancifully of famous speeches John had taught him. Queen Elizabeth's address to her troops before the battle with the Spanish Armada, my loving people I come among you at this time to live or die among you, to lay down for my people, to lose my blood in the dust trod by the feet of my people. He spoke of Agincourt, calling it Arboretum, telling the people that this day will be known as Deliverance Day and lucky are we to be here, our names will be recorded, our feats heralded, and Deliverance Day shall never go by, from this day until the ending of the world, without we shall remember it and be remembered for it, we few, we happy few, we band of brothers and sisters, so that those all over America, those now at peace, shall think themselves cursed they were not here with us upon Deliverance Day.

Imbued as we were with this sense of history, we could hardly wait for the battle to begin.

The way I'm telling it, an old woman remembering from a distance of more than fifty years, of course Tazza's words sound artful and arch. But I beg imagination to put you in that Arboretum during that fierce storm on the day you've been told you will die, listen *now* to words spoken to you by a beautiful man with green eyes talking over a howling wind on the eve of a great battle—our blood boiled to fight with him, to die for him, you would've done the same.

I and my women are with the group that stayed at the Arboretum. Our orders are to run and hide. When you're chased by RATs, you don't have to be told twice to run and hide.

Many of our younger children had never heard or could not remember having ever heard the roar of a diesel engine. They are afraid, their sharp-nailed little hands dig into our adult flesh as, big-eyed, they urge us to run as soon as we heard the RATs, run, run away now.

The storm is rain and wind, blowing, howling—but something worse than a hurricane is on its way. RATs.

We had prepared Molotov cocktails, keeping the wicks dry under our clothes, but who could mount an attack with those terrible trucks bearing down. The fifty-caliber M2 machine guns killed forty of us in the first sixty seconds. I saw one mother carrying one baby, killed by one bullet through both. In five minutes a hundred of us are shot. By then we are in our hiding spots and the RATs have to root us out a few at a time.

Tazza's strike force is repulsed by the RATs held in reserve around the command center. He retreats, the RATs scurry after.

Corporal O. E. Mor served in the command center module where the video feeds from the RAT cameras showed not electronic targets but actual pictures, full color and real time.

Mor is appalled. He and his fellow soldiers had been told they would be fighting armed insurgents, that the women and children had left the Arboretum, that all the TPs—Targets, Personnel—would be legitimate military targets, would be armed insurgents, no women and no children. Mor believed that his beloved Cap would be long gone and somewhere safe. He went to his commanding officer the night before the battle to look the man in the eye and ask the captain if he knew for a certainty that the women and children would be gone from the Arboretum before the battle began. The officer said part of the negotiations with Tazza had been safe passage out of the Arboretum for all noncombatants. Whether the captain was lying or had himself been duped, Mor didn't know.

Because now, look, there on the screens, old women cut in half by rapid fire and children crushed under massive tires and a young woman, sweet Jesus it looks like Cap, running toward a row of columnar junipers, shot across both legs, trying to crawl away, bullets finding her, stitching red across her back and then the RAT running over what was left of her body.

Corporal Mor hurries to another trailer, the technical module—he knows the guard on duty and the three technicians. "We're killing women and children," he tells his buddies. "Switch the video so the crews can see who they're shooting." The technicians look to the guard who shakes his head no. "Get out of here, Ollie."

One of the technicians asks Mor, "Are we really killing children?" He was another one of the hundred and sixty-eight who had spent that night at the Arboretum.

"Switch the feed and see for yourself," Mor tells him.

The guard draws his sidearm and reaches for a radio but Oliver Mor, with the help of one of the technicians, overpowers and disarms him, ties the guard to a chair and gags him—then Mor and the technicians switch the video feeds so they can send that truth into the computers being watched by the crews manning the RATs in the Arboretum.

When the RAT crews realize what they are doing, huge engines are shut down, power to the electrical grids cut, hidden hatches opened.

One RAT gunner looks out to see a half a dozen seven-year-old boys, a cluster of TPs he was about to open fire on—he had been delighted that he had so many insurgents in one cluster, it would be an easy kill and his computer would rack up the credits, earning him and his driver a reward, compensatory time off or another insignia. But now the gunner sees that the TPs are only little boys holding sticks as swords, standing in the rain, soaked to the skin. Seeing him climb out of the hatch, the boys scream like bravehearts and attack. The gunner calls down to the driver to make sure the electrical grid is off as the boys help each other climb up onto the RAT, slipping on the rain-slick armor and making their way toward the gunner who is still half in and half out of the hatch. He takes their blows, stick swords on his heavy helmet and bare feet kicking his Kevlar body armor.

Word comes back to the commanders that the RAT crews, seeing real pictures in real time, have stopped attacking. Another goddamn insurrection, there'd been several over the past year as various troops lost heart for killing their fellow Americans.

The commanders are issuing orders, trying to sound decisive like generals in movies, when they have the sense that something in the room has changed. There was a stir in the back. An odor of outside had come in. Also, that sense we get when people are staring at us from behind.

The generals and commanders turned from their computers to see a dozen young men in outlandish outfits, some of them wearing dresses and others with shower caps and all of them soaking wet and carrying machetes. These Patagonians are eerily quiet, looking upon the officers with mild curiosity. Before the commanders could regain their equilibrium and unholster weapons, the boys were upon them, slashing with machetes, decapitating many, hacking others to death, and leaving some alive but armless.

A hundred federal troops in and around the command center remained loyal to the government and formed a brigade to fight their way out and return to the Mall. These troops killed Corporal Mor.

His name was added to the hundreds of us killed at the Arboretum, women with unlit Molotov cocktails and little boys with wooden swords. Babies. Tazza admitted a miscalculation, he thought he'd be able to achieve control of the command center before anyone in the Arboretum was killed.

John called him a liar. "You used them as bait," John said. "You never intended to protect them."

"I told the people they would die."

"You're no better than the government we're fighting."

"We needed a victory."

"You have that, you have your victory."

"More than that, John, I have my army."

Virtually the entire force that came to kill us had now switched to our side.

Fearing an air attack in the morning when the weather had cleared, we left Washington that night in the rain.

We carried fifty on litters, one hundred walking wounded. I lost ten of my closest friends, my women. But *added* to our number were fifty Rumsfeld Antipersonnel Trucks with their crews, another fifty support vehicles, including ambulances and tankers, and nearly a thousand fully armed soldiers who now wore string around their left wrists.

A few weeks later when we were in the mountains we celebrated the role that Corporal O. E. Mor played in turning the tide for us in the Second Battle of the Arboretum. His lover of one night, Cap, had not been injured in the RAT assault, it had been a case of mistaken identity. Pitifully, she opened a vein while floating in a quiet pool one midsummer's night on the Greenbrier River. It was another tragedy amid a thousand.

26

Tazza had it in his head to retake Washington, but the federal government proved just as adamant about holding the capital.

Striking from mountain strongholds, our forces made assaults along the major highways, through the Metro underground, on the banks and bridges of Washington's rivers. We attacked with our own RATs and we floated in on rafts protected by Boatman, who armored the sides of his red *Boat* and mounted a machine gun captured from federal forces. On two occasions we made it to the heart of Washington and on one of those occasions we were able to blacken the White House yet again.

Back in the mountains of western Virginia where our main force resided, hundreds joined us each week. We women fed, clothed, and cared for these displaced Americans—and then put rifles in their hands. A thousand orphaned teenagers joined us during one summer month, half of them battle casualties the following month.

I talk uneasily about this now, the death of children in battle, but at the time we were a war camp, aware always of being *at war,* judging the sacrifices as necessary for revolution. Our encampment around Monterey, Virginia, was Valley Forge in the winter, the Sierra Maestra mountains in the summer. We were fighters, true believers, and we sacrificed our children with a blithe grimness that shames me today.

As always, John was Tazza's most vocal critic. How can you sacrifice so many so young, John asked him one day as they walked through camp. Nothing's worth this much killing. In answer, Tazza picks up a girl of eight and asks her if she would die for him. "Today?" she asks brightly, hopefully. Tazza kisses the girl's forehead and puts her down. "No, not today," he says, then walks away, John calling after him, saying that the willingness of children to die doesn't make it right.

Later that same night, however, John told a group of us how much he admired Tazza, that a king would allow an outspoken member of his inner circle to keep criticizing him. "This proves we can have personal freedoms, the freedom of speech, under a king— and it shows how smart Tazza is, not to close himself off to voices of dissent."

As our little group was breaking up, I told John privately that, all the same, he should take care how he speaks out against Tazza. I knew Tazza was unhappier with John than John was aware. "Just be careful," I told him.

He told me to go to hell. "You and that bastard you're carrying, both of you . . . go to hell."

Before most battles, Tazza arranged to show the opposing troops the enemy they would be fighting, our young women and our children. He would parade them in a road, at the far end of a bridge, Tazza walking with them, and then they'd return to their positions. Seeing women and children across the battle lines took the heart out of American troops, who frequently refused to fire their weapons. We found out later that federal forces all across the country were crippled by the revolts, mutinies, AWOLs, and conscientious objections of troops who grew increasingly heartsick at the killing of Americans even if the government insisted those Americans were terrorists.

In D.C., the government eventually abandoned most of its outer boundaries, pulling back from the Beltway's western and southern sections and most of the eastern section—setting up defensive lines along the Potomac River to the west, the Anacostia to the east, and the last remaining section of defended Beltway to the north. It seemed we could win Washington after all, Tazza already making plans for the surrender ceremony, for our triumphant return.

But then we suffered a devastating series of defeats from an absolutely implacable force. Parading women and children in front of this new force did not dissuade, in fact these new government troops often opened fire as soon as the women and children showed themselves. You know of course who this was, our new worst enemy—a terrible ally brought in by the government of the United States: *Canadians.*

Resisting our American women was easy for the frozen-hearted Canadians, many of them gay, most of them intoxicated. They had the red-veined faces and white necks of men who came from a place where sunlight's novel. Their foul breaths smelled fishy, of seal blubber, which they also rendered to light their lamps or so it was said.

We took staggering losses from these Canadians. Whatever anti-American resentment had been stored up north across the border over the years, whatever inferiority complex they developed from having a weak currency, all of it paid back to us tenfold. The Canadians, without a sense of humor, were relentless, advancing behind heavy cannon and a wall of Celine Dion drowning out Tazza's war pipes.

Trying to make sense of their evil ways, we questioned those Canadian troops we captured, asking why they had aligned themselves with our government against the American people, why did Canadian troops take such delight in killing American civilians—didn't Canada have enough calamity trouble of its own? Apparently not. They were lonely up there, not enough to do and no interesting people with whom to do it, Canada joining an international alliance to ensure that governments everywhere were reestablished to their former positions. The U.S.-Canada border meanwhile became a sieve as tens of thousands of Canadians migrated south to join the federal army and kill Americans. People talked of building a wall to keep Canadians out but it was futile, so many miles we shared with these conniving Canadians who, once in this country, could fake being good Americans unless they were betrayed by beer breaths and speech impediments that rendered "about" as "aboot."

As winter approached, we made camp in the mountains of an area known as Little Switzerland, in the higher elevations of western Virginia. Tazza said he hoped that the federal government would send a column of Canadians out here to attack us—he would flank them in the mountains and cut their fat northern asses to little pieces. We still had twenty operating RATs and enough fuel for one major battle. But the Canadians never came that winter and all of us—I think even Tazza—were grateful because we had heard how, when exposed to snow and cold, Canadians grow all the harder.

It was in a white tent pitched near Monterey that I gave birth to my only child—the source of my greatest pride and, simultaneously, my greatest shame. I named him David.

27

I had my women around me, they shared in the pride of this birth and scorned jealous eyes. *I was having a baby.* It was thought that no babies would be born during the calamity and yet, at my age, forty-two, I was having a baby. Miracle, blessed event, joy of the ages.

Yet I also cringed for shame at the things I carried, adultery and its sin made visible—I had betrayed my husband with whom I had lived semper fidelis twenty-one years and I had betrayed my Lakota pledge to him, to myself, to my people. All my life I prized a highly developed sense of honor and was ashamed for people who dishonored themselves. I found any form of cheating reprehensible. And now I had become what shamed me the most, I was cheater.

The women around me would've forgiven anything, but when I told John that the infidelity had nothing to do with him and everything to do with me, my age, my biology—he called me a cruel bitch because it was his life that had been ruined. He was right, of course—it had everything to do with him. But I was right, too. It was about me and where my life was. That's how I tried to explain it to myself: that I had lost a sense of who I was or who I could've been and sleeping with Tazza was a selfish form of self-discovery.

It sounds like such bullshit, hearing myself say it now, which is why I never indulged, not fully, the glories of being our people's only new mother. That is, I didn't lord it around that I was carrying the king's only child. Instead, I dressed modestly and did not show off my pregnancy, and I forbade the women around me to talk about it openly, much less brag to others that a woman in their midst was giving birth to this miracle child.

Labor was long and through the night. Being the king's affinity, with dawn I could've had a hundred pipes playing outside my tent and a crowd of ten thousand waiting to hear the baby's first cry but, instead, I gave birth as stoically as an Indian and then sent one woman to go fetch Tazza, that he should come see his prince.

Later I asked her his reaction upon hearing that the child was born, it was predictable for man and king alike: He first asked, "Is it a boy?" And then, "Is he okay?"

Tazza came alone and sent all my women from the tent. He gently pulled the cover back from the bed where David and I lay naked to our king.

"Was it a hard birth?"

I tell him hard enough.

"Your breasts." He meant their size.

"I've come into my milk."

He says, "I'll see my child now."

I hand David to Tazza.

Tazza puts David on his back and uses one royal finger to trace the infant's face and features. When that finger touches the baby's lips, he tries to suckle.

I smile. So conditioned are we by popular culture and tender stories that in my mind there's programmed a stupid scenario that Tazza as the new father will do or say something lovable and goofy.

But Tazza is a king and makes no silly observation, does not appear awkward or adorable as he turns the baby over and smooths the wrinkled skin of the newborn's back, checks his butt for a tail, turns him over again and touches each tiny finger, each tiny toe, each even tinier nail. Who can examine a newborn like this and not comment, oh, look how small and adorable and cute the little fingernails?

After spending long minutes examining all aspects of our child, Tazza announces, "Perfectly formed."

He returns David to my arm and breast, covers us with a Chief Joseph robe.

I tell him what worries my mind. "I know you love children and I know you will adore your own child—but people say there's something wrong with how willing you are to sacrifice children in war."

"We are a *people* at war, not an army at war, you know that, Mary."

"But some say that other leaders would've made sure the children are safe, instead of bringing those children into battle."

"People say, some say—you mean, John says."

I don't reply.

"I will not isolate these children from the reality in which we live," Tazza says. "We're in this for a hundred years, for five hundred years. We will raise generation after generation of warriors."

"I worry there will be none left to raise."

He is exasperated with me. "When the time comes, this one"—he indicates the newborn at my breast—"will go with me to every fight. If I'm killed or he's killed, then so be it and it is what it is—a good day to die."

"It's a miracle you haven't been killed, the way you show yourself, but that's *your* miracle, Tazza. It might not be this baby's miracle."

He stands and puts a hand to my face. "You'll have him for seven years, I won't interfere. Teach him to be strong, to be honest.

Make sure he knows the honor of doing what's right and make sure he knows the shame of doing wrong. Then when he's seven, he's mine."

"We'll see."

Tazza looked at me as if I were the child.

In the days following David's birth, I thought about John and wondered—fantasized—about a reconciliation. In postpartum I take leave of my good sense and consider the possibilities of John being a surrogate father to David . . . John who was great with kids, adored them in a careful and nurturing way so profoundly different from Tazza's willingness to sacrifice children in battle. John would be a let's-take-a-walk father, you hold my hand. He would explain things to David, why the sky was blue and where the sun goes at night. Take him fishing, show him how to build a fire and read to him *brave lad* parts from Jack London books. And talk? John would talk rivers to float David through life.

And if he loved me, if John truly soul-deep loved me, wouldn't he, couldn't he, accept David as being half me . . . did he not have that point of view, that college-professor, well-read, liberal, all-encompassing point of view that would allow him to overlook an infidelity and accept a child who was innocent of wrongdoing?

I sent my women to find John and ask if he would come see me and the boy.

The women told me John was living with the plump redhead and refused to come. I sent them back with instructions to ask again and make it clear the invitation was for John alone, not that young red tart he's been with, because I could imagine John bringing her to spite me.

David was a few weeks old when three of the women came into the tent I was now using as home and said John wanted to see me, would I see him.

"Of course." I start fussing with the baby, meaning to change his diaper and then dress him in a cute outfit one of the women had made for him—but John came in before I got the new diaper on.

"Mary."

"John!"

We considered each other.

I said, "I didn't realize you were here already. I thought you were on your way."

"No, I'm here."

"Yes." I laugh, and say something idiotic, wondering if I should continue dressing the baby or hand him naked to John or maybe I should simply ignore David's enormous existence, at least for the moment.

When John steps in my direction, the three women move forward to block him. They have knives in their hands, they always do.

"Tell these menopausal crones to get out of here," he says.

"John . . ." It breaks my heart to hear him so bitter like this, a hater.

"Or else I leave."

I instruct the women to go wait outside and close the tent's flap.

In the silence of their absence, John and I are old strangers together. I am aware of the ammonia smell of diapers and wonder how I look to him, radiant as people sometimes say of new mothers or has this birth ravaged me in my advanced age, as the mirror sometimes reports?

I tell him how glad I am he's come. "We meant so much to each other for so many years, I can't throw that away. I wonder if there's anything left of it, anything we can salvage."

"May I see the child?"

Perfect, I think. Holding David will melt John's heart. "He's a beamish boy, John."

When I offer David, John quickly reaches out, grabs the baby's ankles, and holds him aloft, upside down, naked. David is too startled to cry, his infant arms shooting out, reaching for something to grasp as his upside-down face looks shocked. John's other hand comes around holding a vorpal blade. I gasp. He places the blade at David's neck and says villainously to me, "Snicker-snack, Mary, *snicker-snack.*"

John please. I have seen so many die, and now I see this death in my mind's eye—one quick slit and then the child, my boy, bleeds out as John, my husband, holds him by his ankles, a rabbit kicking death. John will be executed but look at him, at this moment, death is not of concern to this man I have wounded too deeply to know.

My mind races for things to say that will dissuade him. Meanwhile, I suspect that John is composing the exact combination of slut-skank-Indian-whore-squaw names he will use on me as he cuts my baby's throat.

The three women who were in here earlier must've been watching through the flap because now they come rushing with their own knives drawn.

"No," I tell them. Attacking John will push him into doing it. "Stay back."

"He's going to kill our baby," one of the women says, assessing the look in John's eyes.

By that baby's ankles, John lifts David all the higher and turns the knife blade this way and that at the newborn's neck.

John's character is David's destiny.

And now David, his arms still outstretched in the disorientation of being upside down, begins to cry, not from fear or discomfort, this is his angry cry.

John looks hatefully at me and says, "You filthy fucking squaw."

"Oh, John." What pain he must feel to say that to me.

Just as swiftly as John took the child, he puts him down on the bed, on his back, David howling his dismay.

John flashes his knife at the three women, who could disarm

him and gut him like a pig—they are large women and the work we do has made them muscular, plus their loyalty to me and mine is religious. But I signal them to let John leave.

I wait for his parting words. That he will never forgive me. That I am dead to him. That the child is a bastard. That once he loved me, we were soul mates, he thought it was forever, I broke his heart . . .

But he leaves without speaking, John's river gone dry for me.

28

We spent winter in mountains. Tazza's scavengers made ranging trips like scout bees on searches for new pollen. When something useful was found by one scavenger, the others were alerted and treasures were brought to our camp, where my women took over. We stockpiled what would be needed later, we prepared and preserved the food, we threw away what we had no use for—why would the scavengers bring ballet shoes and tennis balls?

I started thinking of our scavengers as gnomes. Unlike their perfect king, each scavenger seemed in some way malformed—too tall and thin, overly short and round, balding before their time, ears that stuck out, bad teeth a common theme. And while none of us could arrange to bathe daily or otherwise stay minty fresh, the scavengers' disregard for personal hygiene was legendary. I think they had hairy hobbit feet, too, but never confirmed my suspicion.

These scavenger nerds and nebbishes had to learn new skills as the grocery warehouses and department store stockrooms tapped out and we were forced to live off the largesse of the land. Our scavengers brought us root vegetables that went unharvested on farms where families had been massacred by marauders; cattle and sheep left over from herds and flocks; corn left standing; chickens gone feral. The scavengers became hunters and killed the deer that had once upon a time overpopulated these mountain forests. And always our scavengers returned with hogs hung on poles carried by four or more.

I tired of the camping life and grew nostalgic for my perfect house in suburbia, the tile floors and granite countertops, the big sleigh bed so soft, and the deep clawfoot tub, a reproduction but loved nonetheless.

John once told me that our ancestors' mastery of fire not only predated our higher powers of thought but encouraged intelligence and imagination because, after fire was mastered, our human ancestors spent their evenings looking into the flames and *thinking* instead of huddling in the dark trying to sleep, worrying about being eaten. Now, in our camps at night we read poetry and sing and stare at the campfires—but I don't know if it's making us any smarter. During the day, viewing David has become a pastime for the camp. It's as if I had a panda. Singles and couples and occasionally entire families coming to the tent and asking one of my women if the little one can be shown. At a safe distance and never touching him, people were allowed to marvel at David, their king to be. He had perfectly formed tiny toes. I rarely let others hold him but I did offer him to a blind old woman who said she had memories of children and asked if she could please hold the baby and nuzzle his baby smells, cooing and clucking, which David took as a tonic.

With the baby boy as lure, we signed up a hundred more women to devote themselves to the people, each new recruit teamed with an experienced woman to learn our ways—the cooking and nursing, how we wash a body to honor a person's memory before burial, setting bones and feeding fevers, the healthiest placement for dug latrines, and how to salt pork. In the oldest traditions, we were women given to service, and we lived together without the destructive craziness inspired by men. We weren't lesbians. We weren't anti-men. We just got along better and lived healthier lives without them.

Tazza had formed the king's council on which twelve councillors served, advising him on matters of war, of strategy, and of governing ourselves. I thought, John's gone and Tazza needs a dozen advice-givers and river-talkers to take my husband's place—and even so, I'd wager, Tazza never hears half as many sensible ideas as he did when John, my John, was among us.

He's officially exiled. When the king found out that John had threatened our child—I never told but it was a secret too large to be kept—Tazza put a price on John's life.

Only occasionally did Tazza come to check on David and make sure we had everything we needed, he was especially concerned that I ate enough meat, beef specifically. Tazza insisted that beef would make my milk strong. He would, he said, have the boy grow up well-proteined. The battles around Washington had transformed Tazza, who now believed himself heart and soul to be a king. I can't say that I loved him, not as I loved John. But Tazza was my king and Tazza was father to my child.

I'll tell you now something I was going to leave out of these remembrances because it'll sound creepy to you, though at the time I accepted it naturally enough—Tazza asking me if he could taste my milk. I wonder how many other men have requested that of their women. We do so many things together, man and woman, and we think these things are ours alone, but I suspect these private acts are universally shared.

I agreed, cradling my king's head and urging him to be gentle, which he was, gentler than David. Tazza used a finger to push my nipple in his mouth. I wept at this and thought of John, for I would suckle John, too. And in ecumenical lactation I would feed his plump little redhead whore, too. And the starving thousands we saw during the calamity. Let me take them two at a time, one in each arm's crook, while I, Mary, maternal in my old age, feed the multitude.

When Tazza finished, I held his face in my hands to see what he thought. A drip of milk leaked from the side of his mouth, which I cleaned with a practiced thumb.

After that intimacy, I thought Tazza would be back often, soon to share my bed as man and woman, as king and queen, but his visits remained infrequent and he never again tasted me.

At winter's depth I sat at the fire with David under my robe next to my heart and tried not to regret having no man in my life even though I sorely missed my husband, John, and deeply wished my king, Tazza, would stay around and treat me like a queen. I got over that lack and loss before spring and decided that it was the idea of a man more than his reality that made me wistful.

Rumors spread that John was coming back with a group of Cromwellian Canadians to kill the baby, and Tazza assigned a dozen of his Old Guard to stand watch over us day and night. My women wouldn't allow those frightening Patagonians in our tent but the guards stayed close nonetheless, their restless eyes on us always.

People drifted in and out of our camp, pledging fidelity to Tazza and tying the string around their wrists and staying with us permanently or coming only for our food and protection, our medicine and nursing, then leaving when they were full and healed. All were welcomed, none restrained from leaving. We mixed freely all the races and ethnicities but Tazza formed two special armies, celebrating each for its unique talents and heritage.

To his African army, he told stories of the Zulu king Cetshwayo devastating the British army at Isandlwana even though the African divisions, the impis, had spears and clubs, the ikiwi and knobkerrie, while the Brits were armed with 1879 firepower, it was the

Zulus' mobility, their discipline, their fearlessness that struck terror in even a force as well trained as the British. Cetshwayo sent forth the classic Zulu horns, hitting the enemy on two sides, then a crushing rush from the center. Rifles, cannons, Gatling guns against spears, yet on came the Zulus exactly as ordered, more British officers killed than at the battle of Waterloo, six companies wiped out to the last red-coated soldier.

To his white army, he talked of how the Celts loved war and went into battle naked, dyed blue head to toe, men and women alike, tall and muscular, wild blond hair, beating swords on shields, screaming to take the heart out of their enemies, and even the legendary Roman legions trembled before the Celts.

Toward the end of that winter Tazza went among us and told the plan he and his councillors had devised. We would travel west to assemble allies and organize the people scattered by the calamity, we would go all the way to the Pacific Ocean if necessary and then turn around and come back. On the return trip across what had been America, we would collect allies, the people we had settled on the westward leg of the trip. All of us together would march back to Washington, D.C.

Always the District, it was Tazza's white whale and he would have it. At a dinner party back before the calamity, John regaled the table with his explanation that the whale represented evil and the reason Ahab pursued Moby-Dick so assiduously was that he hated and wanted to kill the evil within himself . . . what, then, did the District represent to Tazza that he was so keen on having it under his control? John would've had a theory.

Tazza told us that by the time we made the trip out west and then back east, we would have an army of one million with another million traveling in support, and with this force we would flood Washington and cause the government to capitulate regardless of how many mercenary Canadians had been hired as federal gun thugs.

In March, one of Tazza's councillors came to my women and announced we were leaving. Why hadn't Tazza told me this in person? The councillor issued orders of how the camp should be broken and the packs arranged, declaring who would march with whom and who could ride in one of the few horse carts we had and what cargo was deemed precious enough to be kept in one of the armored vehicles we still had fuel to run. My women looked at this young blond-headed councillor as if they didn't understand his language. He had a small nose and dainty hands and we went about our duties like always.

The councillor shouted at the women, threatened them, he declaimed and inveighed, said he spoke for the king and promised unless we jumped to it he would beat us, flay us, hang us from the highest tree. My women remained unimpressed, one asking him if he had a tiny little dick, was that his problem, and that's the woman he struck with the back of his hand, hitting her in the face, knocking out a tooth, putting her on the ground and then standing over her and saying, "Bitch" and saying, "Whore." Six of my women fell upon him with their ever-present knives.

(We called them finger knives, because the steel broadened out on the top of the blade back toward the handle where you could use a finger there for pressure. Each knife was about seven inches in overall length, half that being a hard maple handle with the tang all the way through to the end and riveted in three places. Scavengers had found a supply of these long ago and the women had confiscated them for our use. The blades were high carbon, not stainless—these blades would stain and pit and rust if not cared for but the carbon made them easily sharpened to a razorness that could shave a man's neck, cut a vegetable into a slice thin enough to see through, scalpel an umbilical cord, clean a gunshot wound. These beautiful carbon blades had to be sharpened often, they wouldn't hold an edge forever like the harder and harder-to-sharpen stainless knife, and all around camp you could hear the snickity-slide of steel on stone, my women edging up their knives before cutting something. We carried each finger knife in a leather sheath wherein fit the blade snug so the knife wouldn't fall out and no strap or button needed to hold it in and impede our access. We strapped these little sheaths at our waists, around a forearm or bicep, one at a thigh, one at an ankle.)

With these finger knives, the young councillor was cut a dozen times, veins opened at various locations, an artery shooting red string, neck and groin . . . he staggered theatrically here and there trying to stem the flow but had only two hands and was bleeding out everywhere.

A huge stink after that. The killed councillor's friends promised that my women would die in retaliation. When the councillor's allies appeared at my tent to demand I turn over those who had killed the councillor, I appeared holding David on my hip, David whom the councillor's friends knew to be the child of their king, and I suggested that they might want to check with Tazza before indulging revenge.

Tazza came to the women's camp, here was his brilliance, settling differences on the spot. I told him what had happened. Tazza assembled his council right there where the murdered councillor still lay, covered with a sheet he had soaked through with his red.

People gathered around as the dead councillor's friends knotted nooses for my women.

Tazza told his councillors specifically and the camp generally that the women who served me also serve the people. "If the women need to do something," Tazza said to his council, "go over and talk with Mary. Do not order women around on your own. Speak directly to the women only to say, 'Thank you, mother, for your service to the people.' Otherwise say nothing. Always respect the women. On the next battlefield, and there will be another one soon—these are the women who will go among you who have fallen, will put you out of your misery with their keen blades if you can't be saved and you will cry out gratitude for their deadly relief. They will strip your body of everything useful and bring back your treasures to honor our camp. Or if they decide you can be saved, they will stay there with you on the battlefield, drag you to a sheltered lee until you are well enough to walk no matter how many weeks they fall behind us or how much danger they expose themselves to. No one, not even my Vieille Garde, will cross these women. What man is fool enough to insult those who prepare his food, shave his neck? I am a king who trembles at their approach."

Always theatrical, our Tazza, but after that particular speech no man in power bothered us. And of course Tazza won my women's hearts, they pledged a devotion to him nearly as strong as the one they had for me and our child.

29

America had been emptied and the ugliest part of empty America was also the ugliest when America was full—the strip mall-franchise-dealership roads that lead into every town of any size. The cheap-ass block buildings are empty, thousands of acres of paved parking lots and service roads blighted with trash and abandoned vehicles, and everywhere nature is trying to grow back through choking blankets of concrete and asphalt. Grass has started in the cracks, trees along the perimeters. But it's going to take centuries, maybe never, before a person or a wolf can cross these areas without feeling the oppression of someone else's horrible mistake. Approaches to our towns should've been made on boulevards and through parks—how did we allow America the Beautiful to become so profoundly ugly?

I grew depressed walking day after day along the strip malls and begged Tazza to take us off the highways, admittedly easier to travel on, and let's go through the countryside and watch for flowers.

He called flowers by their own names, which is another answer I give people when they ask the inevitable, *What was he like?*

You can't travel thousands of people as a straight line through forests and fields; we formed ourselves like the fingers of a hand outstretched with scouts, soldiers, scavengers our fingertips, feeling our way west across America. I carried David in a sling either at my back or around front to feed him as we walked. Everything we did, we did walking.

One day we were crossing meadows and forests, Tazza with us, surrounded as he often was by children. He told them what plants were good to eat, which ones to avoid. "Three leaves, leave it be," he said. "Avoid eating any plant that has milky sap." Tazza would swing a child up onto his shoulder and walk on as she saluted her fellows loftily, king high, Tazza holding two others by their hands, Tazza talking to them as they walked, telling them things, calling flowers by their names.

"Bachelor buttons," he said. "Shirley corn poppy." That one made them laugh. "Sweet alyssum. Forget-me-not." They promised they wouldn't. "Farewell to spring." No, they wouldn't believe that was a flower's name. "Baby's breath." Children picked it. "Bluebell, toadflax, tidy tips, painted daisy, Chinese houses, love-in-a-mist, mountain phlox, and baby blue eyes."

David has green eyes, his father's.

"Johnny jump-up," Tazza said, and a little one nearby named Johnny jumped up, to the delight of all.

"Bird's eye, bird's foot," but when someone suggested *bird's wing,* Tazza said don't be silly. "Snapdragons."

Flowers planted in yards we crossed, yards of homes abandoned during the calamity, how many Americans died, half of us? Before the calamity we thought America was secure . . . terrorists might take down a plane, hurricanes drown a few hundred, but from the true onslaughts of history and nature we considered ourselves immune . . . but estimates later said two hundred million dead and gone, too many to get your mind around but the countryside tells the story, America has been emptied.

In the evenings, Tazza spoke with his council, reviewed his Patagonians, walked among the people seeing to their needs, and spent hours with children, listening to their stories and telling them his. He asked, "Who knows what butter was?" The younger ones didn't, the older ones said it was yellow and went on toast. Tazza said butter was good and someday they'd all have butter. "And pie?" a naughty boy asked. "Will one day we have pie?" The boy said it's been so long since he's had peach pie he can hardly remember, and there ensued a spirited discussion on the relative merits of peach pie versus apple.

Around the fire hot and high, children slumbered and slept. No one had to go home to their parents, the children were with their king. To those still awake Tazza told gruesome stories, he said Blackbeard was a ferocious pirate who twined and twisted tapers in his beard and then, just before battle, he lit the tapers and fell upon his enemies with his beard seemingly afire and his face brightly flamed to show the madness in his eyes. To illustrate his story, Tazza held burning sticks near his face, which glowed in the night, causing children to clasp one another in the delight of fear.

"When the government finally caught up with Blackbeard and cut off his head—to everyone's utter astonishment, Blackbeard's headless body jumped into the ocean and swam three times around the boat before taking off for the vast and endless sea."

To soften the edge of that image, he sang them songs of old Ireland and songs about monkeys and one song concerning a brave little brown mouse what takes to sea in a paper boat.

In further answer to the second of the three questions I'm always asked, *what was he like,* that's what he was like—in peace, as pleasing as pie. In war, no greater despot.

He got evidence someone on his council was plotting against him, Tazza calling out the traitor and, without preamble, cutting the man's throat.

On our way west, we encountered populations unorganized and unaligned, just trying to survive and usually eager to join us, tie on the string, declare fidelity to a king. Those organized under a local warlord, however, often had to be converted by force. We occasionally left behind a number of our own people to farm the land and keep the faith until we came back gathering our million-plus army.

Tazza was the reason we did relatively little fighting, most of the people we encountered falling to our king's charm and his offer, come align with the kingdom. After all, where was their democratically elected government—gone, no army left behind to protect them from marauders. Early in the calamity, before the people were willing to believe what was happening, agents of the rich came through and bought everything so that when the calamity hit in earnest, the people had few reserves. Having survived these betrayals, the people now tied strings around their left wrists and pledged loyalty to a king—village after town, farm cooperative after ranch, camp after camp. Our parades impressed the people, as did the discipline of our divisions, the number of pipers we could field, and the gasoline-powered vehicles we still drove. Tazza sent in women and children to show prospects our softer side. He sent in troubadours to sing epics about the battles we won.

But those few who resisted our offers faced hell's own war, because these local groups were never a match for our armies, the African Corps and the Celtic Tribes, and our professional United States Army soldiers, all of them battle-hardened from the wars back in Washington, attacking to the cry of a hundred war pipes. And as a last resort, to turn any battle's tide, Tazza sent in his silent angels, the terrible Patagonians.

30

I was part of the negotiating team organized to offer Mochs, a small town in southern Illinois, the possibility of aligning with the kingdom rather than fighting us.

The season was late summer, hot and dry in the flat and featureless prairie, and I wished Tazza would allow this particular little town its stubbornness and pass it on by. The town had rejected our initial offer of pomp and circumstance and had sent word by bullhorn that we should take our "king" (a word the redneck speaker placed within sneer quotes) and leave because the town of Mochs was doing just fine without having to pledge fidelity to no goddamn king.

I and several of my women came in under the white flag to negotiate. The modesty and seriousness of our women often convinced the other side to join us—but I could tell as soon as we entered Mochs that we were going to convince no one of nothing, they'd rather die in ignorance than risk being hoodwinked. That's what these country folks feared, that some slicker would come along and cheat them out of something. To avoid that possibility, they hunkered down and crossed their arms and pursed their lips and refused to believe in magic or poetry or kings.

Their women were kept inside, we had to deal with the redneck ignorance of the men. Our women and I wore shirts and trousers and then those long aprons tied at our necks and waists, but in spite of our modest appearance, the men standing around in the streets of Mochs insulted us with rough words and lurid propositions. If Tazza heard you, I thought, in an hour you'd be stumbling on loops of your intestines.

Typical in the towns we encountered, the residents of Mochs had arranged cars, trucks, and buses to form a continuous wall around the center of their village. (Without gasoline or diesel, these vehicles were useless except as barriers.) Immediately inside the wall of parked vehicles, roads were linked up so that personnel and supplies could be shuttled by horse-drawn or hand-drawn carts to whatever section of the wall was under threat from invaders. At measured intervals, the parked and piled vehicles could be rolled aside to form gates through which farmers and others living in the countryside could come to town and receive protection from marauders. After a couple years of successfully defending themselves like a medieval walled city, Mochs had become cocky.

Our team of negotiators, four of us women, met with a dozen of their men, including the spokesman who I believe was their military commander. Said his name was Bo.

We were in the auditorium of the high school, sitting on metal folding chairs at cafeteria tables.

I said to the burly and bearded men, "The offers we're going to make will affect everyone in this town so your women should hear what I'm about to say."

Spokesman Bo said that no one in Mochs actually needed to hear anything I had to say because, in fact, the town's refusal of Tazza as king was absolute and nonnegotiable. Except he said it more in the manner of, "Ain't nuthin none of youse got to say would intrest none of us and that's final." He said if it hadn't been for us coming in under the white flag of truce and them being honorable men and all, we would've long been dead.

I started to outline my case.

He interrupted. "Somebody comes by with some bagpipes and a little fancy marching and we're supposed to turn over our town? I don't think so. You tangle with us, you're about to grab a tiger by the tail." *You tangle wit us'n, you 'bout to grab a tigger by da tail.*

Several of his fellows nudged Bo in acknowledgment of his clever way with words. His toughness came from years ago watching tough guys on TV, talk supplied by screenwriters who abhor dead air. Bo and his gang of burly men had no experience with an army of Patagonians who would walk up and cut off an arm without preamble.

"We had lots come by here," Bo continued, "and try to get our grain supplies, our cattle, our horses. But anything inside our walls is pretty much safe. And anyone trying to get inside our walls . . . they's pretty much dead."

More nudges and guffaws in appreciation of the commander's command of English. He was short, bowlegged, and long-haired—bushy dirty brown hair, his beard growing so high on his face that it seemed only his eyes peeked out. I knew this type of man. Off the reservation, every store I went in, every street I walked—these were the men who made Indian whoops and called me squaw.

If it had been only these men, I would've stood up and left and Tazza would've taken this town without negotiation, but I figured half the population of Mochs consisted of women and children, tucked away at this moment in attics and basements.

"Listen," I told Bo, "I know you men think you're tough, your army strong, I know you've probably fought off marauders and rag-tag wandering groups of displaced persons who were starving to death, trying to get into this town and find something to eat. Whenever the alarm goes off, I bet you grab your guns and mount the walls, and I'm sure you've acquitted yourselves well in battle after battle. But now you're facing something completely different and you don't understand, you don't appreciate, the *inevitability* of the force that's outside your walls at this moment. It's a well-disciplined, murderous fighting force, each man and woman loyal to death to their king. If Tazza says take down this town, we will take it down."

"Yeah we're pretty much trembling," Bo said and spat on the gym floor, a display that I think he thought illustrated ruthlessness.

This Midwest smugness was maddening. These men, what had they ever done in battle, they had shot someone from a distance and thought that made them killers. These men had never confronted the warrior madness of naked Celts painted blue, had never seen the methodical assault of Zulu impis. And yet these hard realities, white and black, were waiting just outside their vehicular walls.

I tried to explain. "They'll take your head," I said, speaking of our soldiers. "And you'll count yourself lucky. Because the other thing they do, if time allows, they'll cut a man from groin to breastbone and reach in and grab a handful of intestine and pull some out and then move on to the next man, leaving their victims to stumble around attempting to get their guts back in the hole. I've seen men frantically brushing dirt and twigs from wet loops of gut before attempting to fold up those intestines to make them fit back inside their bodies. These terrible things, the soldiers outside your walls, they do these things *recreationally*. And you know what? The intestines never fit back inside once they've been unspooled on the ground. So. You folks are dead unless you pledge loyalty to Tazza. And if you do pledge loyalty, you can continue living like normal, you'll simply have to agree to support him when he—"

Bo interrupted me again to say I still wasn't getting it. "We don't bow to no king."

Losing my temper. "Getting in a bar fight or slapping your wife around does not make you a warrior. You have no fucking idea what it's like to engage that army out there."

"You're just a bitch sent in here trying to scare us and it ain't working, I know that much."

"If a woman had come to Tazza and insulted him as I've insulted you, he would cut off her head and send it back to her people. The best you can do is call me a bitch?"

"We might just take you up on that head cutting, you're not careful." The others nodded their bushy beards, shedding crumbs.

"Go ahead, do it," I tell Bo. Hearing this, the three women with me finger their knives.

Bo looks around to the others, no one moving.

"Yeah I thought so," I told them.

"You's lucky we're civilized."

"Oh for chrissakes, you're about to be dead."

"Get outta here!"

As the four of us were escorted through the small town and to a gate, women started to come out and I shouted to those we passed near, "There's a battle coming that will kill all your men and some of you—and maybe your children, too. Come with me, you can avoid this."

To my surprise, twenty women slipped out with twenty children, accompanying us back to Tazza.

I told him that the men inside the walls of Mochs, Illinois, were implacable, unreasonable, and ready to die.

He promised to accommodate them first thing in the morning.

Our army hit the east and west sides of the walls simultaneously, the forces of Mochs ready for this maneuver, defending both sections and still keeping a sizable force in reserve. Their men must've shrugged to one another—this is it, this is the inevitability that that squaw women was going on about?

No, *this* is it: our main force struck the south wall like a tsunami, the soldiers of Mochs unable physically or psychologically to handle a force of Celtic warriors dyed completely blue, screaming like banshees, an assault rifle in each hand. After these Celts breeched the wall, behind them the African impis came pouring in, a murderous wave. The townspeople abandoned other sections of the wall in an attempt to stop the unstoppable come their way from the south, and then as soon as those east and west sections of the wall were undefended, our forces invaded from those points, too.

It was slaughter, an abattoir. The Men of Mochs wept and put up their arms to surrender and still had their guts cut open, intestines pulled out. Tough rednecks in NASCAR hats shit their Wranglers and tried to pledge loyalty to a king, any king, but they got shot, too, and hacked to death. Burly wife beaters in AMERICA: LOVE IT OR LEAVE IT T-shirts put their hands above their heads and had their arms cut off.

It was over in a few hours.

Tazza brought us all in. He wanted his people to see what was done in their name, he wanted our complicity.

The remaining men of Mochs were executed. Teenagers, boys and girls both, were assigned to accompany us on our march west. Half the town's surviving women were to stay here in southern Illinois and rebuild, half to come with us. Several hundred of our own number were to become residents of Mochs, help rebuild it, take in displaced persons, and stay strong for when Tazza would return to collect the army that would eventually retake Washington, D.C.

We had first encountered the town of Mochs in the late morning, Tazza's pomp and circumstance appeal had failed by early afternoon, my negotiations went nowhere a few hours later, the assault occurred at dawn the next day, and Tazza's assignments of who would be executed, who spared, who came with us, who stayed—

all that was completed by noon. We were on our way west again by 3 p.m., less than thirty hours after first seeing the town that we ultimately massacred and converted to our kingdom.

Never once during that first year did I doubt the inevitability of our mission. Doubts would come with winter.

31

We planned to cross the Mississippi River on the bridges of St. Louis, ten thousand of us in five columns, an army as ferocious as any that had ever crossed this river and we feared nothing except bad spirits and overwhelming numbers—if St. Louis still had even half of its population, if the city could muster a force of one million, then, yes, we'd be overwhelmed. It might've been safer to cross the river north or south of St. Louis, but we wanted to see the blackened ruins of the St. Louis Arch where the calamity started. The Arch had become a sacred place for Indians and now for us. Tazza sent a scouting party in, and the members of that party returned a day later with astonishing news—the city was empty.

We crossed the Mississippi and offered our prayers at what was left of the blackened Arch.

Hard to believe that a major city was completely depopulated so we were careful crossing through St. Louis, these urban areas always dicey because of the gangs and the displaced. Evidence everywhere of the wars that had been fought throughout St.

Louis—blown-up buildings and gutted cars, ocher stains on concrete so commonplace that ocher was the thematic tone for American cities, reminding us that people are full of blood and it stains brown. Also we frequently came across scat that had turned completely white, yet we encountered no one. Not a single crazy displaced person begging a handout, no gangs, no wanderers. St. Louis was spooky and many of us had the feeling that someone in this city was watching, keeping just out of reach of our forward scouts.

Rumors ran that the people of St. Louis had been spooked by shapes and shadows, bad medicine from the Arch. We prayed, let us pass through this city.

Our funky scavengers found warehouses and brought back supplies, a few dozen cases of canned tuna packed in spring water and a hundred two-gallon cans of pineapple juice and boxes of paper towels and toilet paper, all deeply appreciated and distributed and then consumed in a day by our thousands. Scavengers even found a few drugstores that hadn't been stripped; they collected medicines for our diabetics and our cardiovascularly diseased, and they found testing devices so the chronically ill could see where they were compared to a baseline established the last time the scavengers raided a drug supply. These wonderful scavengers had a talent for sizing up a warehouse or barricaded store, sending some little guy in through a vent, or putting their diggers to work tunneling into the basement, whatever was necessary to get to the goods, which the scavengers carried to camp with the insouciance of people who expect to do two amazing things every day before noon.

In St. Louis, they came back with stories of finding more of that white scat and seeing glimpses of the devil dogs that shat it, evil creatures with malevolent grins, huge heads slung low, big half-circle ears out to the side, massive jaws like pit bulls whelped by Satan. We didn't put much stock in the scavengers' story, they were the Dungeons and Dragons crowd. But they did scare some of our children with campfire stories about devil dogs that eat the whole body, eye-balls and bones, and it's eating all those bones that makes their shit white, shot through with bone dust and calcium leavings.

As we were passing through the western outer edges of St. Louis, word came that the scavengers hadn't returned from their latest mission and we worried they'd been killed. Rumors circulated that some secret St. Louis force had stayed in hiding until our scav-engers could be ambushed. Or maybe the devil dogs got them. For the first time that night, we heard those dogs, we heard *something*. I don't know what it was, maniacal laughter, crazy people living in the sewers of St. Louis, grunting and squealing when they come out at night. This was more frightening than any battle we'd fought. No one could identify who or what was making those awful night sounds. If an army of marauders attacked, we could defeat them— but how do we fight St. Louis spirits? Patagonians came to where David and I slept and put a double ring around our tent.

Tazza was organizing a search-and-rescue squad when the scav-engers returned bearing a thousand hammocks. "Hammocks!" we told one another, passing the excited word that thousands more waited in a warehouse.

To understand our joy at this scavenger discovery, you have to appreciate the fresh horror of sleeping out on the ground night after night, a thumb-size rock was all it took to thieve sleep as you toss and turn and try to get comfortable, a state never achieved, thankful for morning because you can get off that terrible ground and go ver-tical. I think of a moist and unseen miasma, disease and dander, floating just above the ground, from knee-height on down, so when you sleep on the ground you are sucking in that miasma all night long, the dander and dirt and disease collecting on your skin, your eyelids, lungs. We kept a few folding cots for the sickest among us but most of the people in this traveling kingdom had to rely on tarps to protect against ground moisture and then blankets to pull over us. On that ground were snakes, spiders, hellbenders, and ants that bit—all of these creatures maneuvering in that fog of moist miasma. Sometimes we slept in tents, sometimes under the stars, all the brighter for no competition with electricity, and what can you say about sister moon except she's always a joy but, still, under canvas or not, in view of the moon or not, night was awful for being on the ground.

But with hammocks, with *hammocks,* we'd be up above miasma and snakes, able to swing, sway yourself to sleep, Rock-a-bye Baby, hammocks of hand-twisted cotton twine, strong as steel, large hammocks you could sleep three crossways. Tazza approved the hammocks because they were easy to roll and stow, light to carry—his restriction being that we couldn't tote with us the heavy metal frames that had been found with the hammocks, we'd have to ask the standing people if we could suspend the hammocks from tree to tree among them. But we didn't always camp near trees, at least not a thousand closely spaced trees for all the hammocks we had, so our scavengers and engineers rigged up wooden poles that worked fairly well but not like being able to suspend your hammock between two big trees that would swing you peacefully to sleep and then stand sentry the night.

One of the nights passing west of St. Louis found us in a grove of mature hardwood trees, some park whose name I never saw signed, and I remember waking at dawn and seeing our camp as thousands of hammocks strung from every available tree, no swing or sway at this early hour, just the pacific *picture* of it, all those hammocks filling the forest with sleep.

After getting through St. Louis without being killed by devil dogs, without having our bones ground to dust that would whitewash our killers' scat, we talked, many of us, how much safer we'd feel if we had dogs on guard while we slept.

Except for the summer of love, when dogs came out from wherever they'd been hiding to wear bandannas and chase balls and get girl hugs, we had traveled without our best friends. They disappeared (we suspect poisoned) when the government arrived, many killed when we fought the hated Canadians. West of St. Louis is when dogs began to show up again, a few shepherds and beagles trotting along our marching perimeter. Then packs of mixed breeds running in among us and then back out again to test whether we were going to kill them or reconcile.

It was up to Tazza. Rumor had it that he thought dogs were detrimental to a traveling army, extra mouths to feed, or that they should stay at our edges and live off our scraps in exchange for barking if anyone approaches our lines. But then a Border collie with one brown eye and one blue came for Tazza.

We were setting camp in an old cornfield, our scavengers picking among the standing stalks to salvage nubbins, is how dedicated they were to their art and call. Tazza among us telling stories, listening to complaints, singing softly—each time he came near me the thrill renewed, even though I should've been unimpressed by now, having seen him unkinglike back when we were sleeping together, whimpering with a little death suffered eyes closed. Or farting as he got to his feet of a morning. Yet still, dark and green-eyed, walking with such fluid grace, his hair fingered back, Tazza strong and perfectly formed. If he was my portion, I considered myself well served. This particular evening people laughed and pointed behind him.

Tazza turned. A whip-thin black-and-white Border collie trailed Tazza assiduously and only Tazza, the collie undistracted by sly offers of food off to the side, he was tracking a king. The dog's coat was matted and mangy. You could only guess how long it'd been since last he'd eaten. Still, it wasn't food this particular dog had in mind—he had something for Tazza.

Tazza faced the dog, we waited expectantly, God knows how

Tazza will react, the anti-dog rumor in all of our minds. As Tazza stood tall, the collie approached creeping, head down, less in submission than in that classic Border collie herding position. When he reached Tazza, the dog dropped a chewed-up old discolored once-red rubber ball that none of us even knew he had in his mouth.

How long had he carried it! And through what unimaginable travails? Did the dog leave the ball when he got hungry and went off hunting, returning to find the ball again and resume the journey? Who last threw the ball for the dog, what wonderful child can the dog still smell in his dreams and what terrible story had the dog lived to lead him here where he offered his treasure to a king?

To our relief and cheers, Tazza picked up the ball and threw it. The dog fetched the ball and dropped it at Tazza's feet. Tazza laughed—and ordered a tub, water, clippers. He cleaned the dog himself and doctored torn pads on the dog's feet, disinfected foul ears, and pulled ticks by the dozen. We gathered around and watched and helped but this clearly was Tazza's dog and doing. Throughout all the doctoring and washing and clipping of matted fur, the dog had blue-brown eyes only for Tazza.

Tazza named him Buck.

After that, the people started acquiring dogs. Tazza said only large ones, the minimum size being Buck, but the rule was stretched and much abused.

It was lovely having dogs in camp and seeing the children play. We became a happier people. Dogs were our sentries, they took up some of the space in our hearts left by friends who'd been killed and they loved us unconditionally. We made packs for them to carry our things, and this burden among many others the dogs accepted in exchange for renewing their contract with the human race. If we are ever threatened by those white-shitting devil dogs again, we will have canine allies to fight them.

Away from St. Louis, into the countryside, we came upon a huge ranch, a thousand acres we later discovered, well guarded along its river and fence perimeters, fat cattle grazing, and horses, too. Tazza sent a force over a fence to investigate and his spies came back and said there were singers at the main house and actors and women famous for being famous. It was the first we'd ever heard of a ranch established for the protection and preservation of celebrities, financed by rich people and guarded by mercenary federal forces.

Tazza, always the actor, he dresses in his finest battle gear, surrounds himself with a personal entourage of Patagonians and pipers—and goes calling. The rest of us wait outside the fences.

Tazza came back two days later, mesmerized. John had always said that in post-apocalyptic America the underclass would never again serve the privileged class because the underclass could simply take whatever it wanted from the outnumbered privileged class. John said only the military, through mutually agreed upon discipline, and religious orders, devoted to God, would still operate hierarchal systems.

John was wrong. In fortress enclaves all over America, the common people worked for the rich and guarded the rich in exchange for food and housing and a taste of the commodities the rich had amassed. Why didn't the people just take everything? Revolts require coordination and unification, which the people have trouble with unless there's a unifying force like a king. Also, the people who worked for the rich took comfort in the orderliness of their lives, being told what to do by those who had more than they did.

The people apparently were also willing to be subservient to celebrities, to serve them and protect them in exchange for the reflected glory that celebrities provided even in the post-apocalyptic era.

Tazza told us who was there, living there at the ranch, big names from the entertainment world, and we asked if we could go see, too. He said there were lecture halls where the celebrities got up and talked to others of their kind about their work, their art, their goals, their dreams—while the service crews, that is, all those who worked the celebrity ranch to make sure the celebrities were fed, watered, and warmly housed, the service people could stand at the back of these halls and up in the balconies. The service people were needed for more than just feeding, watering, and caring for the celebrities—the service people were the fans. In fact, as they were told nightly, you're the best damn fans in the world. Can we please go see them, too, we asked Tazza. He said there were celebrity ranches all over America. We pleaded with Tazza, can't we go and sit in those balconies and see famous people and get thanked for being the best damn fans in the world?

He said no. I was ashamed of him for being ashamed of us.

Tazza's councillors were all for raiding the ranch, taking everything, all the horses and all the cattle. Kidnap the biggest celebrities and use them as negotiators to get people to surrender to us.

Tazza said no to that, too.

I knew he hated the rich so I reminded him these celebrities were rich, they lived on this ranch in luxury while the rest of America starved—let's take everything they have and leave them beside the road.

He said no.

As we marched by the main entrance to the ranch, a dozen celebrities came out, but I can't tell you their names, they were dressed in robes with deep hoods that kept famous faces back in the shadows, denying us even the opportunity to gawk.

I hated them.

For weeks after, Tazza told stories of his two-day stay at the celebrity ranch. I can't pass those stories on to you because I never heard them. Whenever he started telling one, I'd get up and leave.

My women listened to the stories, however, and told me what the celebrities had heard about Canadians, that Canadians were our government's shock troops, that Canadians were trying to train war dogs to track Americans through our swamps and up our mountains, but the dogs refused to work for Canadians and kept running off first chance they got. The story was undoubtedly apocryphal but we got a lot of Canadian jokes out of it and then later on, to show our own dogs how we appreciated their good judgment, we fed extra rations and slept with our arms around shaggy necks.

32

As winter approached and our march took us onto rocky ground, we urged Tazza to find a town where we could spend the dark months living in houses, then we could launch out again in the spring. We passed several likely candidates, towns with enough houses to house us all. But instead of settling down in any of these places, Tazza converted what few residents we found, had them tie on the string, told them to watch and wait because we'd be back to march on Washington, and then he took us, his thousands, farther into the west and winter. He told us we'd stay more alert and harder to our mission if we kept traveling, kept camping on the trail instead of living in a town somewhere.

We found cities empty, small towns half populated with residents starving—these were bad months. Snow caught us, then melted, then miles of mud. Winter rains came. Everything got wet and stayed wet. We slept in the wet and were covered by it. Until now, cold had never been our biggest problem. We bundled up and walked and stayed warm. When we were stationary in camp, we built large fires. Cold was not a problem until now when we stayed wet and felt cold down to bones and internal organs—and I remembered back when I was starving to death and felt like this all the time. Our shoes and boots stayed wet and newly dry socks soon were wet. Foot funguses were rampant so that you didn't want to be around when someone took off a boot at the end of a day of marching, the socks we wore so foul they had to be thrown out—you didn't even want to see what had grown between your own tender toes. Mold covered tents and clothing. The blessed hammocks were useless on the rocky ground—no trees to hang them from, the ground too hard to drive in stakes from which to suspend our hammocks. Back on the miasmic ground we slept, made all the worse by stones of all sizes in divers places and of course the constant wet of the ground. The skin of my fingers and toes cracked open and I never felt truly warm, truly dry.

We sent our scavengers out for dry socks and waterproof boots, they came back with nylon dress socks and tennis shoes.

Everyone grumbled except the Patagonians, silent and unreadable as always. Watching them soldier on without expression made me both angry and curious—why didn't they bitch and moan like the rest of us? I wanted to get one in our infirmary where I could slip a needle under a nail and see if a word came out, a curse, a plea, something showing that Patagonians had humanity in them. Not that I would've really harmed one of them, they had taken to David.

We came to Denver, why not stay in Denver, water and shelter could be had all winter long in Denver, what's wrong with Denver?

Tazza said Denver was indefensible. What if the Canadians came down from Canada? Denver was too close to Canada. What if the Canadians came down from Canada and attacked in the depth of winter, a time when they thrive like demons, where would we make our stand, we can't defend a city of Denver's dimensions.

Urban warfare, we urged. No dice, he said.

We asked Tazza, how will we make a stand if the Canadians catch us camping? Better out in the open, he insisted. We will form a perimeter of Patagonians, he said—and who has the power to break through the Old Guard, no one does, not even Canadians with their icy hearts. Upon hearing this declaration from their king, Patagonians stiffened with pride. Besides, Tazza said, there have been no overflights so the government doesn't know where we are, won't be able to locate us as long as we keep moving and stay away from obvious settling places . . . like Denver.

Can we at least go in and scavenge, we need shoes and wool socks.

He said what if a million armed residents are living in Denver and come pouring out to overwhelm us, not even Patagonians can defeat an army that outnumbers us a hundred to one. But the same could've been said of St. Louis, yet into St. Louis we marched—why not Denver? No, he said. *No.*

You can mark down that this was the first time that the people came close to revolting against Tazza—we were winter weary and wanted to stop.

Tazza finally agreed it would be worth finding out what's in Denver, so he sent in a spy squad, twenty-five scavengers who were gone an entire week.

What took them so long, they later explained, was that Denver, like St. Louis, was empty. Vast areas of the city had burned to the ground, high-powered gunfire had pocked the buildings still standing, and the stench of death wafted every street and cul-de-sac. They had found the zoo. Someone had been keeping the animals alive, but barely. Exhibits and cages had been opened but most of the animals stayed in the vicinity. Whoever the caretakers were, they left or went into hiding when our scavengers got there.

"We stayed at the zoo feeding the animals," one of the scavengers reported. "Then we took down all the cage doors. We don't know if any of the animals will survive. Maybe they'll scavenge the way we do."

I thought of all the zoos in all the cities across America, all the pets in millions of households, all the farm animals—what happened to them during the calamity? Did monkeys die in their cages, dogs in their crates? Did Samaritans in cities across America go about setting free the bears? Are elephants foraging old peanut farms in Alabama? Has America eaten everything that it once zooed?

"There was a place at the zoo called Predator Ridge," another scavenger told us. "According to the signs, they rotate African predators through there, lions, hyenas, wild dogs. The hyenas had already gotten out, they'd attacked some of the other animals. The hyenas invaded Primate Panorama and ate the shit out of those monkeys. Bones and all. The calcium turned their shit white and they scared us, those hyenas, they didn't run away when we approached. Scavengers my ass, they're devil dogs and they must've been in St. Louis, too, escaped from *that* zoo."

We won't scavenge Denver, Tazza said.

He decided we would turn south and march toward better weather. We came in from the countryside to make faster time traveling major highways. It was arid country that had been picked over by others. Hyenas or no, Tazza should've let us go into Denver and replenish our supplies. We were down to nothing. Our scavengers went out every day and kept coming back empty-handed. Some of the scavengers were gripped by depression, hardly able to function, taking hard their failure to provide for us.

Unlike haunted Denver, the towns and smaller cities we passed were populated, if thinly, but we no longer bothered converting the residents, we needed to get somewhere we could find food and water for our thousands. Often the starving residents stalked out walking funny to greet us, asking if we had supplies to spare or something to sell—did we have flour or coffee, did we have sugar, did we have bread, did we have soup? We asked what they planned to use in trade. They offered knives and guns, which we had plenty of. What about ammunition, we asked. But at the mention of ammo, they turned sly. Everyone had guns, it was ammunition in short supply all over America. Give over a hundred pounds of gunpowder for us to load our own cartridges, we told them, and we'll give you a hundred pounds of potatoes. But they didn't have a hundred pounds of gunpowder, they didn't have even ten. All they had were a few cartridges each, weighing down their pockets. When that ammo was gone they were defenseless. We didn't have food to trade them in any case—at least no food to spare. Which is why we were confused that Tazza agreed to take any children offered us. We couldn't properly feed those children already marching with us, why take on more? Tazza said the children we raise today will populate tomorrow's armies. His willingness to consider children our current and future soldiers troubles me now but, at the time, marching on a crusade, I wouldn't have argued the point. You think you will act reasonably in any situation but then you get so enmeshed in a movement that you can't think straight and when the Kool-Aid comes around you decide you have no choice except drink it. I know now that one of the reasons John left—in addition to the main reason, my betrayal of him—was because John could never accept, as Tazza did, the death of children as necessary casualties in our royal war.

But nobody's going to populate nothing if we all starve to death or die of thirst.

My own child was robust, intelligent, perfectly formed. The Patagonians are always bringing him treats, giving up parts of their meals. Of all the burdens I carry this terrible winter, David is one I carry joyfully.

We marched through knee-deep snow and then there was no snow and then no water. We had cut back on our food rations and we became skilled once again at starving, but our need for water was unforgiving. What we carried we went through every few days, scavengers sent out for more. They kept coming back with less.

We needed at least a quart a day for each of us and even that amount, hard to come by, kept us dehydrated. We found ponds and wells, our needs draining them dry. Some of the people hallucinated, all of us were irritable, our tongues coated and developing a trench line down the middle. We stopped peeing and then, when we did, it came out dark and it stank.

Towns had been stripped bare, water towers drained dry, evidence everywhere of mass starvations, dehydrations.

We began finding bodies facedown on the ground. They were fully clothed but those clothes had been sliced away from the lower back, the buttocks, the legs. Slices of flesh had been taken from these prone and chilled bodies. As we had discovered during the starvation following the calamity, when people turned to cannibalism, this was how they arranged the bodies they fed from—facedown, steaks cut from the back, bodies never turned over. People who had survived for months on the back and leg meat of friends refused to turn those bodies over to get at the meat on the front side, horrified to see the face of those whose flesh they ate. The cannibals sometimes starved to death right next to bodies that were never turned over, pounds of good front meat going unused.

At the edge of a cold desert, Tazza halted the columns until water could be found. At this point, to go on without water was to perish. Scouts and scavengers were sent in all directions, many of them never returning. Tazza himself went out looking, claiming he possessed the ability to hear water singing underground. He took along a dozen women, a dozen children, and me with David slung on my back. During the search, Tazza lectured us about the ways of water. He reminded me of John. I suppose we should've come to expect miracles from our king—two and a half days marching and camping in the desert, he threw himself upon a rock, listened for a few minutes, and then stood to tell us, "You'll know the purity of water by the way she sings." He told our engineers to dig at the base of this rocky hill. From their digging emerged a sweet spring that eventually watered us all and filled our containers, with water left over.

Two nights after the spring's discovery, I overheard a young man telling others that one of the scavengers had found wet sand at the bottom of that rocky hill, that the scavengers dug out enough that they could determine the water's source, but then Tazza had them fill everything back in so he could, in front of witnesses, discover the spring. I called the young man aside and asked how old he was. He said fifteen. I asked if he'd like to experience the joys and challenges of sixteen. "If your king says he hears water singing underground," I told the boy, "I advise you not to go around whispering about how scavengers found the water first. Such talk undermines our belief in our king—and it'll get you killed." He knew who I was and became terrified that I'd tell Tazza. I didn't say I wouldn't. Such is how we protect the divinity of kings.

After the desert, we spent a month in a forest, able to use our hammocks, which was heavenly, but we remained desperate for food. One of the scouts found a lake of several acres, and our scavengers set up poles and nets. The lake was full of fish but we had so many mouths to feed that Tazza ordered our engineers to cut the lake's earthen dam. We stayed a week, collecting fish that had flowed out of the lake with the water and then we dug through freezing mud for hibernating turtles, frogs, snakes. When we were full, we cut and dried amphibian meat on racks of sapling sticks arranged over smoldering fires. We departed well provisioned, thanks to the unnamed lake, but that lake was gone, the woods around the lake had been fouled with our latrines, the trees cut for firewood, and virtually every living creature put in our bellies or our larders. This kingdom of Tazza was a mobile bio-vacuum sucking up and consuming all things edible, drinkable, burnable. I was ashamed of us and thought that when David was older I would teach him to live in harmony with nature—but I also realized that if one day he inherited this kingdom and marched an army of thousands, his soldiers would eat what they would eat and harmony be damned. His father would teach him how to define exigency.

Among the items we packed from that forest around that lake were mushrooms our scavengers found in woodland caves, under logs, stolen from fairies and sprites, I don't know, but whichever scavenger was in charge of checking to make sure these particular mushrooms were safe to eat got it wrong. The mushrooms had been cut up to flavor whatever mulligan amphibian fish stew we were making those days and a hundred of us went into convulsions, ten died including our only set of twin girls, twelve years old, beautiful and dead. Even those of us who didn't convulse suffered hallucinations that plagued our minds off and on for a day and a night. A severe ringing in the ears was accompanied by voices telling us (depending upon the individual) we were marching to doom, devil dogs over the next ridge, or that angels had been sent to deliver us. We saw things, especially over the fires at night. After two days of this, Tazza issued an extraordinary order. He said the hallucinations and deaths of children were caused by the bad spirits living in the place we were then passing through and that the only solution was to get out of there as quickly as possible. I think this was a corner edge of Utah, contaminated by Mormons who sinned against Indians. Tazza ordered us to march all day and through the night, which we had never done before. Some of us carried torches, hard to keep lit. Through that night, I swear to you, a yellow dog shadowed David and me, keeping just at the edge of our light.

I'll tell you what I remember but I can't authenticate what was true versus what was inspired by mushrooms—because what I saw on our perimeter during that night march I saw an elephant and an ape and huge muscled angels leading warhorses twice the size of any earthly horse, muscled giants like those at the end of Memorial Bridge back in D.C., and I took David over to see horses and warrior angels and he, still a baby, marveled at them. Toward dawn, the yellow dog trotted in close to speak in plain words, *"Quelle horreur."* And then it said something nasty about Canadians that I didn't catch exactly but agreed with wholeheartedly.

33

Before that winter was over, we found Ozwee, a town suited to what we were to become, with rocky ridges all around we could mount like walls to defend ourselves from Canadians, a town of ten thousand souls, with only a few thousand remaining by the time of our arrival and they are starving and diseased and living in cold houses, though the town itself was unravaged, nothing's been bombed or burned, a dozen white church spires piercing the clean mountain air, hundreds of houses, woodstoves and windows, a town where we could live as if civilized.

The residents of Ozwee converted quickly to our cause, shakily tying string to their left wrists, not really understanding why, interested primarily in the food we laid out for them from our modest supplies. When word spread that we newcomers had food to share, the remaining residents came stumbling blinking out of their unheated attic places to beg for something to eat, they pressed their fingertips together and repeatedly pointed at their mouths as if they thought we spoke a language different from theirs.

Our scavengers were contemptuous of these starving residents, why not forage the countryside and bring back carts of wood for your stoves, game for your larders? The townspeople couldn't explain what had happened to them except to say that at some point during the calamity they'd lost heart.

At our tables and under our tutelage, they put weight back on and regained their enthusiasms. They showed us their hidden, rock-basin mountain lake a mile from town, and we repaired pipelines so the town once again had gravity-fed water. They showed us houses where their diseased neighbors had gone to die, though some of these houses had been nailed shut, window and door, from the outside so we knew the isolation wasn't voluntary; we burned the houses to ensure diseases wouldn't spread. They showed us hidden trails and passes through the surrounding ridges; our scavengers used the trails to go hunting while our Regular Army sent guards to the passes.

Tazza oversaw the settlement of Ozwee, which he renamed Oz. Tazza decided who would live where and how guard duty would rotate and the intricate placement of sentry posts in the surrounding countryside to ensure no force could ever sneak up on us. My women established a hospital and school. We made soap with animal fat and wood ash, insisting that everyone stay clean as a first step in preventing disease. The engineers ensured the water was potable, the sewage system working. Our various warriors divided their time between hunting parties and guard duty. Tazza decreed that dogs had to stay outside on our porches (we had porches!) or in our sheds, although many of us snuck dogs inside to sleep at the foot of our beds. Tazza's dog, Buck, got fat. We enjoyed a lovely winter, what else would you call it when you stay dry, live in a house, sleep in a bed, and your stoves radiate wood heat? Even our beloved hammocks were stowed away.

Come spring and beautiful warm hopeful it was as our thoughts turned to Tazza, that he would soon order us to provision and march west toward California. To leave our comforts now that spring had sprung! While we waited for word to leave, O dreadful day, we planted gardens (foolish hope, we knew, but the residents had hoarded enough seeds to feed an army if only they'd had the gumption and optimism to plant them) and we pruned fruit trees and cut paths to wild berry brakes. Maybe Tazza, seeing our earnest domesticity, would spare us a single year of staying put. Let us remain in Oz for this next year, we told him in council, then gladly we will march west, convert more to our cause before reversing course, collecting all our people, and descending a million strong to take Washington, D.C.

In the surrounding hills, scavengers found domesticated animals that had survived their own holocaust. By April we had corralled a few hundred sheep and goats then one day in May scavengers came home with two dozen *milk cows*. Children who couldn't remember ever drinking milk drank milk and my women churned up the miracle of butter. Yet we could see Tazza had grown restless, swanning around town in a scarlet cape. His dog, Buck, trotted along, that ruined red rubber ball still in his mouth. Tazza had once directed battles and ordered armies but now he ordered a fence to be painted, directed the demolition of an eyesore shed and was morose. To cheer him, we baked blackberry scones served with clotted cream and served by our most beautiful young women in white dresses with scooped fronts and faces scrubbed clean and hair brown and blond shiny from shampoo and barefoot and laughing the way girls will as they leaned over to serve their king who, clotted cream on his perfectly formed lips, said, yes, then, we'll stay in town another year and come next spring resume our march and complete our mission.

We worked through the summer fixing up Oz and provisioning our larders. As we harvested our gardens, piled our firewood, and put up hay for our stock, many of us became giddy with the idea of staying put forever. The ridge wall around us was impenetrable except for the passes that we guarded day and night—we can defend this town from any force on earth save an air force. And we hadn't seen a plane fly over for more than a year. If all the oil-based fuels have at long last been burned up, no airplanes to fly ever again, then our town was a fortress for the ages. We could grow our own food, raise our own stock, nurse our sick in our own hospital, and teach our own children in real schools. Tazza could still be our king, David his successor. Better to rule in Oz than serve this quest to conquer Washington.

But none of us dared argue with Tazza about staying put, he suffers dark moods now that we are stationary. He put one man to death for fermenting grapes into wine, an offense we didn't know was capital until we saw the vintner hanging by the neck.

That next winter many of my women left our communal life to go off and live with men, and some returned with black eyes and weeping accounts of abuse. What did you expect, I wanted to tell them—you should've stayed with us. A woman walking alone at night was raped, the first rape in our community. If the rapist had been caught, Tazza would've hanged him, too, but meanwhile men didn't respect us the way they once did.

An Oz police force, formed from the ranks of our Regular Army, wore jackets with emblems showing lightning bolts and got a reputation for clannish brutality.

A new group was formed, the artisans. Their skills ranged from metallurgy to tonsorial. Instead of cutting one another's hair, we now had barbers and hairdressers. The fashion had turned again to clean-shaven, the younger women finicky about kissing men with facial hair. Many of my women began shaving their legs and under their arms. I never resumed the practice, not to this day—I did not live through a holocaust to become dainty about my underarms.

Come that spring, Tazza didn't issue the order to make preparations for our departure so we planted another year's gardens, having kept seeds back from the previous harvest, and we continued our domesticated ways. Windows got washed and flower gardens planted. The elderly among us were revered for what they remembered about pickling and putting up preserves.

I spend my time with my David and my women, the world of women comforting me in the old ways that now make life with a man—Tazza or John or any man—remembered as manic and overly dramatic. And although we women spend our days cooking and nursing, it is my old life living with a man that seems one of servitude. We women talk as we sew buttons and snap beans, recalling life before the calamity as indulgent, America the site of the largest accumulation of wealth in human history with the gap between that wealth and the poorest Americans widening every year, was it any wonder that *that* America became unsupportable, we owned too many things, too much smug wealth, rich people spending more on remodeling bathrooms than most of America ever spent on a house. One of the women remembers cleaning a house with his and her toilets in the master bathroom. I tell stories of my own suburban house, how the university got it for us, and how I thought losing that house was the worst thing that could happen to me—and how very wrong I turned out to be.

We tell stories of teenagers, how they acted before the calamity, profane and spoiled, then they became frightened and humbled during the starvations, and now they're getting haughty again, my women telling stories of being sassed by teenage girls around town, they're worse than the boys, my women say. One of those girls mouthed off to a Patagonian, mocked his sign language. He walked up to her and cut off her left forearm without warning beforehand or comment afterward.

"What was she thinking of," one of the women asks, "making fun of a Patagonian?"

"They just don't know what a Patagonian is capable of."

"Kids these days, since we've been here in Oz, they don't respect anything."

"Like they don't remember how bad things were during the calamity, the march."

"They remember but they don't care."

"That girl who got her arm cut off cares."

"Now she does."

"What happened to the Patagonian who cut her?"

"What do you think? They made him stay over in that part of the town where the Patagonians live, is all."

We talked of many things, life without coffee and how more women are moving in with men. A thousand couples got married, Tazza officiating at multiple weddings. By his order, the entire kingdom showed up for these group weddings, which became drunken revelries now that Tazza had allowed the brewing of our own beer, the fermenting of our own berries to make wine. No one mentioned the executed vintner. Again, only the Patagonians kept apart, staying silent and hard and as weird as ever, no one trying to talk with them or daring to disrespect them.

Through another winter then and we became ever more domestic, more comfortable, and more like what we were before the calamity. The pre-calamity troubles that we'd been free of during the march now plagued us—men hurting women, another rape, adultery that had people at each other's throats, a woman set her husband's bed afire while he slept, our first domestic homicide. Tazza was forced to set up a court system. Our new police force added bars to the windows and doors of a house and declared it our jail—then filled it and converted another house and filled it and converted another.

Even so, we kept rooting for Tazza to allow us one more year and one more year. He gave the order, however, to start provisioning for the march, and surely we would've left with the warm weather had it not been for horses.

Our scavengers discovered in some isolated canyon a hundred horses, not wild mustangs but domesticated horses that had gotten loose or been set free and survived. Apparently they were happy to follow the scavengers for memory of a meal and a stall.

Although we saw horses back east and used them at various times, we hadn't seen any here in the west, the horses' own home. Had they all been eaten during the calamity, that's what we suspected. During our march, Tazza often said if he had horses, we could conquer America. But we *didn't* have horses—not until the scavengers brought them into Oz, down our residential streets, people coming out to marvel at the thundering herd numbering a hundred or more.

For the first time since settling here, Tazza's mood soared and he gave speeches and concerts, sang cowboy songs and told us again how we were going to take Washington and establish an American kingdom, all the old enthusiasms regained as he imagined himself riding at the head of a mounted army, a king's dream come true.

Our scavengers said there were more horses, they had seen signs of hundreds more, and Tazza told them to round 'em up, boys.

We would require another year, maybe two, to condition and train the horses, teach our armies to ride, and convert from a people afoot to a horse-based kingdom. This was huge undertaking, galvanizing everyone. We manufactured saddles and built wagons, gathered wild oats and plotted fields of corn. Those among us who had horse experience were exalted, farriers became famous as did those who could teach horses to follow closely. Tazza, good at everything he tried, was a natural horseman who loved to ride hellbent for leather. He came around for David to ride in front of him, and they left me with my heart in my throat. David took to horses too and at age five was riding bareback, one hand holding reins, the other twisted around in the horse's mane, David screaming with delight and giddy-up. I was thrilled and proud but too afraid for him to watch.

Some of the women who remained with me talked fondly of the day we would pick up and leave Oz to return to the old ways. I couldn't believe they were saying this, the same women who were so desperate to get off the march and settle down. But they didn't like what was going on in Oz. I discounted much of the women's talk as the peck and bite of bitter hearts, but when they told me the third time that our king was up to no good with young girls—I went to see.

I found him in a large bathroom with two girls whom I knew to be ages fourteen and sixteen. Tazza was in the tub, the girls were clothed, wearing long skirts and white blouses and no underwear that I could see and I could see everything because the girls were soaking wet. One was white with long blond hair, one was black with short curly hair—I heard them laughing and squealing as I climbed the steps to the second floor, listened briefly at the door, then opened it and caught the girls kneeling at the tub with their hands in the soapy water. They were initially terrified of me. As well they should be. On the way over to Tazza's house I had used my finger knife to cut a switch and now without speaking, I closed on them quickly and switched their bare wet legs as hard as I could, crisscrossing their calves with welts and chasing them out of the bathroom, still switching them as we three descended the porch steps. I told them, "Go report to my women. You'll be working and living with us now."

"You can't make us," the black-haired sassed me as she lifted her hem to squeeze out the bathwater. "Tazza won't let you."

"If you're not with my women by the time I get there, I'll give every woman in town a switch and send them all to find you. And if you ever come back here to this house, I'll arrange to banish you."

Banishment was serious, it was a death sentence. The girls weren't sure I could pull it off, though. They knew I was powerful, mother to the future king, but they also had tasted the surprising potential in the power they had over Tazza, the man—how they made him silly and how their antics put a glaze on his eyes and how like hunger his expression became when they did certain things to him and to each other and to themselves. But neither were they sure I *couldn't* arrange their banishment, so they settled finally for giving me hateful young-girl looks over their shoulders as they headed barefoot and still dripping toward the section of Oz where I and my women lived.

I went back in to see Tazza. He held up one finger to warn me, but I spoke anyway, "If you're about to remind me that you're a king, then I say act like one."

He rose naked and sudsy from the tub, making sweeping motions with his hand, shooing me out of his house like a fly.

Life in town proceeded up and down for another year. We trained on horses, groomed them, fed them, watered them, mucked out after them, rode them, doctored them. We celebrated marriages, mourned deaths. Someone started a dance club. Nearly every house had a fire pit out back and that's where families spent evenings in all but the worst weather. It was a hard life, we still had to heat water on woodstoves even in summer, wash clothes by hand, butcher our own meat—but it was the most convenient life we had lived since the calamity began.

Why, then, did we let everything go bad? I don't know. We went overboard a thousand different ways, small and large. Our simple rituals became elaborate and showy. The king wore a robe and a crown. I laughed out loud the first time I saw such a thing; people gave me horrified looks. Reverence toward your king became no laughing matter, some people were whipped for cracking jokes. He appointed dukes and viscounts. We heard rumors of perversions,

243

sickening if true. Cliques got started. Drugs were manufactured and widely used. We started seeing daytime drunks, which we'd never had before, no matter how heavily some of our residents drank deep into the night when despair gets too heavy to bear. The number of women in service with me became ever smaller, who wanted to work so hard on the behalf of so many when others were just having fun? Appeals to Tazza fell on deaf ears, he was off training cavalry or appointing barons or meeting young women on the sly, the only concession to me being that they met now in secret places and took pledges of discretion, more violated than not.

Another year passed like this, good and bad in Oz like the years good and bad before the calamity. David grew into a strong, curious, intelligent boy. He was about to turn seven, the age when he would stay with his father who would train him in the ways of warriors. But for now I had him and the women had him and we taught him how strong a boy and man must be to be gentle. With the women, David read books and recited poetry. It seemed we might be here for the rest of our lives and we forgot about tipping points and how quickly things can change. The engineers talked of building a steam-operated generator that would restore electricity to Oz. Kids started bands. Older people went on morning walks around town, you could set your watch by them. We had joggers, we had a theater group.

One morning in May, a hateful month for all its promise, I was with a woman who had served with me from the beginning, starting back on the National Mall. We were in the living room of one of the houses we women occupied, my friend seated while I stood behind, brushing her hair, beautiful, long, and gray. Kathy was one of those women who look all the more radiant with age. I told her often she had the face of a saint. We talked of the usual things, who was doing what with whom, tsking about the foolishness of young women and the wayward ways of men—while nearby on the floor David built wooden block buildings that towered and toppled. In the kitchen, bread baked. The wood burning and the bread baking combined their smells with the day's quiet to produce a narcotic effect and I didn't register the importance of something Kathy said until several moments after she said it.

I asked, "Pigs?"

"What?"

"You said something about pigs?"

"Oh. Apparently, dozens of them began wandering into town this morning."

"Just wandering in of their own accord?"

"That's what I heard."

"Where?"

"What I heard, they were seen all over—not just one spot but they were seen in different sections of town, all over town. Just wandering around, rooting in yards. People were upset about their grass getting rooted up. On the other hand, when's the last time we had pork? I think the pigs are being corralled—"

I interrupted Kathy by dropping the brush and kneeling in front of the chair, grasping both of her hands and looking hard into her saintly face so she'd know how serious I was. "Listen to me. This is an emergency. Get Tazza. If you can't find him, tell any Patagonian, any officer in any one of the regiments you see. *Tell them we're being invaded.*"

"By *pigs?*"

"No, Kathy—by *Canadians*. I'm taking David to one of the safe houses. If I see anyone, I'll spread the word, too, but my first obligation is to make sure David is safe so it's up to you to notify people, you'll have to hurry."

Then I remembered the bells. We had bells on posts all over

town, bells that could be rung in emergencies, except it had been so long since any were rung that many were missing ropes rotted away or had had their clappers stolen as pranks by kids.

"Ring every bell you can," was the last thing I said before the explosions began.

34

Sneak attack!

Toque-wearing, beer-belching, pork-obsessed Canadians!

We were criminally unprepared and would've perished one and all, king and scavenger alike, had it not been for our terrible Patagonians, who, unappreciated by the rest of us, had remained vigilant throughout our years of indifference in Oz, Patagonians who had never stood down or gone off guard duty, and who counterattacked the Canucks with such over-the-top ferocity that the thick-waisted Canadians were stopped long enough for our surprised forces to regain their equilibrium, regroup, and counterattack.

A marriage made in hell, pigs and Canadians—they employed their hogs as kamikazes with explosives strapped to their undersides. The pigs were kept hungry so that when they were released at the outskirts of Oz, the starving hogs quickly began exploring town for something to eat. Either by timers or remote control, the explosives were detonated, disrupting everything, preventing our various brigades and corps from assembling, this confusion made worse because our soldiers weren't at their posts to start with. Not all the pigs were blown up at the same time. By staggering the explosions, the Canadians kept us in chaos—we never knew when or where the next one might go off. Look, there's a pig! Do we try to catch it and remove the bomb or chase it away or shoot it or will the shooting cause the bomb to explode or what?

Several hundred of these porcine devices invaded us, Canadian bacon in the making, pork in the trees of Oz, our fighting forces running around trying to avoid hogs, forgetting what they were supposed to do, where they were supposed to assemble, what the plans were for repelling invaders.

The Canadians invaded our corrals and killed our horses. They grabbed Tazza's old dog, Buck, and strapped him with explosives, thinking Buck would go to his master and blow up both of them. In the confusion of the initial attack, one of our elderly couples saw Buck trotting around with that old ball in his mouth, something strapped to his back. The couple brought him in their house to protect him during the battle. The house exploded, killing the couple and Buck. I know what you're thinking, what kind of people would blow up a dog and an old couple and shoot horses wholesale. Canadians, that's who.

The Patagonians were always on the streets of Oz—we simply hadn't been aware that they were *patrolling*. When the first hog exploded, a Patagonian recognized instantly what this meant and signaled another Patagonian who signals another until their main force, always on alert, assembles in less than twenty minutes and a hundred Patagonians, with machete and gun, meet the first thousand Canadian shock troops.

The beer-bellied northerners are seasoned fighters but they don't know what to make of our Patagonians, attacking with an assault rifle in one hand, razor-edged machete in the other, the first ten shot and killed in an instant, ten more behind, getting closer to the Canadian lines, this second wave killed too, the third ten reaching the entrenched Canadians and wreaking havoc and malice in total silence.

Tazza never said where he was when that first pig exploded but we all suspected he was with one or more of his young girls on the outskirts of town. Our other supposed protectors were similarly preoccupied. The Celtic tribes were hungover from the previous night's debauchery. The African Corps were scattered, sleeping, napping, toking. Our Regular Army troops had furlough that day, at home with their spouses, preparing barbecues and throwing horseshoes. Engineers were out of town repairing water pipes, scavengers on whatever adventures occupied them. The brigade that had guard duty that day, that were supposed to be manning the forward sentry posts and the secret mountain passes that led into town, most of them were in a drug haze when the Canadians snuck in and quietly slit their throats.

In kitchens and gardens and on sick wards, my women were working when the Canadians attacked. We immediately set up a field hospital and then armed ourselves to defend it.

When Tazza finally arrived and found out that a handful of his Vieille Garde were holding off more than a thousand Canadians, he rounded up what fighting men and women he could find and rushed to relieve the Patagonians. Tazza *leads* soldiers into battle. And to make sure his men and his women and his enemy know who he is, Tazza wore red.

The house-to-house battle is savage. Our remaining soldiers are trying to find their units, waiting at their assembly points, looking through boxes for gas masks, for helmets. Tazza grabs them, sometimes literally by the collar, you fucking idiot, shoulder your weapon and follow me. He throws another twenty into the battle, another fifty. We have no radios, no way for Tazza to know where the rest of his forces are or to call them to war—though with all the explosions and gunfire, it would seem everyone should know a fight's on.

When the force fighting with Tazza has been cut in half and then in half once more, *that's* when he orders an attack and when that one fails he orders another. How Tazza survived leading those attacks dressed in red is anyone's speculation. He took seven wounds, stopping to plug the holes with linen rags soaked in olive oil before resuming the battle over street rubble and through cratered yards. Men who make history, Caesar and Alexander, are blessed with more than charisma and leadership—they are born under lucky stars and wear good fortune like a cap right up until the time they end badly.

Here come the Africans, newly assembled, then the Celts. You know what they say about Canadians, yellow as the snow they leave in their wake—and when the numerical odds shifted from their favor to even-steven, they turned their big fat asses and fled, with Tazza, the African Corps, and the Celtic Tribes in hot pursuit.

Hit with a flanking maneuver just as they were leaving town, the remaining Canucks bunched up in a cul-de-sac that became a killing field. We think—and hope and pray—that not a single Canadian survived.

In the days to follow, we women nursed those among our soldiers who would live and we comforted those who would die. Our engineers buried bodies around the clock, Canadians in open unmarked graves and our own brave dead in individual plots with stones that said their names.

Some among us expected Tazza to go on a rampage about how criminally unprepared we'd all been, all save the Old Guard, but he knew we carried in our hearts the full measure of our disaster, so he used his energy to rebuild our defenses and set up a massive provisioning for when we would leave and resume our march. We were all aware now that leaving Oz was inevitable, just a matter of how long it takes us to prepare.

Only twenty-three Patagonians survived the battle, all wounded, some severely. Within a month, fourteen of those would die from their wounds—leaving in this world only nine living Patagonians. The women and I cared for them, wet cloths on fevered brows and hands held when they became delirious.

A few weeks after the battle, Tazza asked me to go for a walk. He wanted to know why I fled with David to a safe house during the fighting, why I huddled with him in the basement.

"You always told me my first obligation was to David. What was I supposed to do with him, didn't you want your son safe?"

"I wanted him to see and hear and smell a battle and feel the explosions and see the faces of men at war. This would've been an invaluable experience for a future king, but he missed out on it, hiding behind concrete blocks in a basement."

"So I should've sent him into battle?"

"Don't be flippant with me, Mary. You should've taken him to the attic of that house and told him to watch out the window. You should've opened that window so he could hear men screaming, smell cordite burning. You should've sat with him and explained how the battle was going, who was on the attack, who was retreating, who got flanked. I think you don't appreciate, Mary, that you're not just raising a boy, you're preparing a king."

We stopped at a large long mound, the fresh mass grave of Canadians, the disturbed earth still an odor in our noses and the back of our throats. "You used to be such an interesting man," I told Tazza. "And now you're such a prig."

"I warned you before about talking to me like that."

"I know who you are."

He paused a long time and then said, "I wasn't going to tell you this but John was among the Canadians."

I didn't believe him.

Tazza insisted it was true. "He became a turncoat after he left us.

The Canadians figured he knew enough about our thinking that he could track us down—and they were right, weren't they, Mary? He was a hollow old fool, nothing but talk—and a coward when it came to war."

I asked Tazza how he could be so cold toward the man who made him king.

"He didn't make me nothing. I was born a king."

"I was there, Tazza. You can create whatever legends you want for yourself, you can make up whoppers about divine hurricanes, but *I was there*."

"And now John is *there*," he said, kicking dirt before walking across the covered pit, casually spitting as he went.

When I was alone I knelt there to tell John I loved him and, upon doing this, I sensed his presence and was overwhelmed by it, throwing myself facedown on the dirt of his grave, wishing it the warmer, sweeter be as I turned my head and listened for the faint murmuring far below, John talking to Canadians at his elbows, speaking to them of sausages and Celtic kings and the property of mercury under pressure, talking and talking as I remembered floating in the rivers of his talk.

What a pathetic and sentimental old woman you must take me for, to tear up at memories of throwing myself on the grave of a man. Women don't do that anymore, do they?

After that, the kingdom was lost for me.

35

Life in Oz was grim, our energies directed toward provisioning the march. Never again, we told each other. To get caught like that.

What horses we had left we trained to the cart and travois. Our men grew beards again and bristled. We put an edge on our dogs, no longer bedmates and ball fetchers but recruited now as war dogs fighting as Buck's Brigade. Those dogs who didn't have the heart for war were shot. We had become a hard people once again.

We had lost half our number in the attack. We needed more of everyone but especially we needed more Patagonians.

A week after the battle, Tazza commandeered a building and brought together our most talented metal artisans. He had them set up their residences in the building, no one would be leaving until the job was done. Tazza had in mind exactly what he wanted and told the artisans exactly how to create his vision. We could smell the forges and hear the pounding but none of us knew what commission the artisans were working on in shifts around the clock.

One month later, Tazza assembled a meeting to celebrate the Patagonians. He called the nine survivors to the high school auditorium stage and presented each with a kukri.

This is what the artisans had been working on, had labored in shifts day and night to follow Tazza's instructions and get it right. It was a knife made famous by Nepal's Gurkhas, the kukri shaped roughly like a boomerang, the blade bending forward. The ones Tazza had forged were nearly two feet overall, the blade fifteen inches long and powerfully thick, made from leaf springs taken from the town's long-abandoned trucks—this was high carbon steel, virtually unbreakable, capable of being sharpened like a razor. Each kukri weighed about two pounds. The ingenious design had been used in one variation or another from five hundred years before Christ. Because the blade angles forward, the edge is always shearing whatever it cuts, whereas a straight-bladed knife will strike head-on, like trying to push a paring knife through a tomato instead of slicing through. The people of Nepal use kukris as a combination knife-sword-machete; a Nepali boy is given one at age five and by the time he's a man, his kukri has become an extension of his arm. The Gurkhas made the knife famous in warfare, most especially as a tool for severing limbs and heads.

Our Patagonians knew nothing of Gurkhas and kukris but immediately recognized this weapon as brilliant in design, deadly in intent. For them, seeing a kukri for the first time was like an art lover seeing the *Pietà* for the first time, like me seeing David for the first time. You think I'm exaggerating, but had you been in that auditorium that night and seen those silent faces, nine left from a hundred, you would know some small portion of what it was to be a surviving Patagonian seeing a beautiful kukri for the first time. To hold a kukri in your hand was a kind of bliss if you were a Patagonian, how the blade-heavy weight makes the instrument feel like a spirited horse that can barely be held back—this is a knife that was forged to cut and eager to lead you toward the act of cutting, blade first, toward the very destiny of cutting.

When Tazza told them that the kukri can never be returned to its scabbard without drawing blood, all nine Patagonians immediately tilted the blades across their forearms, bringing blood. "No," Tazza said, "I meant to say *in battle*. If a kukri is drawn in battle, in anger, it can't be sheathed again until it tastes blood." Tazza told them to look at the hilts of their knives. Each one had been engraved:

The Patagonian
Ever vigilant, his honor as keen as his blade

Rumor has it that several people saw Patagonian eyes glistening but this was never confirmed and none of us was so foolish as to inquire.

"I'm having one hundred and one of these made," Tazza said. "The first nine are those you hold. The next one forged will be mine. The remaining ones we will hold for when you fill your ranks."

The Patagonians spent several weeks becoming accustomed to their kukris. We heard that it wasn't unusual for a Patagonian to go for days with his kukri never out of his hand, he would eat and wash with the other hand—and sleep with his kukri in his dominant hand even if that meant awakening to sheets stained red from shallow razor cuts left accidentally here and there over his body.

These nine surviving Patagonians quickly became Gurkha-like in their talents with kukris. Success at filling their ranks, however, was elusive.

We set off in the spring of the year that David would turn eight. Tazza put out scouts to ensure we wouldn't be surprised again. Our vulnerability had always been that we traveled as a people, with our children and elderly and stock animals and everything a people need to survive, while the forces arrayed against us were soldiers who traveled as an army.

We left Oz burning behind us. We marched, we walked, we set up camp, slept in hammocks that we women had repaired because so many of them had rotted in storage—and then we broke camp and marched again. Our bodies with aches and pains and strains eventually accustomed themselves to this new old life. We were grimly aware that Canadians might attack again at any time. At night we listened anxiously for the snort and snuffle of their pigs.

It turned out that we never saw another Canuck that winter, though we did come across a remnant herd of their hogs. Our scouts determined that the hogs weren't strapped with explosives but they were clearly Canadian swine because their ears had been notched in a particularly Canadian way.

We were camped on either side of an interstate highway. Our cattle and horses grazed the medians and berms. Who would've dreamed when these highways were laid and when thousands of cars and trucks traveled them racing both directions each day that eventually the roadways would be *grazed* like ribbons of pasture crisscrossing America?

The herd of hogs, maybe sixty, were foraging ahead of us in the forest, making their way in our direction. In the old days we would've butchered as many as we could and merged the remaining with our stock—but you never know what diseases the pig-fucking Canadians might've given these animals so we were determined to shoot them or chase them off.

David said to his father, "Let's see what the Buck Brigade can do against them."

Tazza agreed, find out which dogs were game.

We had a hundred. Their owners led the dogs barking crazily into the forest where they were sicced on the pigs. It was a rout. Whenever a fleeing pig was cornered, however, it fought like a Patagonian, and our dogs got torn up bad. All that night we heard barking, baying, squealing, howling. From dawn until noon we whistled them in—fifty came back, cut up and limping and lop-eared but all the more ferocious. This was not a major happening in our history, things like this happened all the time—but I was asked to tell about it because of the annual celebration we hold to this day, Dogs & Hogs. How is it that certain of these events live in history and become festivals while others, equally important, are never heard of again, I can't tell you. Maybe it's the alliterative sound of Dogs & Hogs—but today's festival, games and races and chases, bears little resemblance to the original event on which the festival is based. When I was more mobile I would be invited to Dogs & Hogs festivals as if people thought I would get a kick out of the festivities. I never did. The original was bloody and cruel.

When David saw so few dogs returning and so many of those injured, he apologized to his father.

Tazza said, "It's better this way. Find out which are game, which aren't. Now we have real war dogs."

We resumed our march south. We needed well-populated towns to replenish our numbers but we found few. In the Malthusian world of a hundred years ago, who would've guessed that the future's biggest problem would be running out of people?

In Arizona we encountered a phenomenon stranger than anything we'd come across so far. One of our scouts came back with news of a community called Ultra. "You know what the people are doing in Ultra?" the scout asked, bug-eyed with disbelief as we waited for him to supply the answer—what are the people in Ultra doing? He said, "They're playing golf."

36

Before the calamity, Ultra was a sprawling gated community of millionaires, self-made, white, retired, and golfers. At the beginning of the calamity, a contingent of the very rich, that top tenth of one percent in wealth, came to the merely rich of Ultra and offered a deal: let us bring our stockpiles into Ultra, pharmaceuticals and footwear, canned goods and guns. We'll build warehouses. We'll hire poor white trash from the trailer parks to guard the warehouses and police the perimeter. You've already got the Mexicans doing yard work and household chores. We'll be fine. We'll last out this calamity—and be better golfers for it.

Astonishingly, while America starved, the merely rich and the very rich residents of Ultra lived in luxury including access to four of the most beautiful eighteen-hole golf courses in the Southwest. No house in Ultra was less than seven thousand square feet, all were designed by architects, most had swimming pools.

In the earliest days of the calamity, guided by the very rich among them, the merely rich of Ultra withdrew their money before the banking system collapsed. Once again ahead of the curve, they took that money and invested in tangibles such as gold coins, stock-piled gasoline, firearms, ammunition, and sheep and cattle. The residents of Ultra elected their own president, one of the very rich who had moved in. John Bett was one of the most successful and notorious corporate executives of the early Twenty-first Century, famous for taking old-line companies like General Electric and turning them into profit machines by squeezing employees for more work, fewer benefits. A ruthless negotiator, Bett was famous for his declaration: "Loyalty is just a word." What counted was performance. What counted was the deal. In his corporate career, Bett cut costs, broke unions, and made a billion-dollar-a-year salary doing it. In retirement he got a third wife—because his second trophy wife wasn't making the cut any longer, performance was what counted. Number three was an avid golfer half his age, they were writing a book together before the calamity hit.

To prepare for life in Ultra during the calamity, Bett sat down with the workers who kept Ultra running. He convinced them it was in their own best interests to stay, to keep working, to take firearms training so that along with grooming greens and cleaning houses they could also help defend the community. "Because otherwise where will you go if you leave Ultra?" he asked the workers. "Society is breaking down. Marauders will take everything you have. You'll starve. Stay here in Ultra and you'll have housing." Some of the rich residents had departed for back-East homes when the calamity began in earnest, leaving several ten-thousand-square-foot houses that could be used for workers, ten couples to a house instead of just the one couple who lived in each of the houses originally but, still, Bett told the workers, you'll be living in what you must think of as a mansion, and who among you would've ever guessed that might happen? The workers would share in the food being stockpiled, in the water being pumped from Ultra's own wells, in the protection afforded by Ultra's walls and armaments. My husband had been wrong about workers taking by force whatever the rich held; in Ultra, the workers were thoroughly domesticated.

Similarly domesticated cattle and sheep pastured on the golf courses, which broke the heart of golf purists but sacrifices had to be made, it was a jungle outside the walls of Ultra and the natives in that jungle were restless, starving, desperate.

The residents of Ultra, meanwhile, had come out on top again. Being self-made, they had none of the modesty or chagrin and precious little of the *noblesse oblige* occasionally displayed by those who've inherited their wealth. In fact, the residents of Ultra believed that no matter how you shook up the world and started over again, they would keep coming out on top. They were winners. If you weren't wealthy, you were one of the losers. The reasons you didn't end up rich ranged from not being smart enough or hardworking enough or just not wanting it enough. Need proof of this? Here's the bottom line, which the residents of Ultra were fond of referencing: In the midst of a calamity so profound that half the population of America died and the most powerful modernized nation on earth was reduced to a primitive existence of bartering and warlords, *we play golf every day.* So you tell us, are we winners or are we winners?

And what happens when the barbarians show up at the gate and want to take everything we've worked so hard to accumulate? We just send out John Bett and he either runs the barbarians off or *negotiates* our safety.

If the people at the gate were starving and lightly armed, presenting no significant threat, Bett told them to leave or be fired upon. Seventy years old, he still had the balls to back up his threat and more than once ordered his guards to shoot into the crowds of men, women, children—effectively getting rid of the people *and* establishing a ruthless reputation that would help keep future beggars away.

If marauders showed up and seemed to have the numbers and firepower to threaten Ultra's own guard force, Bett came out under the protection of a white flag and negotiated.

Yes, you can fight your way in to Ultra, he told marauders, but you'll take heavy losses because our men are well trained and well armed.

And if you get in, what will you have won? Our women left as soon as you showed up, and they took with them all our wealth, whatever gold we had. These women have scattered into hiding places we worked years to prepare—you'll never find them. We've also prepared what we used to call in the corporate world a poison pill that makes takeover unpalatable. In our case here at Ultra, the poison is literal. I have men waiting for a signal to contaminate our wells. Gunners have been stationed to kill our sheep and cattle as soon as any invader wins an upper hand. People in each household will poison as much food as they can.

So you win a victory and what does it gain you? No food, no women, no wealth.

On the other hand . . . and here's where Bett clinched the deal . . . if the marauding force would just move on and leave us alone, the residents of Ultra would pay them a cigar box full of Canadian Maple Leaf gold coins and several sheep and cattle, maybe a few horses. Sometimes, Bett had to give more; often he got away with paying less. It was his call, he was an expert at sizing up those on the other side of the negotiations. Never would he offer firearms or ammunition and always he was willing to walk away and fight. In every single negotiation that Bett conducted with groups threatening Ultra during the calamity, he won. No marauding force ever invaded and, in Ultra, John Bett was as famous and valued as he'd been in the pre-calamity corporate world. In fact, the residents of Ultra would've paid whatever it took to keep Bett working on their behalf, just as boards of directors once did.

So now comes this latest threat, a ragtag group of people, some on horseback, led they say by a king. Bett had heard stranger things—marauders led by men calling themselves emperors and czars. He set in motion the usual preparations, people ready to poison food and water and shoot stock while the women of Ultra departed through well-practiced escape routes, carrying with them the vast majority of Ultra's gold. Ultra residents told Bett that these preparations were no longer necessary, he always won the negotiations so what was the point? No, he said, you can't bluff about something like that, if you threaten to swallow a poison pill you have to be prepared to swallow the poison pill.

All the same, it was with a certain weary smugness that Bett, carrying a white flag and accompanied by a few of his executive assistants, left the front gate of Ultra to get rid of this latest group of marauders who, if they had worked hard and worked smart, would've been living in a gated community instead of threatening to pillage it.

"Who's your leader, your negotiator?" he asked. Bett wore golf slacks and a knit shirt, on his head a white cap with the Nike swoosh in black. He also wore his golf shoes, intending to get in nine holes before dark.

Tazza dismounts a stallion. "I'm their king."

Bett suppresses a smile. "Your majesty." He really shouldn't have said that so snottily—sarcasm doesn't sit well with these megalomaniacs. And this one, with his long black hair and brooding face, unnaturally green eyes, his red cape and haughty manner, he looks like a crazy person by way of community theater.

"I've brought out some coins to show you," Bett says, looking over at one of the assistants, who opened a cigar box to show the gold Maple Leaf coins. "Now let me explain to you how you can get those coins all for yourself," Bett continues. "By making a choice. Yes, you can fight your way in to Ultra but you'll take heavy losses because our men are well trained and well armed. And if you get in, what will you have won? Our women left as soon as you showed up, and they took with them all our wealth, whatever gold we had, everything except those coins in that box. Our women have scattered into hiding places we worked years to prepare—you'll never find them. We've also prepared what we used to call in the corporate world a poison pill—"

Tazza reaches behind his back and draws his kukri and with a wide powerful horizontal sweep of his arm brings the boomerang-bent blade around and through Bett's neck, causing the Nike cap to fly off, Tazza hitting hard, putting his weight into it like a home-run hitter, raising his left arm so the kukri blade can continue its momentum, Tazza's left hand jumping forward over the top of his right arm, his left-hand fingers open like a cobra's mouth, striking out to grab Bett's hair before the decapitated head can drop to the ground. Decapitation with one blow is difficult, Tazza made it look inevitable.

He holds the head leaking blood high for all those back at the Ultra gate to see. Bett's body collapses shooting a string of arterial blood twenty feet. The administrative assistant who'd been holding the gold coins drops the box at Tazza's feet, and Tazza kicks box and coins into a nearby drainage ditch, full of water and snakes.

We thought, good God, look what our king does. And on the other side, the people of Ultra thought here is a ruthless man who comes to us like a Viking, a pirate, a barbarian. To him the flag of truce means nothing. To him the sanctity of negotiations is a joke. Here is a man to whom decency and rules mean nothing. Imagine what he will do to you and yours once he's inside the gate, inside your house. Even our precious gold means nothing to him, he kicks it away into the ditch—which was maybe the hardest message for the residents of Ultra to hear because they measured their power in gold and if gold is worthless to someone, then what power do you have over him?

One moment John Bett is a powerful negotiator about to brush off another group of ruffians, the next moment his leaking head is held in a man's hand as his golf-clad body slumps to a pile and twitches as if trying to figure out how to get up again.

Those witnessing this from behind the gates of Ultra immediately flee, abandoning any thought of making a stand. The working-class defenders were not about to fight these particular barbarians on the behalf of rich golfers—and the rich themselves, having never seen anyone as pitiless as Tazza, run quick-like to their golf course mansions.

Ancient Celts had a fondness for severed heads and our own Celts put Bett's head on a pole for Tazza to carry into Ultra.

The hired guards and the groundskeepers and the domestic workers and their families lived in the outer ring of non-golf-course houses, and they surrendered to our main force led by Tazza carrying Ultra's corporate hero's head on a pike. Tazza offered to accept their surrender if they told us all they knew about the community, where the commodities were and any secrets about booby traps and poisons and anything else we should know. The workers agreed enthusiastically to betray the merely rich and the very rich because, in Ultra, loyalty was just a word.

Riding along the beautiful tree-lined roads leading to the mansions flanking golf courses, Tazza turned to the warriors around him and gave an order he'd never issued before, not even against Canadians: "No mercy."

No mercy to those who golfed while a hundred million Americans starved to death.

We attacked mansion by mansion. Some of the rich fought for their lives, sticking rifles out windows, but each house proved too big for two people to defend, just as they were too big for two people to live in, and our warriors broke into back rooms and bathrooms and game rooms and media rooms, eventually making their way to the homeowners. The rich were disarmed and dragged out in front of their mansions to be decapitated. The executions went quickly when done by Patagonians wielding their kukris. The decapitations were a horror when done by one of our other warriors with a machete or Bowie knife hacking through neck and spinal column or letting arms get in the way so they had to be hacked off before the neck could be reached—nasty business that I regret ever seeing and regret even more that my son saw.

If the rich of Ultra surrendered and came out of their mansions with their hands up . . . they were decapitated, too.

The tough ones to dislodge were those who locked massive mansion doors, lowered and locked steel storm shutters, then locked themselves in all-steel safe rooms with food and water and separate ventilation. We burned those houses, a process that sometimes took all day and night, many of the houses steel and concrete so our engineers had to pile in wood from Ultra's own supply of firewood, pile in hay that'd been cut from the golf course, and eventually the houses burned to the ground. As the grand houses burned, the residents often came out coughing and begging for mercy that wasn't ours to give—we decapitated them in their scorched yards.

Tazza ordered all heads of the rich collected, he ringed the greens with them. And when the greens were full, we took them to the tees.

We spread through the gated community to pillage what we could, and we merged our cattle and horses with the herds of Ultra, all the animals grazing on fairways and roughs.

Some of the Ultra women—first wives and trophy wives alike—came back after a few days even though they could see their community had been torched, where else were they to go? Tazza had them decapitated, too. I know books have been written about his trajectory into insanity. The Canadian attack on us in Oz had shamed him. He was angry with himself for agreeing to stay that long in one place. And he had turned forty without conquering Washington. Are those the reasons books give for Tazza having gone insane?

After a few days, we left Ultra a smoldering ruin.

Word of what we'd done spread throughout the Southwest, Tazza now bypassing regular towns to target gated communities. Some surrendered immediately. We took everything they owned and cut off their heads. Many fought us but the gated community guards had no experience with an army like ours, with warriors like Celts, like Africans, like Patagonians, who had finally filled their ranks and were once again a hundred strong. Also, these sprawling gated communities were too large to defend; we hit in multiple places until we found a breach. Many times we came to a gated community that had been abandoned, the very rich and the merely rich fleeing into the countryside where they tried to pass themselves off as common folk, as the people, but they were easy to spot, betrayed by soft hands and manicured nails and by a lack of denim in their clothing. The dead giveaways, what always got them killed, were pockets full of jewels, gold coins taped to their bodies—they couldn't bear to give up their things. Whenever we found the very rich hiding among refugees, Tazza had the rich stripped of their valuables and decapitated.

We sometimes spent a week or more in a gated community, packing up what we could carry, destroying what we couldn't. This was taking forever. Our numbers were still down from the defeat at the fat hands of the Canadians in Oz, but Tazza wouldn't ask the rich to join us—he just kept cutting their heads off. We became so ashamed at what we were doing that the Regular Army refused to participate in the executions, leaving decapitations to our Patagonians. Dozens of our people simply left, depleting our numbers ever lower.

I was recruited to talk to Tazza. I asked him bluntly why he was executing everyone. When would these constant, awful decapitations end?

"When we can spare the rope to hang them."

"Tazza. We need people if we're ever going to retake Washington, why don't you offer the residents of these gated communities an opportunity to join us?"

He said they can't be trusted. "The others who've joined us, from towns all across America, they were victims of the calamity. But these rich people, they abetted it. And then when the calamity came to pass and America began to starve, these rich played golf and lived in big houses with swimming pools and they had cocktail parties and they danced, Mary—they danced and played golf."

I grabbed him by his long hair and made him focus those green eyes on my face so I could tell him the truth even if it got my head separated from my shoulders. "You can't keep doing this. The people will leave you if we continue these mass executions. Killing during a battle, yes—even savage killing during battle, we understand that and we've become a hard people. But not this. Not this systematic slaughter of the rich men and the women, too, even after they've surrendered, after they've been disarmed. Did you know that our people are already leaving? Twenty of my most loyal women left in the last month, and I didn't even try to talk them into staying. They took their men with them, their children, they'll live as best they can in the countryside because they won't be part of a people who do what we've been doing, who tie up the rich and cut their heads off the way we do. You've made us into monsters. One of these days you'll turn around and see it's only you and the Patagonians left, everyone else gone to get their humanity back."

"Give me a thousand Patagonians and I'll take Washington without any of you sheep to slow me down."

"You limited the number of Patagonians to a hundred for a reason, they're too dangerous. I know they love David and would do anything for him but—"

"What do you want, Mary?"

I made the mistake of threatening him. "I'll never turn David over to you while you're conducting this holocaust. If I have to, I'll leave with him and you'll never see your son again."

Tazza struck me.

When he steps close to hit me again, I draw a finger knife and cut him across his left cheek.

He jumps back, surprised, one hand holding his bleeding face, the other drawing his kukri.

Still holding my finger knife, I wait to die.

But after a moment, he laughs. "Mary, you've just committed a capital crime, assaulting your king. And you're standing there with that little *kitchen knife* as if it's going to protect you when I could cut off both your arms and then decapitate you before your arms hit the ground."

Still waiting to die, I am ferocious and demand of this man, "I am the mother of your child and you will respect me for that."

He goes to his pack and brings out a first-aid kit, then sits in a camp chair, handing me what I need to dress his wound. "Here, before I bleed to death."

It's a shallow cut, he won't bleed to death—but I could make it deeper. I stand behind him, cotton dressing in one hand, the finger knife in the other. He puts his kukri away, I could easily cut his throat and I can't tell you how close I came to doing it, close enough to picture it exactly in my mind, a swift deep cut severing his carotid artery, then step back out of his way and watch the bull stagger and bellow.

When I reach over his shoulder to put the cotton on his wound, he grabs my hand and draws the kukri so quickly I couldn't have stopped him from killing me. But all he did was touch that blade to his bleeding cheek, explaining, "If it's drawn in anger, it has to taste blood."

"Yes, I know." I dressed the wound with the cotton and moss and ointments.

He tells me he has thread for sutures.

"We'll leave it open so it won't get infected," I say. "And also I think every king needs a scar across his face, don't you?"

"Preferably one earned in battle."

"Isn't that what we just had?"

"Who won, Mary?"

37

It was a draw. Tazza agreed not to go out of our way to attack every gated community in the Southwest—but we would test those communities we came across in the course of our march. We would send a family to the community's gate. The people would ask for food, whatever could be spared, a loaf of bread, a can of peaches. In all our travels we had never refused anyone who came to us for food. And if the residents of the gated community gave our test family some food, no matter how little, we would pass by and let the community live. If they refused our people, would not give even a single can of peas to Americans they thought were starving, then we'd attack.

I argued against even this compromise and asked Tazza why don't we march fast to the south and see what the calamity had done to Mexico? Yes, I was the one who first suggested Mexico to him and, no, that's never been acknowledged, but my reason wasn't to create an alliance with Mexico, I wanted to stop the mass executions. Trust me on this one, there was only one reason we took so long to get through the Southwest, Tazza wanted to find more rich people to behead.

In the month after Tazza's concession, we came upon three gated communities. Tazza was surprised that the first two, while not inviting our test family in, did fill a basket of food and give it to the people with their prayers and blessings. "Ultra would never have given food to travelers," Tazza said, defending what we did there.

Then we came to the third community, bigger and richer and better guarded than the first two. I was helping assemble the group to go up and beg for food—four women and four children. We didn't include men because we didn't want to intimidate the guards or make them suspicious. Two of the children would go up to the gate and ask for food, the rest of the family staying a hundred feet back. To play these roles, we dressed our people in tattered clothing and dirtied their faces—almost literally sackcloth and ashes. I was in the middle of making these preparations when Tazza came in.

He orders David to be one of the kids in the group and, more than that, he wants David to go up to the gate and ask for food. "Two will go to the gate, David and that girl," Tazza said, indicating a twelve-year-old.

"But David's only eight," I said.

Tazza said that was old enough and he didn't want David getting a pass because of who he was.

I didn't argue the point. Tazza was right, David had to take his turn at whatever task came up, but I sorely did not want my son to go up to that gate. What if the community had a policy of shooting beggars? We'd heard of such things. I decided to join the four women in the group and I armed us with short-barreled assault rifles that we kept concealed beneath blankets we wore like serapes.

I took David aside. He had witnessed so much for being eight. In his green eyes I saw composure and strength but none of the innocence of being eight. I gave him one of my finger knives, telling him if he's grabbed he should slash their faces first, a man who's face-cut will let go of you long enough to escape. "If you're not sure, then don't do it. But if you do decide to do it, cut quickly and without hesitation." David nods. Like a Patagonian, he says, Yes, I agree, exactly like a Patagonian, without discussion or hesitation. This is how far the journey had taken me: when I began, I mourned never having had a child and I was terrified of the Patagonians and their chilling capacity for violence—and now I have a son whom I urge to fight like the beasts I once feared.

With a leather band, I tied the knife around his thin waist so all he had to do was reach in his shirt.

The other women and I and two of the children stood off from the gate so the guards could see us and know we were not a threat, David and the twelve-year-old girl approaching slowly. David asked one of the two guards for food. "Just enough for me and my family," he said, looking back at the rest of us. "A few cans of whatever you have. It doesn't matter how much, just something." Give us something, anything, and your lives will be spared, is what he meant.

The two guards were sympathetic but had strict orders about dealing with beggars, the leaders of this community fearing that if they got a reputation for generosity, people by the thousands would line up with their hands out. As the guards were debating giving this kid a few things from their own lunch pails, one of the community leaders came up in a golf cart and demanded to know what the hell was going on.

David and the girl were fascinated, they couldn't remember ever seeing a really fat man. He wore a golf shirt and white shorts. His face was apple red and spidered with broken veins around the nose, a nose so large that David stared at it when the man talked.

The fat man reamed out the guards for even allowing the kids to approach. "You go to the briefings, you get the memos, and *still* you talk to these people," he told the guards. "If we start putting out corn for rats, what do we get—more rats! God knows what diseases . . ." He turns to David. "No food, understand? Go back and tell your mommy and daddy, if in fact you know who your daddy is, tell them that the nice man told you if they had worked just a little bit harder in their lives, they wouldn't be starving. 'Cause I started out poorer than you are now, I guarantee you." His lecture stops when the girl looks at him and he seems to see her for the first time, realizes in fact she's a girl and not a skinny boy. His piggy eyes glisten as he puts a pudgy hand to the side of her dirty face. "I bet you'd be a looker if we took you in and gave you a bath. Would you like to come and see my house?"

She stares at the ground and shakes her head no, David keeping his eyes lasered on the pig man's face.

"We've stockpiled fuel," the man tells the girl as he drops his hand from her cheek to her shoulder, "so I get to ride around in this golf cart. Have you ever ridden on a golf cart?"

She doesn't answer, she wants to leave.

"Why don't you come with me? I'll send you back in a couple hours, all freshly bathed, new clothes, a basket of food for your family out there—isn't that a good deal all around?"

She looks to David.

David takes her hand. "We'll go now, mister." He is signing the man's death warrant.

The man casually pushes David aside and puts his hand on the girl's budding breast, rubbing back and forth with one sausage thumb and whispering, "You like that, don't you?"

The guards have turned to look elsewhere.

When David tries again to take the girl's hand, the man backhands him and grabs the girl's upper arm, intent on dragging her away. Without hesitation, David takes out the finger knife and quickly slashes twice across the man's eyes. The man lets go of the girl and falls back, his fat ankles tangling and tripping, the guards hearing the commotion and turning around to reach for the boy, David slashing their arms and then leading the girl away from the gate, running for those of us who are waiting.

Other guards come out, armed, and I motion for David to take the girl and run wide so they won't be in the line of fire, then the four women and I lift our blankets and let off bursts from the assault rifles, annihilating those who were chasing our children.

We escape into the woods and send a runner to a group of our warriors stationed nearby. Meanwhile, a contingent of armed guards leaves the gated community to capture or kill what they assume is a single starving family—and we meet them with a force of one hundred from the African Corps who set posts and engagement lines and then so quickly kill the pursuing guards that the action seems casual.

To Tazza's credit as a commander, he doesn't act impetuously even though he's enraged. Instead of attacking immediately, when everyone in the gated community is on alert, we wait until after dark, until midnight, when Patagonians and Africans slip over walls and slice open the necks of sentries who die without crying out, and like rivers of night our black-clad soldiers flow into the community and flood open gates to let in our forces, and deep in that night we awaken the rich from their dreams to their nightmare of glass breaking, our warriors' running hard and fast across tile floors, then it's a blade at their very rich throats, hacked to death as they try to get out of bed, they knew, didn't they, deep down they knew that to be vastly wealthy in a world of devastating poverty represented a moral imbalance that could not last forever—so that by the time the sun comes up all are dead save one, a very fat man with broken veins along his nose and who is bandaged, a wide swath of white cotton around his pumpkin head, across his eyes, our soldiers bringing him out blind to the third tee which is right there at his house where before the calamity he would gather with others of his kind on the balcony to sip alcohol and fruit drinks while commenting on pitch shots that overshoot the green and putts that die too soon.

He stumbles around asking who's there, where's his wife, what's going on. Tazza approaches with David. I'm watching from a cart path. Tazza draws his kukri and I cringe that David is going to see this close up but, no, it's worse than that, horrible, Tazza hands the kukri to eight-year-old David, leans down to whisper in the boy's ear, instructing him in the swing and heft and hit of a kukri. David nods, he can do this.

But he can't, he *shouldn't*, he's a boy, and I want to cry out, No! David! Even if he has the will to do it, which would be tragedy enough, he doesn't have the strength to cut off a man's head and it'll end up a butcher's job. But if I say something now, criticize Tazza in public, he'll have me killed.

Thank God Tazza takes the knife back, walking quickly to the fat man and swinging hard, the kukri lopping off the head so cleanly it seems to pop up like a chip shot before dropping with a thud to the green as the man's fat body flops and his feet scrape and his clawed hands attempt to crawl in the full mania of death throes that dig up divots all over the place.

Tazza tells David to take out the finger knife he had used to blind the man, my heart sinking again as I think Tazza is going to have my son go over to that decapitated head and slice off a trophy ear but, again, I am wrong and Tazza lifts David to his shoulder as David holds the knife high for everyone to see. The people have heard the story, how an eight-year-old boy attacked a man and two guards to save a girl, and now Tazza parades David among us to tell the story again, David on his shoulder and showing the little knife that did the big job. "Here's your king!" Tazza tells us. He's screaming this declaration, weeping openly with pride and joy. "Here's your king!" The people crowd around, making way for a special delegation of the Old Guard—and when those silent and unsmiling Patagonians come up to touch David's leg, Tazza tells them with emphasis, *"Here's your king."*

38

After that, David was never returned to me. Tazza had warned
early on that when the boy turned seven, he would start the training needed to become a king, he would live with the African
Corps and the Celtic tribes. The Regular Army would teach him
the theory of war. He would go out with our scavengers. And
most frightening of all for me to think about, he would bunk with
Patagonians and learn their ways. Knowing all this and resigned
to it, still I expected David's transfer to his father would be
orderly. I thought I would have opportunities to say good-bye and
remind my son of things I didn't want him to forget, things my
women and I had taught him, and also I'd have plenty of chances
to kiss him good-bye and hug him and kiss him again. Instead,
the last I see of David is being paraded on Tazza's shoulders and
then someone from Tazza's camp comes over and gets David's
clothes and things, and I am not told when I can see him or if I
ever will again.

I talk with the women, those who've been with me longest, those

279

who are most trustworthy. I divide them into four teams of twelve each. I warn them that if we're caught doing what I propose, there will be no trial or warning, we will be decapitated. All but four agree to go with me and those four promise not to say anything to anyone. Forty-four women and me. We will kidnap David and go back East. They ask me what I think our chances might be, and I tell them sixty-forty against, which is a lie because I'm thinking we have one chance in ten if we're lucky. But my son is gone, to be raised by a murdering madman. My son will grow up ruthless, already he is fearless but without humor or the tomfoolery of a boy. I imagine how different David would have turned out if he'd been raised by John. John would have taught him poetry and principles and how the selection of one word over another matters. John's dead but I will have David back or die trying.

My women and I bide our time. I occasionally send someone to spy on David. I am told he lives among the Patagonians, who worship him more as a god than a king to be.

Another few months, another few gated communities, another thousand rich people exterminated—and then we are in Texas of all places, then we cross the Rio Grande into Mexico.

Now I tell you plainly what I can't explain, Tazza was a hero in Mexico from the very beginning. *As if the Mexicans had been waiting his arrival.* Tazza rides through villages and cities already converted. Everywhere we go, thousands gather to hear him speak and then as word spreads those thousands become legion.

The man astonishes me once again by addressing these crowds in Spanish, referring to himself as Tazza Emiliano Zapata. He tells the Mexicans, "Before the calamity, you were accused of crossing the border into the United States but I tell you now, it was the border that crossed you! For a thousand years the people lived here. Texas, Mexico—these were names of states, not people, and the states were defined by borders drawn by conquistadors and those who followed them. You did not move. You did not cross a border. The border crossed you!"

Each time he said that line, ten thousand Mexicans cheered him. They loved the pageantry of this Tazza Zapata. He took to growing a fierce mustache and the Mexicans took to wearing string. They traded their machetes for kukris, which they learned to make for themselves because everywhere in Mexico there was a surplus of old truck springs. Tazza came into his own and said he felt more like a king in Mexico than anywhere else he'd been—these people, he said, were peasants and Indians whose very DNA yearned for a king.

They had their own leaders, however—elected mayors and powerful warlords, men of the people, politicians. Some of these threw in with Tazza Zapata, others refused to give up their power and told followers that this American king was another invader from the north. Tazza argued back, telling the Mexicans to look at his face and see his truth.

He was forty-four years old, more magnificent than ever. Even though I was against him, against what he'd become and what he now stood for, I could still appreciate how he was every inch the king. He'd become thicker, more muscular than before and moved less like a dancer now and more ponderously with more power. His black hair had grown long and full. Battle injuries to his nose made it appear larger than before as it hooked over that great Zapata mustache. His face was crossed with scars, one of which I gave him. He was a man who could talk to you in the language your heart understood or he could cut your head off with one sweeping blow. When he rode in on a black horse, red cape billowing behind, black boots to Tazza's knees, his hair around his head like a black and bristly crown—I cheered the glory of this man even though I knew he was a murderer who had kidnapped my son.

Meeting with my women, I told them that with Tazza busy trying to convert a million Mexicans to his cause, now is when we will get David back. I waited until David was with the Regular Army, I could've never gotten him away from the Patagonians and probably not from the Africans or Celts either. I convinced officers in the Regular Army there was no harm in releasing a boy to his mother and I promised to have him back by nightfall.

I kept my emotions in check when I saw him, not wanting David to become alarmed. I told him, you're just coming with me for a visit is all. But hurry.

Getting the women and me and David out of camp and on a road north wasn't the problem, I knew that. The problems would start when Tazza found out David was gone. He would send patrols after us, men who could track the wind across the desert. My only hope was foolish hope, that I would leave half the women on the trail to bushwhack whoever was chasing us, giving the rest of us a chance to make good the escape, or we would slip our pursuers through dumb luck.

It didn't take David long to figure out what I was doing, he might've known from the beginning, and he finally demanded that I take him back or just turn him loose, he'll find his own way back.

"No, you're coming with me."

"He'll send patrols."

"We'll outrun them."

"No you won't."

"David—"

"You'll end up getting killed, do you understand that?"

I did. Of course I did. David wanted to go back so I wouldn't be killed, I knew that.

"If you won't give me permission to leave, I'll slip away first chance I get," he said. "That's the only way you'll make it out of here alive—if I get back to Tazza."

I realized I had no threats powerful enough to stop David, no ropes he couldn't cut or untie, no number of guards he couldn't escape. But I did have one weapon in mother's arsenal. "If you go back, I'll kill myself, I swear to God I will."

"No."

"You know I will, David. How well do you know your mother? You know I will. Listen, when you're of age, when you turn twenty-one, you can go back to him and be the king in training or whatever you want to be. This is an absolute promise I make, you can go back. You know he'll accept you, no matter what. I'm just begging you to give me the chance to give *you* the chance for another ten or twelve years away from this life. Grow up *relatively* normal, then go back to this ongoing fantasy, kings and Patagonians, that your father has created. In the meantime, until you're of age, have a life, play baseball with other kids, practice on a guitar, hold hands with a girl . . . Jesus, David, real life is not the kind of life we've been living. I'm begging you. As your mother, I'm begging you."

Who can withstand a mother's guilt, not my David. He agreed not to escape.

I had split the women into four groups of eleven, each group with a string of twenty horses. We took separate roads away from Tazza, planning to meet up after three days of riding. One of the groups never made it and we never found out why, ambushed by marauders or caught by one of Tazza's patrols? Only much later did we find out that Tazza never sent anyone after us.

The story is in all the books. How Tazza's advisors came in eager to pursue me because if David falls into the wrong hands, he could be used as a bargaining chip for a rival faction, Tazza might have to pay a ransom or make concessions. They were adamant that Tazza send someone after us, bring David back. But Tazza knew me, knew I wouldn't give up my son, a Lakota woman fighting for her only child, it would be a hell to pay and I had my women with me and in terms of loyalty they were my Patagonians. In other words, I would die in the battle and there was a chance the boy would be injured, too.

One of the advisors was brave enough to say David was better off dead than used as an instrument of insurrection.

Tazza said no.

The advisors said if Tazza was afraid of David being hurt, the patrols could be told not to take risks, no explosives, no firearms, just go in there and engage the women hand-to-hand, kill them all if that became necessary, just don't hurt David.

Tazza said no.

His people kept asking why.

You know what he supposedly said, it's famous now, true or not, it's in all the books so it might as well be true—he said he wasn't sending anyone to get David because that's not the way this story ends.

And when they asked him how does the story end, he said, "His mother is still alive and David is there when I die, weeping and cradling my head, and the Patagonians are all around him, protecting him, because he's the new king."

39

I wrote my book about our trip back East, the thirty-three women, David, and me, so I'm hoping you'll let me off the hook about having to remember everything about all that. This remembering has made me weary. I will, however, repeat one point of pride that I covered in the book. As you know it took more than a year for us to get to Washington, and I'm very proud to say we didn't lose a single person on that trip *nor did we take a single life.*

When one of the women broke a leg after her horse fell, we stopped and set her leg and waited for her to heal, the months it took before she could ride again. Tazza would've given her a rifle, a jug of water, and his best wishes—he didn't stop the march for anything. There were only thirty-five of us plus our horses so we obviously made a much smaller footprint than all those thousands on Tazza's march but, still, we caused minimal damage, nothing at all like the march west where we drained lakes and burned forests. On our trip to Washington, we collected downed wood, already dead, already dry. We fished and hunted only what we needed and mostly we lived off the plants and berries and roots we gathered and what we could barter from the people we met. Also, when times got bad, we simply didn't eat. David always got food because he was growing but we women just stopped eating and went days without food. For me, it was nothing to go a month, I was a hunger artist and a month without food made me peckish is all. Ride all day and night, live off air and sunlight, is what the women said of me.

David and I talked of many things around our nightly fires. We talked of John. I tried as best I could to tell the truth and to teach David the principles John would've taught him and explain who John was and what he stood for, though I didn't mention that John had gone over to the Canadians before his death, a betrayal that made me ashamed on John's behalf. I also didn't come right out and say that I was married to John when David was conceived. And David never revealed what Tazza had told him about John.

David carried his own kukri knife, which the Patagonians had given him. I asked him, when he was living with the Patagonians, what were they really like, did they use sign language with each other or write messages or what. He laughed and said they talked. Patagonians talk? I didn't believe him. I said the Patagonians love you. David said they will die for me. But I didn't want to hear any more talk of someone dying for someone. I asked David if he knew any good Canadian jokes. He said do you know the words to *O Canada*. *"God keep our land full of the black fly and flea. / O Canada, we stand on pork for thee."*

But you know all this from my book. Yes, even the photographs. Several of the women took pictures the entire time we were marching west, living in Oz, and then on our trip back East. It was an act of faith, taking photographs when you have no way to develop them and don't know if they'll ever be seen by anyone. Our very lives back in those years were acts of faith.

David was nine by the time we reached Washington, it was strange seeing the place up and running. We didn't tell people who we were because there were signs everywhere that the United States government was in control again. Everyone was voting when we got there. They used the method of dipping a finger in ink to show you've voted, prevent you from voting twice in the same election. They had lots of elections going at the same time so people had three or four fingers inkstained, an index finger for the mayoral election, middle finger for president, thumb for dogcatcher, it was bewildering, all the posters and signs touting candidates or more generally exalting democracy—one person, one vote, power to the people, don't tread on me. When we left all those years ago, democracy was corrupt, an agent of oppression, and now it seems people can't get enough of it.

I guess another big surprise, how few people there were. Fewer even than when we all lived on the National Mall. You hardly ever saw a baby. But we knew it wasn't like that everywhere in the world—in Mexico, for example, women were having babies all over the place.

I wanted David to see where the adventure began, so while the women set up camp in one of the empty parks, I took my son to Memorial Bridge. I had told him about crossing that bridge with John all those years before and how we didn't know what to expect except John had the strangest intuition about meeting our American king.

David and I couldn't get across the bridge, closed for security reasons. Certain boats had been authorized by the government to ferry people across the Potomac. We went down to where they were loading. I chose the line waiting for a red motor launch because it reminded me of—and then oh my God there he was, the one we called Boatman, twelve or thirteen years later and he's still motoring around the Potomac on a red boat.

David and I had just reached the head of the line for the next load when I first got a good look at him, the butter and eggs man who had gotten thick the way those men do. I held David back to prevent him from stepping on board even as Boatman told us to hurry up, hurry up. "Come on, lady."

"I'm waiting for your hand to help me aboard."

He glanced at my face, recognition flickering in his eyes.

"Boatman," I said.

"*Boat.*"

He told me later that we never got his name right but he had never wanted to correct us.

I said, "You can't believe it's me, can you?"

He agreed he couldn't.

"It is." I came aboard with David and threw my arms around Boatman.

He closed the gate and indicated to the waiting passengers that he was making a private run with just two people, everyone else would have to wait for the next trip. They booed him, someone tossed a bottle.

"We could've gone across with the others," I told him.

"No, I want to talk to you in private." He shook David's hand and said, "I guess I know who this one is, the spitting image."

"Yes, Tazza's—"

Boatman interrupted me, that was what he wanted to talk about. "Certain names you shouldn't be saying out loud. You just get here?"

"Yes."

"Don't say who you are and especially not who that one is," Boatman said, indicating David.

I asked David to go up to the bow and take a look around while Boatman and I talked. Boatman explained that the United States government had two declared enemies. The Canadians, of course. And Tazza's kingdom. "For twelve years we've been expecting he's going to come back and try to take over."

"Well it might take him *another* twelve years but eventually he will be coming, with a million Mexicans this time. You said the other enemy is Canada? I thought Canada was *aligned* with the U.S. government."

"*Was.*"

Character is destiny so of course the Canadians turned on the old government and brought it down. Now the U.S. has a new government, supposedly a better one.

Boatman asked if I was there in Washington to spy for Tazza.

"No, just to show David D.C."

He looked doubtful. "You can trust me, Mary."

"Trust you?"

"I'm a loyalist," he whispered, pulling up his left sleeve to show the string still tied there.

"I took David's and mine off a long time ago."

Boatman nodded that it was a smart move to keep the string out of sight, someone could see it and turn you in, you could do jail time for treason. Boatman said, "But if you're on the king's business, you can count on me. Others of us, too. Are you going to see John while you're here?"

"John?"

"Yeah."

"John's dead."

Boatman laughed. "Not as of yesterday when I had lunch with him."

"He's here in D.C.?"

"He's a senator, Mary."

"They got Congress up and running and John's a senator?"

Boatman laughed again.

I couldn't believe it. "Tazza told me that John was killed in a bat-tle we had with Canadians, that John had gone over to their side."

Boatman said that was crazy, John hated Canadians as much as any true American did.

"I wonder if he'll see me."

Boatman shrugged.

I asked him how John was.

Boatman took a breath, there was a lot to say. "He's what they call our elder statesman. Everyone respects John. He fights against the censorship laws and . . . for example, he thought it was wrong to jail people for wearing the string and he was the only one in Con-gress to vote against the string law, but it passed because people are still that afraid of Tazza."

"But the people loved Tazza when he was here in Washington."

"Used to be a friend, now a terrorist—you know how that goes."

"What does John think?"

"Of Tazza? John was for the kingdom but now he's for democ-racy."

"He's Irish so mainly he's against whoever's in power. God, he's in his sixties."

"Piss and vinegar like a thirty-year-old."

After we landed on the other side of the Potomac, I asked Boat-man if he was going to spend the rest of his life here on this river, waiting for a king.

He said yes as if that was the easiest question he'd been asked all day.

Over the next week, as David and I toured Washington during the days and camped with my women at night, I tried to get used to the idea that John was alive and I considered ways I could get word to him, to tell him that David and I were in Washington, to find out how he felt about me—would he have us arrested as enemies of the state or would he give safe passage to me and my son and my women?

In the end I decided to go see him. It was amazing, we encountered so few people in or around the Capitol and you could walk right in and find a senator's office and knock on the door. Which is what I did, holding David's hand.

An aide opened the door and stepped out. "Hello," she said, shaking my hand and bending down to address David. "Hello there, young man." Then to me, "My name is Christina, may I ask what business you have with the senator?"

"Tell John his wife is here."

Her big hello-constituent smile was quickly replaced with an uh-oh-a-nut frown.

I told her again. "His wife. Mary. And her son, David."

"Uhm . . ."

"Is he in the office? Just go tell him, you'll see."

"I think you may want to talk with one of our guides, you might have the wrong senator."

But just then John came down the wide hallway with several more of his aides, stopping when he saw me.

I was surprised. He looked smaller than I remembered. I guess my expectation had been corrupted from so many years of looking up at Tazza. John braced himself at the sight of me but I couldn't read how he felt. Would he curse me again? Or deny he even knows my name?

And the longer he stood there and stared, the more foolish I felt for springing us on him like this. He might have a legal obligation as a U.S. senator to have us taken into custody and use David against Tazza for when Tazza and his million Mexicans show up across the

Potomac, who knows how things work in this reconstituted United States.

One of the aides with him finally broke the silence, asking me, "And you are?"

John answered, "That's Mary, my wife. And that's her son, David."

I started crying. Me! *Lakota.* Crying because he had called me his wife. I covered my weeping face with both hands, the tension there in the hallway making me feel underwater where I couldn't move or breathe.

But when John put his arms out and I went to him, the water drained away and I could get air again.

We stayed hugging for the longest time, David waiting like a junior diplomat who had been trained not to show emotion or react to that shown by others.

John finally turned to him. "How do you do? I know your father well."

David shook John's hand. "My father is king."

The aides were alarmed to hear this but John laughed. "Indeed he is. I knew it before he did."

"Yes, sir, he told me that story many times."

"He did?"

David nodded.

I couldn't believe it and asked David, "Tazza spoke to you about John?"

David nodded again. "He said John was a man who always knew the truth."

"Not always," John said, looking at me. Then he addressed all of us, "Let's go in the office, get everyone a Coke."

"You have Coca-Cola?" I asked.

"It tastes different." On the way through the door, he asked David, "What books are you reading?"

"None right now, we've been on the road a very long time."

"We'll remedy that. Have you read *King Arthur*?"

John, laughing again, how I missed the sound of my John laughing, putting his arm around my shoulder.

40

I'd like to stop there. I realize I've left out how it all ends but my memories of that hardly add anything to the *public* record. Thousands saw what happened, it was videotaped for godssake.

Yes, the years leading up to it, I could tell about those—they were among the very happiest of my life.

John introduced me and David to his woman, Linda, who was as gracious as she could be, considering she was meeting her man's wife and all. I offered to sign whatever papers were necessary for a divorce so John and Linda could get married, but she said it wasn't necessary. We eventually became friends, Linda and I, and of course I had long before stopped referring to her as the cow. Did you ever read or see *Gone With the Wind*? Linda was Melanie. A saint except with red hair. Having your long-ago husband living with a saint can be intimidating.

I nursed Linda when she got the cancer and, a year after she died, David and I moved in with John. We were lifelong friends,

John and me, and living with him again was a delight even if we didn't live as man and wife. We stayed together until the very end.

John tutored David in a thousand things, let's-take-a-walk, you hold my hand. He explained things to David, why the sky was blue, and they went fishing and they read the *brave lad* parts of Jack London books. I'd meet them coming back from a walk and John would be talking rivers, you know John's rivers, deep and fast you can barely follow the flow, rivers Everglades slow, over topics you can't see the bottom of, cutting deep into a subject's bedrock, John in his advanced age all the smarter and more articulate and even more well-read, wise enough to float coal barges on what he knows, maddening but never boring, always talking, always knowing, while David listens and listens and absorbs entire rivers of talk.

I thought at times that the talk and the books, the poetry and painting, the yearning for doing what's right which John instilled in David, that all of it might be taking the edge off the boy. The women and I had tried to civilize David, too, but our work was done in contrast to Tazza's brutal realism. Now there was no contrast, no one putting an edge on David, just the gentle intellect of John. When David was fifteen, a bully demanded that David give him the finger knife that David still carried and I would've thought that my son would slash the boy rather than be bullied but, in fact, he handed the knife over and then just talked to the bully. I told John that maybe David has become overly gentle when he should be learning to fight for what's his in this world. John asked me, "What would you have had him do, kill the boy?" I said I would have him remember his father is a king. A few weeks later, John told me that the bully was now David's staunchest ally, that the boy followed David around like a bodyguard, willing to die like a Patagonian for David.

I know what you must think of me, that I'm a blood-soaked old woman who wanted to see her son slash another boy—but you'll never understand what it was to live the life we lived all those years and witness so many deaths, so much violence, always under a threat. A life like that takes the soft parts of you and makes them hard.

In Washington, we kept waiting for word that Tazza was coming but the years passed and all we ever heard was that he remained bogged down in Mexico.

I suppose it was inevitable that John would groom David to run for president, David with all of Tazza's charisma but a more principled man than his father ever was, more patient and, with John's help, wiser, too.

As soon as David turned twenty-five, the youngest age the new Constitution allows for anyone to be president, he ran and won. John was in his early eighties by then, health problems but still sharper mentally than anyone else in the Senate, anyone else advising the new president.

I was proud not only that my son won the presidency but proud that the people loved him for being a leader, for the way he acted and walked and spoke, for being his father's son and my husband's student. David is one of those people, when you meet him you don't wonder so much if you like him or not, you're hoping he likes you. So I thought all along that the election was pretty much a foregone conclusion, my greatest pride was in the way David ran the country—the way he *changed* the country.

Like instilling a sense of shame and of honor in America so that if you did something wrong you were ashamed of it and if you did something good you were honored for it, you can't pass laws for that, it has to come from appealing to the people's better nature.

Life was good until we heard Tazza was coming. Tazza and his kingdom had existed as boogeyman and myth for so long that the prospect of actually confronting the great Tazza terrified our people. There was panic, genuine panic in Washington. It had taken Tazza almost two decades but he had finally put together his invincible army, the people across America who had pledged loyalty to him plus a million Mexicans—and they were on their way here to conquer Washington, Tazza's obsession for nearly thirty years. We had been foolish to think he had ever just gone away and forgotten us or had been killed or had given up, not Tazza, no.

John had died, he wasn't there to advise David at this moment of our greatest danger, Tazza on the way and people streaming out of D.C. David's cabinet wanted him to order the army to engage Tazza before he reached Washington. "Do not let the enemy reach our capital," they kept telling David. Do you know how he answered them? He said I don't define my father's kingdom as the enemy. Wow, that put people back on their heels. Suddenly, David's loyalty is being questioned. The *terrorists* are coming, a million strong, and our president doesn't define them as the enemy? People talked of impeachment. Washington insiders said once you're part of the kingdom you're always part of the kingdom and maybe David will ride out and hand the United States over to his father, is what people were saying.

I stayed in Washington, of course I stayed. I was an old woman even back then. And my son was there. And I had lived too hard to panic at this late date.

An army of a million or more invaders assembled around Washington, some of their divisions stationed miles away as reserve units, some mustered right across the river. People had heard that they rape and pillage and murder, people were terrified. What was the president thinking, why did he let them come right up to the river?

And then . . . it's in all the books . . .

David rides out by himself, his aides begging him not to go, he rides around the Lincoln Memorial where Tazza converted the Patagonians, he rides onto the Memorial Bridge, David on a pretty little Andalusian mare, all prancing and head shaking. I guess word had been sent to Tazza because he came across from the other side, riding one of those big warhorse stallions he was partial to, and although David, nearing thirty, was a tall, strong man, he seemed like a boy on a pony next to his father who, past sixty now, was massive, shoulders and chest, long bristly black hair and still that Zapata mustache, scars everywhere, he was like an old bull still able to intimidate all contenders.

We watched through binoculars and telescopes and the zoom lenses of video cameras.

I am asked if I felt anything seeing Tazza on that bridge after all those years. I suppose people mean did something flutter in me and spark the memory of sleeping with a king—no, I felt nothing except fear for my son's safety.

They rode toward each other, meeting in the middle of the bridge, David alone, Tazza there with a hundred Patagonians, some of them old enough to remember David personally and all of them steeped in the legend of David.

David and Tazza got off their horses but did not embrace. The world on our side of the bridge watched closely each step they took and of course we know now each word they spoke.

"I'm your son."

"I know who you are."

"I didn't leave you willingly all those years ago."

"I know that, too. I let her take you, did you know that? I could've sent my soldiers after you, killed her women and taken you back. But I figured she'd come to Washington and raise you with John's help."

"You wanted that?"

"I permitted it."

"Why?"

"It would be good for you, raised by those two."

"I've been elected president."

"I know. Proves my point, they raised you right. Have you ridden out here to offer me terms?"

"A war between us will cost a million casualties."

"Then surrender your city."

David walks past Tazza to go among the Patagonians, asking them if they know who he is. "I am Tazza's son. I will be your king." They knew, the younger ones had been hearing about David all their lives, how as a boy he attacked grown men and armed guards, David with nothing but a little knife in his hand. The story inflated over the years, that David killed a dozen men and saved a dozen children. The older Patagonians remember touching his legs when he was a boy being carried around on Tazza's shoulders and then living with him when he was training to be king. To the elders, he was a living god.

After threading among the hundred Patagonians, David made his way back to his father. "I'll take command of your armies now."

Tazza—surprised, wary, and a little proud, too—laughs, telling his son, "Join me and we'll conquer this country, then turn north. Canada is our real enemy."

"I know it is. And I need your Mexicans to fight Canada and repopulate America. So I say again, I'll take command of your armies now."

"Not just yet, son. I'm still king."

As fluidly as a dancer, as powerfully as a matador, David draws from behind him the kukri that these Patagonians had given him twenty years before and with one wide horizontal sweep, putting his body into it like a home-run hitter, he cuts off his father's head and then reaches out quickly with his left hand to catch the decapitated head before it hits the ground.

First, there is a collective gasp and then silence as David holds up the king's head, the silence broken by Tazza's warriors at the far end of the bridge, shouting rage as they advance.

Watching from our end, we are astonished, appalled, disbelieving. Our gentle young president decapitating a man, no not just a man, his *father,* a king, and doing it while they were just standing there talking, negotiating—we wondered what else our president was capable of, he could cut off a man's head like that with one blow. And I think . . . clutching myself, I think, now I will see my son killed and torn apart by Tazza's soldiers.

And then those soldiers will *still* sack the city, what was my son thinking?

Holding his father's head by the hair, David tells the Patagonians, "I am your king."

His calculation could've been fatally wrong. Patagonians who had followed Tazza all those years could've been so outraged to see him killed in front of them like that, they could've charged David and cut him into pieces. But David knew the Patagonians and relied on that part of Patagonian lore that said David would be their king and, somehow, this vicious act of succession now made perfect sense to them.

In unison and without a detectable signal, they turned around to face their own forces, indicating they would protect this new king. The soldiers on the bridge stopped. Who among them would charge into a phalanx of Patagonians?

With the Old Guard around him, David rode to that far end of the bridge and among the armies. Weeping, cradling his father's head, he told the warriors he was their king. He told them this for two days and two nights. He spoke to them in passionate speeches reminiscent of his father and he spoke to them in quiet wide rivers that went on and on like John's did. He talked to the armies at the campfires that night while still cradling Tazza's head and he was in saddle among them at first sun the following day. And then he led the armies away, led them from Washington. He didn't even come back to tell his mother good-bye and I was convinced I would never see my son again.

He was gone five years, as you know—time during which his vice president, Carl, took office, then Carl was elected president, then David returned. People weren't sure what David would do, would he take up where his father left off and try to conquer Washington? Instead, as you know, he declared his candidacy for president. And this was in spite of David still being king. During the election, David argued that by being leader of both the Kingdom and the United States, he would bring peace to both. He'd already settled the Kingdom's million-plus population along the U.S.'s northern border as a buffer against Canada. David explained that now the Canadians have to go through the Kingdom before they can ever get to the United States and, as bad-ass as the Canadians are, the Kingdom is badder still. David said we had every reason to make peace with his Kingdom, it was already protecting us. He also campaigned on the platform of recruiting Mexicans to come to the United States because otherwise we'd never have enough people to be a prosperous country again. David had already sent recruiters throughout Mexico, paying incentives if families would agree to come north and settle.

Did you know that I was the one who came up with the response David used during the election, when anyone asked how he could be president of the United States and king of the Kingdom of America both at the same time, and his reply was, "How can I not?" That was my line. *How can I not?*

David being president and king both was the right thing to do, it was the inevitable thing to do.

And now? Goodness, now everything has changed. Now, instead of considering Canada a morally corrupt nation and constant threat to our security, mostly we just make jokes about how cold Canadian kisses are and how Canadians are holding onto their tire money hoping cars come back.

Eventually David retired the Patagonians, they didn't fit in with the new world, and now on Halloween people think it's funny to put on shower caps and wedding veils and dress up as Patagonians. Please believe me when I tell you there was nothing ever funny about Patagonians.

The rivalry between the United States and the Kingdom is limited to sports—and making fun of each other. People in the States say that people in the Kingdom are uptight, dull, no imagination. People in the Kingdom accuse residents of the U.S. of being libertines. But we're a good pressure valve for each other, conservatives in the States can move to the Kingdom when things get too pink here and artists and rebels in the Kingdom can come to New York City instead of mounting a revolution back home. Worrywarts say the alliance between a democracy and a kingdom can't hold forever. Nothing holds forever.

I told you in the beginning that there are three questions people always ask me, but you never asked the third. *Which do I prefer, a kingdom or a democracy—which do I think is best?*

I've lived in a democracy and I've lived in a kingdom, and, at their cores, like all governments, they are both corrupt. We form them as necessary evils to protect us against other corrupt governments, but governments are not *the people* and they never have the people's best interest at heart, they have the government's best interest at heart. Regardless of what protections we put in place, a Bill of Rights or Magna Carta, governments will oppress the people, censor the people, exploit the people. Governments do not trust the people, governments are contemptuous of the people. Governments build concentration camps and cathedrals, the people plant gardens. We feed and breed, we nurse and harvest, and if you want advice from an old woman, I say put your trust and love in the people, never a government. Ask not what you can do for your country, ask what you can do to save and promote and protect the people even if that requires treason of king or country, because the people, your family, friends, neighbors, we are the conspiracy that has survived a million years, and we are alive today not because of governments but in spite of governments. We endure. We are *the people*.

The end.

David Lozell Martin's previous novels include international best-sellers *Lie to Me* and *Tap, Tap* and the critically acclaimed *The Crying Heart Tattoo, The Beginning of Sorrows,* and *Crazy Love. Our American King* is his twelfth book. He lives in the Washington, D.C., area.